Praise for

WHERE THE BIRD SINGS BEST

"*Where the Bird Sings Best* is Alejandro Jodorowsky's brilliant, mad and unpredictable semi-autobiographical novel. Translated by Alfred MacAdam, this multigenerational chronicle introduces a host of memorable characters, from a dwarf prostitute and a floating ghost-Rabbi to a lion tamer who eats raw meat and teaches his beasts to jump through flaming hoops. Fantastical elements aside, *Where the Bird Sings Best* is a fiercely original immigration tale that culminates in the author's birth in Chile in 1929—a complicated time in that nation's history. Combine that with poetry, tarot and Jewish mysticism and you have a genius's surreal vision brought to life."

—NPR, BEST BOOKS OF 2015

"Wildly inventive.... Jodorowsky's masterpiece swirls around the reader, lurching from violent episode to mystical encounter to cosmic sexual escapade as we follow our narrator's grandparents' journey from the old world to, refreshingly, South America. As the drama unfolds, the reader's response veers from incredulity to awe, from doubt to delight. The momentum holds for the length of the novel as a cavalcade of outsized characters careen across the page in a frenzy that seems for once an adequate and just representation of the living fury that is history.... the images possess an extreme yet striking beauty."

—ASKOLD MELNYCZUK,

LOS ANGELES REVIEW OF BOOKS

"This epic family saga, reminiscent of Gabriel Garcia Marquez's *One Hundred Years of Solitude* in structure and breadth, reads at a breakneck pace. Though ostensibly a novelization of the author's own family history, it is a raucous carnival of the surreal, mystical, and grotesque.... It weaves together Jewish philosophy, passion, humor, Tarot, ballet, circuses, natural disasters, spectacular suicides, lion tamers, knife throwers, Catholic devotion, farmers, betrayals, prostitutes, leftist politics, political violence, and the ghost of a wise rabbi who follows the family from the Old World to the New."

—PUBLISHERS WEEKLY

"First, a hard-boiled fact: No one alive today, anywhere, has been able to demonstrate the sheer possibilities of artistic invention—and in so many disciplines—as powerfully as Alejandro Jodorowsky.... His new semi-autobiographical novel *Where the Bird Sings Best*, translated by Alfred MacAdam, is his magnum opus, a fantastical something that in many ways mirrors the author himself: It is brilliant, mad, unpredictable.... It's not difficult to see why *Where the Bird Sings Best* has been compared to Gabriel García Márquez's *One Hundred Years of Solitude*. But Jodorowsky's saga stands firmly on its own.... Reading Jodorowsky is not suspending reality; it is allowing yourself to believe that with imagination, anything and everything is in the realm of possibility."

—JUAN VIDAL, NPR BOOKS

"In his ancestral adventures, Jodorowsky brings to life not just the engaging story of his own family, but the mechanisms of engagement underlying story itself. Each paragraph pulsates, threatens to burst from its burgeoning body of details. Jodorowsky relieves pressure as necessary. But time after time, he proceeds to build up and dazzle all over again.... Each individual section is endowed with Jodorowsky's full vitality."

—BENJAMIN ABRAMOWITZ,
THE JEWISH BOOK COUNCIL

"Jodorowsky is today's true Renaissance man—a master of many mediums that all point directly towards a towering and imaginative vision replete with profound insights into the real by way of the surreal. The stories told in *Where the Bird Sings Best* contain deep moral lessons, giving his mythic immigration story the feel of a modern day *Sefer-ha-Aggadah*—the classic collection of Jewish folk tales drawn from the Mishnah, Midrash and Talmud. This long awaited and brilliantly evocative translation is a must read—frightening, hilarious, outrageous, touching, and (as is always with Jodorowsky's work) filled with a deep core of mystic truth."

—JOHN ZORN

"A sweeping tale of personal, philosophical, and political struggles. It's an immigrant's story of Fellini-esque proportions. . . . For the self-proclaimed atheist mystic, the sacraments are memory, dreams, family, wisdom, the grotesque, and the reinvention of the self. . . . As with *Where the Bird Sings Best*, Jodorowsky's non-film works are conduits and biographical keys that further reveal his mesmerizing process of imaginative self-fashioning."

—ALISON NASTASI, FLAVORWIRE

"The legendary filmmaker has taken his lineage for inspiration in this twisted meditation on existentialism flavored with Jewish mysticism, incest, and some honey for good measure. This supposed biography works more as a jumping off place for a truly wild literary ride. Graphic, ambitious, magical, demented—Jodorowsky's visual virtuosity showcases a whirlwind of occultism, cultism, sex, and death across time and space. Truly striking, psychedelic, and one of the more surreal books I have read in a while. But what more could you expect from the man who adapted Frank Herbert's *Dune* into a 14-hour film and created his own tarot?"

—ASHANTI WHITE-WALLACE,
WORD BOOKSTORE (JERSEY CITY, NJ)

"I find myself impressed by his dilatory imagination, love of pure spectacle, and puckish sense of humor. . . . Sober, dressed, and with all the lights on, I ripped through *Where the Bird Sings Best*—the first of Jodorowsky's many novels to appear in English translation—in just a few enraptured days. The trick is to eschew caricature and give yourself over to the experience, at which point the wondrous strange takes over. The mind—and, god help me, the spirit—finds itself traveling in realms it could not have otherwise explored, or even dreamed exist. . . . *Where the Bird Sings Best* is electrifying."

—JUSTIN TAYLOR,

THE BARNES & NOBLE REVIEW

"Alejandro Jodorowsky [is] a superb novelist. *Where the Bird Sings Best* [is a] gloriously readable, fantastical autobiographical novel. . . . [A] deliciously far-fetched, multigenerational saga. . . . One outrageous set piece follows another with an exhilarating density of imagination as Jodorowsky juggles the tale within tale with *Arabian Nights* agility. . . . Exuberant, unrelentingly creative in its folkloric style of heightened reality, the book serves as one gigantic prequel to 2013's *The Dance of Reality*, his first film in 23 years and a visually dazzling masterpiece in which Jodorowsky recreates his childhood with his parents. A master of both film and fiction, he expertly harnesses boldly surreal images to capture the gorgeous, brutal essence of life."

—NICK DIMARTINO,

SHELF AWARENESS (NICK'S PICKS)

"A wild, fantastic, autobiographical family saga. The writing is impossibly beautiful, the story is epic and magical. I couldn't take my eyes off the page. One of the best books of 2015 by far."

—BRIAN CUDZILO,

HARBOR BOOKS (SAG HARBOR, NY)

THE SON OF
BLACK THURSDAY

FICTION BY
ALEJANDRO JODOROWSKY

Where the Bird Sings Best
The Son of Black Thursday
Albina and the Dog-Men

THE SON OF BLACK THURSDAY

Alejandro Jodorowsky

Translated from the Spanish by
MEGAN McDOWELL

RESTLESS BOOKS
BROOKLYN, NEW YORK

First published as *El niño del jueves negro* by Siruela, Madrid, 1999

First Restless Books paperback edition September 2018

Paperback ISBN: 9781632060532
Library of Congress Control Number: 2016940777

Cover design by Richard Ljoenes
Set in Garibaldi by Tetragon, London

Printed in Canada

1 3 5 7 9 10 8 6 4 2

Restless Books, Inc.
232 3rd Street, Suite A111
Brooklyn, NY 11215

www.restlessbooks.com
publisher@restlessbooks.com

CONTENTS

INTRODUCTORY NOTE

I N *Where the Bird Sings Best,* I told the origin story of the Rabbi, a hermit from the Caucasus who threw himself into kabbalistic studies and, searching for the wise saints who, as Zohar says, live in the other world, lost himself in the labyrinths of time. He was unable to return to his body because, after he'd abandoned it in the woods, it had been devoured by bears. Eventually the disembodied Rabbi came upon an orphan child: Alejandro Levi, my grandfather, and he proposed that he accompany and advise the child, because "the other is a form of nourishment" and "man without man perishes from spiritual hunger." Later I was asked: "Is the Rabbi imaginary, since he can't be seen and there is no proof he is real?" All I know is that my grandfather passed him on as a kind of legacy, so that in our family he has gone from one brain to another; he haunted my father, Jaime, and me as well.

When I asked the Rabbi to tell me about his life, he didn't answer, but he started to cry. Neither my grandfather nor my father had ever thought to ask what his existence had been like before the bears devoured his body. I was the first to take an interest in that past. I understand my ancestors' attitude: Jaime was never sure the Caucasian was real. It could have been schizophrenia and not a real out-of-body existence that, in making us heirs of madness, passed him down to us. Still, hallucination or not, the Rabbi changed our lives. Without him, I never could have put down roots in this world that is made largely of aggression. My grandfather made

xi

an accomplice out of the Rabbi, my father made him an intruder, and I a teacher, because I lost Jaime when I was two years old and saw him again only when I was ten. And so, though my reason says otherwise, I prefer to believe that the Rabbi and everything he said about my country and my family is true.

To the question "Is the Rabbi real or unreal?" I can only reply that I feel him in my heart.

ALEJANDRO JODOROWSKY

THE SON OF
BLACK THURSDAY

ONE

THE LOVERS' STORE

F AT BALTRA, owner of the Everything-for-Forty bargain store—a dusty warehouse where he sold every kind of object for forty cents each—barged like a hurricane into Ukraine House. Sara Felicidad, my mother, was there—six feet nine inches tall, with blond, almost phosphorescent hair, pearly skin, and enormous eyes of a deep oceanic blue; she didn't know how to talk like human beings but only like the angels, in musical notes. Fat Baltra blew right past without greeting her and went behind the counter to pound desperately on the bathroom door. Inside, my father Jaime—a short but robust man, communist and atheist, believer that the only ideal worthy of man was that of having a full stomach—had placed a radio in the urinal, where it was emitting news censored by the police department. Jaime cursed the dictator Coronel Carlos Ibáñez del Campo and urinated toward the announcer's voice, whose dry tones belied a military brain and spoke little of the disastrous economic situation of Chile in 1928, but much of the growing prosperity in the United States.

"Come quickly, Don Jaime! Basilia's escaped again!"

In the bar at the port, a marine who'd wanted to keep his binge going had traded fat Baltra his pet monkey in exchange for three bottles of pisco. The animal, no bigger than a cat, was named Basilio—with an *o* at the end and not an *a*. He knew how to search his master's head for lice, do somersaults, scratch his belly while sticking out his tongue, or show his teeth while he let out little shrieks that imitated human laughter. . . . He was a tame monkey, but—and who knows why, maybe it was the smell—he hated Baltra. Once they were back at the bargain store and Baltra was overcoming his drunken stagger, he offered Basilio a piece of banana, and the first thing the monkey did was bite his hand. Ow! Though the monkey was male, the fat man slid the B of Basilio toward the B of Berta, and in full-on delirium he conflated the monkey with his mother, the woman who had hated him since his birth and had handed him off to a blind maid while she, the slut, spent the day seated before her round mirror, observing her face and praying no new wrinkles would appear.

"Basilia, you ungrateful monkey! I won't let you try to seduce Time like Berta did—because Time was my mother's only lover. She seduced it so that her body aged only on the inside. Outside, she was a young woman, but through all her pores seeped the rancid-chicken smell of decrepitude. She ordered a coffin lined with mirrors. I didn't go to her funeral; it was attended only by thousands of flies. . . ."

The little monkey, as was its habit, responded by imitating human laughter. Enraged, Baltra undressed his gypsy doll, and, protected by thick leather gloves, dressed the animal in the green silk blouse and long red skirt. Then, dragging him by the chain attached to a leather belt around his waist, he brought him out to the patio and tied him to a plank wall separating Baltra's property from the small square of earth behind Ukraine House.

"There you'll stay, Basilia, forgotten like you deserve, evil whore that you are! If you want to eat, find yourself a blind maid to wait on you. I certainly won't do it!"

4

Basilio, smelling the fat man's insanity, tried to bite him, jumping furiously but cut short by the chain, which lashed him against the ground and raised a cloud of dust. The fat man let out a couple of peals of malicious laughter, and returned to his counter. After many hours, the animal, thirsty, hungry, his skin cracked by the implacable northern sun, dug a hole at the base of the wall. Making the most of his long chain, he passed over to my father's land, where he found a little shade beneath an old chair.

Jaime, who occasionally went out to the patio to smoke a cigarette, found Basilio in agony. Convinced that animals attack only when someone is afraid of them or wants to hurt them, he brought a bottle of water outside and took the languishing animal in his arms, then filled his own mouth with the cool liquid and pressed his lips against the monkey's open mouth, obliging him to drink. When he regained consciousness, Basilio thought Jaime was like Baltra. Baring his fangs, he threatened to sink them into his savior's neck. Jaime didn't shrink from him, but rather brought him to his chest very calmly, petted him, took a caramel from a pocket and placed it in his mouth. In one second the monkey went from fiend to angel. As he chewed the candy and asked for water-bearing kisses, he hugged the man who was now the love of his life.

Though he was aware that the animal did not belong to him, Jaime grew fond of it. As soon as Basilio heard his friend's footsteps, he would roll onto his back and grunt in affection, raise his red skirt, and start rubbing his belly. Jaime would come closer and show his empty hands. The monkey didn't believe him and would search through all his pockets until he found a piece of toffee, some fruit, or cracked nuts. When the snack was over, he climbed up onto Jaime's shoulders and spent a long time searching his hair, inch by inch, for parasites. Jaime had earlier spilled grains of sugar in his hair, and Basilio would devour them as if they were lice, immensely satisfied. To Jaime, every attitude the monkey struck was a lesson. When Basilio didn't believe him as he showed him empty hands, it taught him to believe in his ideals without ever losing hope. When Basilio ate grapes or any juicy fruit and lifted his face toward the sky so the squirting liquid would run down his throat, he taught Jaime to be attentive, to not waste a single minute: each action was essential and you could lose everything in an instant. And finally, when he gave the monkey a piece of onion to snack on, and he rubbed it over his whole body until it turned black to eliminate the burn, he demonstrated that it was possible to overcome adversity by integrating it into oneself, not rejecting it.

On the 18th of each month (the date when Berta had begun, with stomach pains, fetid sweats, murderous breath, nausea, and demented tantrums, to suffer the eight days of her period), Baltra got dead drunk. Yanking at the chain, he'd pull Basilio from his neighboring refuge and drag him into his own yard where he tried to pulverize his bones with the shovel his mother used to use to block her bedroom door on nights of ocean storms, when Baltra had been terrified by the waves crashing on the coast and would try to climb into bed with her. The animal dodged the blows, letting out deafening shrieks. The fat man, yelling like a hysterical woman, insulted him as always: "Take that, for being evil and a whore!" This ruckus would last for hours until finally Baltra collapsed, exhausted and snoring. Then Basilio would urinate in his face and, satisfied, cross back over to Jaime's yard. . . . However, there were times when, from so much pulling, a link of the chain gave way and the monkey would get free. Then he would climb up to the rooftops and disappear into Tocopilla. Only then did Baltra realize how attached to the animal he was. Cold sweat broke out on his brow and an inner claw yanked his heart into his guts.

Conflating his emotions, when he asked Jaime to go with him to find the fugitive, he hiccuped: "What can I do? I love-hate her from the bottom of my heart! Without the grief that she-monkey gives me, I can't live!"

Basilio, having nowhere to go—not a wisp of a weed could grow in the hills, and opposite them the boiling waves of the Pacific hammered the cliffs and rocks—ran berserk and took refuge in any house he could find. The terrified Tocopillans threatened him with brooms as if he were a rat. His shrieks drowned out the sound of a fire truck's siren, but the firemen, axes in hand, didn't know how to get him down from the closets, the lamps, or the skylights.

Jaime, impassive, his mouth full of water, would get as close to Basilio as he could get and then stand motionless. When he saw Jaime's swollen cheeks, the furious animal would come slowly down, climb my father's body as if he were a sturdy tree, and press his mouth to his lips to take a long sip; then he was calm. Next, whining like a greedy child, he probed Jaime's pockets, triumphantly extracted his caramel, and, sucking it delicately, started to search for the sugar-grain lice. . . . Thus, with the monkey on his head, the proud hero and the admiring crowd that followed him went back along the streets toward the Everything-for-Forty store.

Baltra always received the monkey by offering him a peeled banana. And the monkey always bit his hand! Ow! Then Baltra cursed him, tied him up in the yard, and it was the same thing all over again!

†

But that morning, something was different.

"Basilia ran into the hills, Jaime! Why? She won't find anything or anyone in those hundreds of miles of dead land!"

Jaime pulled on his boots, stuffed some caramels in his pockets, scattered some sugar in his hair, filled a canteen with water, and, shielded by an umbrella, set off on the hot ascent.

The road was sown with rocks sharp as razors, and it rose in a zigzag. After an hour of walking, far ahead, he saw Basilio emerge from a crack in the rock and wait for him in the middle of the road. When he was about to catch up with him, the monkey ran a hundred yards ahead and waited again. The same game repeated, over and over, for another hour. The black cloth of the umbrella began to smoke, and Jaime's boots seemed to shrink. In those lands it had been three centuries since the last rain. Jaime was stupefied by the heat and let the Rabbi come to him. Free of corporeal anxieties, the Rabbi observed the imposing landscape in amazement. He saw that herds of animals formed by lines of stones decorated many of the hills. "Ancient sites of sacrifice," he said to himself. "The hills used to be gods. Now the only sacred thing left to them is their shadow." He looked toward the desert immensity, ignored the masses and focused only on the darkened places. He sighed in satisfaction: "Material rots, but not its shadow. . . ." Jaime, recovering control, expelled him in rage: "Cretinous parasite! When will you leave me in peace?" Just then, Basilio left the road and took a detour, jumping over a rusted barrier: "Military zone. No entry. MORTAL DANGER."

What danger could there be in that isolated and barren place, where not even lizards would deign to dwell? Jaime jumped the barrier as well and kept on chasing the monkey. Ten minutes later, he stopped. A change in the wind carried to his ears the sound of an out-of-tune chorus singing an old bolero:

> *Ya sé que soy*
> *Una aventura más para ti*

Y que después de esta noche
Te olvidarás de mí. . . .

He closed the umbrella and ducked into a crevice that ran along the path, and, nearly hidden (hopefully they weren't highway robbers willing to murder a man just to steal a gold tooth), he approached the place from which the song came.

He stole a look, peeking out from between two heavy rocks. He saw an army biplane parked on a cement runway. Next to the plane were four drunken soldiers muttering filthy jokes as they attached a heavy chain to the feet of six women, heavily made up and wearing seductive dresses covered in sequins, feathers, and fake jewels, their breasts crossed by red silk sashes. Miss Chillán, Miss Curacaví, Miss La Serena, Miss San Fernando, Miss Copiapó, and Miss Talca. In a truck, also army-issue, were four more of these lovely women, Miss Maipú, Miss Osorno, Miss Calbuco, and Miss Colchagua, plus a fiftysomething fat woman with a long blond mane, and a bald man in a tuxedo who had Basilio in his arms. They were all intoning the bolero as if it were a canticle offered up to God.

Jaime bit his lip to hold back a cry of surprise. That man who had not a hair on his body, nor on his scalp, his face, his armpits, or his pubis, that man who was smooth all over like a tortoiseshell doll, was his younger brother, Benjamín. Yes! The poet so disgusted by the animal part of himself, he who would have liked not to have teeth or fingernails or fecal matter, he who aspired to be translucent like a jellyfish, he of subtle speech and exquisite gestures, the faggot who, like a scourge on Jaime's virility, filled him with shame! What was he doing there, among those—he now realized—ridiculous transvestites?

†

Helping the six misses carry the heavy chain, the four soldiers loaded them onto the plane. It rose and headed off toward the sea, disappearing beyond the hills. The song ceased. The soldiers got into the truck cabin, uncorked two bottles of wine, and went on drinking. Miss Calbuco took off her underpants, adorned with a felt heart, to fan herself with them. Jaime, taking advantage of the soldiers' distraction, looked out from between the rocks and made cautious signals. Basilio greeted him with indiscreet shrieks. The soldiers looked up. The fifty-something woman, to cover for my father and at the same time to transmit a message to him, opened her arms wide, shook her blonde wig, and began to give a speech to the hills:

"Ancient witnesses: we are the victims of unjust abuse! We were in holy peace, celebrating our annual Miss Chile competition, when the soldiery fell upon us and, after they raped us, they sent us away from Santiago to this wasteland. Don Carlos Ibáñez del Campo has decided to purge the country of communists and homosexuals. The former he packs into concentration camps, and us he throws into the water."

The soldiers dissolved in contemptuous peals of laughter.

"Go ahead, whores, complain to the hills all you like, until your well-traveled asses swell up! I'm sure the hills will gallop off to the capital to beg the president to save you, fucking faggots!"

The drinking continued. The fake blonde, with the infinitesimal consolation of having found a witness for her inevitable demise, went on speechifying. The other transvestites clung to her, shedding black tears. Meanwhile, Benjamín took a metal box from his pocket, opened it, took out a notebook and a pen, and, looking occasionally at the bit of Jaime that peered from the crevice, began to write.

"And so it is, noble bluffs: seventy-six competing misses were taken prisoner, plus me, Camelia Chalimar, organizer of the event, and Mr. Benjamín Jodorowsky, distinguished poet and president of the jury. All morning, in groups of six, the airplane has been carrying us off toward the blue mother to throw us into her insatiable maw, tied to the fatal chain that drags us to the bottom. Please, dear hills, tell this injustice to the world, so our deaths will not be in vain!"

With a metallic purr, the light plane announced its approach before it appeared. Basilio ran to take refuge in Jaime's arms. The soldiers, hardly able to stay on their feet, didn't notice him. The monstrous bird produced a giant gust of wind and perched on the cement runway. Benjamín stopped writing, returned the notebook to its steel case, and put it in his pocket. The uniformed men, hitting their prisoners unnecessarily, marched them down from the truck, linked them together with a chain as they had with the others, and boarded them onto the plane. Jaime's eyes met his brother's in a look that was fleeting but intense, a look that, being the last, seemed to him to be the first. In that moment he realized that they had never really laid eyes on each other's faces, prisoners as they were of aggression and pride: Jaime with a mortal fear of sodomy, Benjamín guilty for his lack of virility. Now, finally eye-to-eye, an immense affection issued forth. . . . Jaime, realizing his respect for his brother's bravery, his authenticity, his dignity, had to hold back his sobs.

†

When the plane disappeared behind the hills, the soldiers set off back to the capital, making S's with the truck. Like an emanation from the scorched ground, a dense silence inundated the landscape. With the monkey settled safely on his head and munching away at false nits, Jaime descended toward Tocopilla. Through Benjamín's veins flowed the same blood as Jaime's, and maybe that was why the animal had gone to such lengths to find him. . . . He handed

Basilio off to Baltra and, not waiting for the master's hand to be bitten yet again, he went to the port. There he hired Don León, owner of a diving suit, and, in his boat that was equipped for just such tasks, they set out to sea. After searching in circles for a long time, the boatman pointed toward a yellow spot. Jaime recognized the transvestite's blond wig!

Encased inside a diving suit and receiving oxygen Don León sent through a hose, Jaime descended through the vast ocean, not expecting to touch bottom. . . . Luckily, they were still near the coast and it wasn't as deep as he'd feared. Soon, an immense dance appeared before his eyes. In that marine cemetery there were at least a thousand cadavers. All with their feet imprisoned by a weight, floating vertically, swaying slowly, in pairs, in trios, in groups. My father thought he could hear the music that he'd heard before on the radio, the sad Sibelius waltz. The groups of multicolored fish reminded him of the flames of old lamps, and the treelike seaweed, columns of a royal palace. The dead were not decayed; pale, yes. Their paleness gave them the look of sleepwalking princes. . . . Jaime moved among the lines of dancers, searching for his brother. In the midst of the brilliant misses, whose sequins attracted clouds of little sardines that came to float motionlessly around them like hummingbirds sipping from giant flowers, there was Benjamín, dreaming, tranquil, finally in the unreal world that befit him. An octopus resting on his bald head let its eight tentacles undulate, giving him a violent mane. Jaime desisted from rescuing his brother to give him a normal burial; he only searched his pockets to extract the metal box.

Back on the dock, as soon as he emerged from the diving suit, he took out the notebook and began to read:

"Jaime, dear brother, my mirror: do not fear poetry. She, who is pure love, transgresses prohibitions and dares to look head-on at the invisible. The poet descends, like Orpheus into the fires of hell, into the depths of language to recover his soul. Thanks to the miracle of your appearance—the Muses wished for you to be our witness—I want to give you my portrait, that of a poet foreign to virtue, reputation, law; without name or age, nation, race, or history; pilgrim in the abominable enchantment of shapes, messenger of the essential—that is to say, of himself—disdaining the illusions of thought, making all paths his. Dry leaf that in a sigh of time comes to grant hope to the bonfires, he is the fire burning in the center of the mind. Who could define him? With his red feet he erases all boundaries. He does not seal himself off, he does not hide, he does not flee; like the clouds, ceaselessly he transforms himself. He runs from words because they are only memory, yet his silence sustains them. He is the content that escapes forms, the land where the stars germinate, the true, unspeakable root of beauty, the resplendence that betrays his invisible action, adding the insanity of the unthinkable to the object that hides every name and to the name that hides every object. He is the flight before the birth of the bird, the celestial chorus of the worms already inscribed in the body being born, the fall that gives meaning to the wall, the kiss that brings all lips into being. He goes to the essential, to the center of the world and from there . . ."

†

With feverish fingers, Jaime flipped through the pages in search of one more phrase, a word, a sign, something that would help him better understand the truncated message. Nothing! He felt the notebook burning his hands. It was a relic he had stolen. If Benjamín had truly wished to give it to him, he would have sent it with the monkey. No, that Jaime-mirror was not him! The poet, inventing a brother capable of understanding such language, had sent a message to himself! He, Jaime, flesh and blood, in no way wanted, or should, or could escape the limits of "real reality": in his world, political in essence, matter was queen.

He wanted to throw the box into the ocean, but an immense sorrow stayed his hand, as well as a strange feeling of responsibility and a secret wish to someday understand the posthumous writing. . . . As if he were fooling invisible witnesses, he stashed the notebook and threw the metallic case into the sea. . . . His hatred for Coronel Ibáñez grew until it turned his blood to acid.

✝

He reached Ukraine House brooding on his desire to set every police station in the country on fire. While Sara Felicidad sprayed water over the cement floor—a material that brought him the painful and appalling memory of the landing strip—the radio talked incessantly about the power of those to whom Ibáñez had sold out:

"Mr. Ford's car factory triumphs! Its annual production has gone from five hundred thousand vehicles in 1914 to five million in 1928! Our president applauds this giant of industry and wants Chile to open up to foreign capital, so that we too can produce more with less effort. . . ."

Jaime leapt over the counter, determined to launch a yellow stream toward the cop's imperious voice. He opened the door to the bathroom and found a Jesus Christ urinating on the stinking radio. He was perfect, in every way like the illustration of a religious calendar. His sandals, his blue robe and red sash, his long hair and beard down to his chest, his good-dog eyes. . . . Without the least bit of modesty, he shook his appendage, lowered his tunic, spread his arms as wide as he could, and leapt at Jaime, encircling him in an embrace scented by two damp and hairy armpits.

"My brother: your wife is as pure as my sainted mother the Virgin Mary Chamudez. I, her miracle child, am Jesus Chamudez, the Christ of Chañaral. I have come to these arid lands because my Father, and yours, who art in heaven, conferred unto me the sacred mission of turning them into the mirror of the Edenic Gardens. Yes, dear brother, here fructiferous waters will fall, the hills will turn green, and in their trees will live millions of canaries that never cease to warble in praise of God! The concert of my birds will be heard throughout the Americas, and that song will make the hearts of men flower, so that they can finally cease to be evil and will follow the paths that their divine savior—yours truly—shows them! Today they laugh at me; tomorrow they will build for me, out of eggshells, the grandest cathedral that has ever been seen! This I promise you, child of my soul!"

"But, Sara Felicidad, where did you find this madman?"

My mother fell to her knees and pressed her hands together in prayer as she emitted sweet, clear, fragrant sounds that Jaime translated like so:

"For once, accept that the universe is for us a generous cradle. Every day, the Creator sends nourishment for our helpless son. Only a miracle can nourish a soul that fasts in the garbage heap men have created in place of the marvelous garden God granted us. In this perverted world, where everyone demands or takes and no one gives, as demented as it seems to you, a saint filled with love has arisen. What does his tattered appearance matter, or his naive words: he is a messenger of the miracle, he brings us hope, he shows us the way! Jaime, the hour of the Jesus Christs has come! One will appear in every town! Very soon we will see file past, instead of sinister armies, interminable ranks of prophets again fulfilling the sacred duty to fertilize the earth!"

Jaime wanted to throw out the clown with the same fury with which he'd expelled the Rabbi, but, enchanted as always by his wife's voice, he kept quiet. . . . Jesus Christ's canine gaze filled with fire; he lowered his voice to more guttural tones and began a vibrant oration:

"You need not say a word to me, my son. With your eyes full of the scum that plagues the world you cannot see me, but your wife can. Trust in her because her pupils are clear. Have you realized she is an angel? Her mouth, a celestial trumpet, gives life to the dead. With her song she will announce my coming, leveling all paths. She shall be my spiritual wife. . . ."

A flat *la* from Sara Felicidad rang out like an amen. Jaime's jealousy colored the store red.

"My wife will go with you, you say? She's your spiritual wife, you say? I'm going to smash your face in, you cretinous clown!"

Jesus Christ smiled, showing an incisor covered in silver, and he raised his right hand in a soothing gesture.

"Peace, brother man! My Father sent this woman from heaven for you! The two of you are one. If you do not believe in me, she cannot follow me. You must come together. And so, to vanquish your incredulity, I shall now work some miracles."

Sara Felicidad, widening her large blue eyes, nodded. Jaime stifled a mocking peal of laughter.

"All right, Señor Lord Jesus Christ! Work a miracle in front of me and we will follow you to the end of the world!"

"I didn't say one, I said some! They are various, the wonders you shall shortly see! With the help of the Father, the Son can do all! I am going to levitate! Watch!"

And the bearded man, slowly, bent a knee and lifted his left leg, keeping the sole of his foot parallel to the floor, and waved his arms in an undulating motion.

"You see, dear brother? My body is floating in the air; nothing holds it up!"

"You call that levitating? And your right foot, what's it doing still on the ground?"

"My Father wants me never to abandon my brothers, not for an instant. That is the blessed reason for which, though the rest of my organism is floating in the air, I must keep one foot stuck fast to the earth. Do not worry about the details; if you have eyes to see, look, and be amazed!"

On my mother's white face appeared the pink shades of a sunrise. She moved closer to my father, leaned toward one of his ears, and poured a melody into it that seemed to come from the depths of the centuries.

"Jaime, please, do not doubt. If he says that his body is weightless, it is because he feels it to be so, and that is enough. If all of us were to decide to feel light, life would be different. Pain and sadness are weight. The birds always sing because they know how to feel themselves to be lighter than air."

As if he knew the layout of Ukraine House, Jesus of Chañaral gestured for them to go outside with him to the small yard. They followed him. Basilio grabbed handfuls of dirt, and, shrieking with fury, he threw them at the Messiah.

"It's nothing," said the latter. "The adorable monkey, since he has no flowers, throws this offering of earth to me. All animals love me."

Without giving my father a chance to contradict him, he raised an index finger toward the heavens, where a considerable flock of seagulls over the nearby sea were monitoring a school of sardines that could soon run aground.

"Tell me, dear brother, how many of those hungry birds are flying up there?"

"They move constantly and there are many of them. How do you expect me to count them?"

"The divine gaze sees all: there are exactly two hundred and four seagulls! Now, look well!"

He raised his other index finger, made a cross with his hands, and sang out:

"I am not I, I am You, infinite Father! I open myself as a channel, send your torrent of love! Let it be! Amen!"

And embracing Jaime and Sara Felicidad, he let out jubilant cries.

"Praise God! From nothing, life has arisen! Now in the skies two hundred and five seagulls fly! I have performed the miracle of creating a bird with its beak, its feet, its little wings and feathers!"

Jaime, looking at Jesus Christ but addressing his entranced wife, clapped a hand to his forehead.

"A person would have to be as crazy as you and your mother to believe there's one more bird in that flock!"

Sara Felicidad, engulfed in her own sweetness, caressed my father's neck with a song.

"The primary attribute of a spiritual being is the power to identify the individual in a crowd of things. God has made no two things alike. Each ant is different, with its own character, physiognomy, feelings. Each grain of sand is different, every leaf on a tree, each square inch of land. Where you see a group of seagulls all alike, he can distinguish his, which has just appeared. And he can, for the same reason, see in each one of us human beings the difference God has given us, which is our signature, our treasure. Throughout ages of ages, there will be no one identical to you or to me. Thanks to that difference, we will be inscribed in eternity.... Ephemeral life is a rushing river that we must cross in a solid boat. He is that boat! If he helps me across the current, what does it matter whether he is a true Messiah or a madman?"

Jesus Christ burst into tears. He explained in stuttering words that he was not crying for himself, but for Jaime.

"The faithless man walks wrapped in a shroud, and his funeral is the world's. It is a great sorrow that a man with the soul of a hero makes of his every step a repudiation. Just to convince you, dear son, I shall disobey my Father. I am going to leave the ground entirely, and I'm going to fly in circles with my sister seagulls!"

He rolled up the sleeves of his robe and climbed onto the little garden's wall. Once at the highest point and balancing on the edge, he opened his arms, looked for a few seconds toward the heavens, and leapt. Plop! He fell belly-first to the ground! Amid the clouds of dust, letting out cries of pain that did not drown out Jaime's laughter, he moaned:

"You see, you naughty child? The Father has punished me. . . . He wanted me to break a rib or a bone in my leg. Your incredulity obliged me to sever my rootedness and abandon humanity for a second, and you see what happened. This punishment must prove to you the existence of the Creator. If God does not wish it, the saint cannot do it! Intone a hallelujah with your wife and carry me to the store so that I can lie down, pray, and mend my bones. I do not need doctors. I am my own medicine. . . ."

"Ribs or bones, my ass—you have broken nothing! You jumped from less than six feet and you fell onto soft ground! You're complaining to mask your failure, that's all!"

"Jaime, your Marxist ideas are keeping you from entering the dimension of miracles. This good man trusts in God; if there had been a deep abyss here, he would still have jumped. Respect him, because he is able to let faith and hope into his heart. The illusion of flight is worth as much as the flight itself. And it is worth as much as God, who guides us toward Him."

This time Sara Felicidad's vocal cords had produced hoarse, dark, harsh sounds. Jaime swallowed: it was the first time he had ever seen his companion angry. He bent down, lifted up the Messiah as if he were a beaten child, and went to deposit him faceup on the store's counter. To avoid curious onlookers, he lowered the metal shutter. In the gloom, the phosphorescent numbers of alarm clocks shone. All of them, unwound, pointed their long hands to the ten and their short hands to the two. Jesus Christ smiled beatifically:

"The ten is a one with the halo of the zero. The sainted unity, that is to say, me, Jesus Christ of Chañaral. The two is the receptive duality, both of you. The long hand, when the clock is wound, will move to cover the short one; it will transport the unity to the duality. This shows that if we are patient and believe in divine generosity, we will be married. The man and his wife, the bride; Jesus Christ, the husband. Please, go and return in ten hours! You will find me like new, with all of my bones in perfect condition! . . . Do not close the shutter, the brother of all should not be imprisoned. Leave it halfway down, without fearing for me: no thief will dare to bother the Son. The Father protects me with cherubim carrying burning swords. Go in peace! Use the night to meditate and return just after daybreak! An immense task awaits us! From my hands will fall rivers of seeds! I will sow the earth as well as souls! The two of you, my dear wife, will herald my arrival and help me to open the way!"

Jaime did not dare kick the madman's ass, as he would have liked to do. He growled a hypocritical "So shall it be, Master," and left with Sara Felicidad, turning bitterness to honey, to spend ten pleasure-filled hours in their iron bed. . . . Determined to demonstrate that his wife was very much his, swinging between the chords emerging from that beloved throat, intense and harmonious as those of a whale, he possessed her eight times in a row. Then he murmured a couple of phrases dictated by the Rabbi: "What I remember of myself is what you are. . . . I reach your shores like an invisible sea. . . ." And he collapsed, snoring.

At dawn, Sara Felicidad, adding her happy song to the roosters', woke Jaime. He got dressed and turned bitter as the coffee being poured in the kitchen when he saw two large backpacks, gravid to the point of bursting, announcing their definitive departure to follow the visionary.

"But, my little china doll, have you truly taken this clown's ravings seriously? Do you really want us to leave Tocopilla behind, only to lick the dust trodden by his hardly aromatic sandals? Don't tell me you've been bitten by the same bug he has!"

Sara Felicidad, without exhaling a single note, placed on his back one of the heavy backpacks. She took the other. Then, taking him by the hand and skipping happily, she dragged him to Ukraine House.

✝

They found the metal shutter entirely open. Inside, there was nothing left: no merchandise, no shelves, no counters. Everything had been taken. In the middle of the cement floor, a pile of fecal matter poisoned the air with its effluvia. From my mother's mouth flowed a long, violin *fa*. Fat Baltra came in wearing his pajamas to contribute to the sadness.

"I looked out the window, because it was after midnight and all the lights in Ukraine House were still on. I saw the bearded guy tossing back a bottle of aguardiente with a woman who was old but robust, perhaps his mother, and a young little thing with big tits and ass, surely his lover. When they started to load all the merchandise onto a truck, I knew I had to run and warn you, but, having also imbibed more than my share, I fell asleep. Forgive me, even with the best intentions, sometimes the body can't keep up!"

With all the lightness produced by the misfortune of others, the fat man returned to his Everything-for-Forty store. Under Jaime's severe gaze, Sara Felicidad—because they'd taken even the broom and dustpan—pulled a board from the patio wall and swept up the excrement, never ceasing to emit the long *fa* of a violin. Jaime, understanding what she wished to say, had to force himself to maintain his accusing gaze.

"More than blood, it is faith that keeps me alive. You, who lack that essential root of the soul, I can sustain with my immense belief. And by supporting you, I transform you into my structure. If you were not at my side, I would become a torrent, I would flow without boundaries until I was swallowed by the world! When that Jesus Christ appeared, I believed in him not as a god made flesh, but as a man who had developed within himself an overwhelming faith, capable of breaking through the obstacles built by human selfishness. Who can say what difference there is between a madman and a visionary? Both are capable of seeing the miracle—because miracles are not worked, they are accepted. Everything is a miracle: the smallest fly, the slightest pebble, every being that is born, every flower that wilts, every feeling, every desire, every spark of awareness, everything. All manifestation is a wonder. He who recognizes the miracle of the days and realizes that every instant is an unprecedented gift loses the desire to destroy, to separate, to rise up in a single reality, an armored island floating in the middle of the void, and instead he wants to sow, to share, to cultivate the thirsty earth into the garden that he holds inside. . . . What hurts me is how this swindler discovered that in a dark corner of their hearts, human beings hold the hope of the paradise to come, an anticipation that allows them to bear the yoke of this lie called 'reality,' and he goes around taking advantage of such a beautiful sentiment. Instead of sowing hope, he sows disillusion! I don't suffer for us, Jaime, because united as we are, we will always survive. I suffer for the weak people, in families or couples but alone, the ones whose faith he will destroy when he extracts their very last cent, desiccating their souls. And when souls wither, the earth becomes a darkened wasteland!"

†

Before Jaime could say a single word, the radio—which the thief had surely disdained because of its stench, leaving it on in the toilet—began to declaim the first news of the morning.

"The Chuquicamata deposit, mined by the North American company Grugenstein, produced eight million tons of copper in the year that has just ended! Their miners are the best-paid in Chile; they are given houses, good food, optimal pay. Much is the metal and too few the arms to extract it. You—what are you waiting for, citizen? Copper is calling you!"

Grumbling, Jaime went to the toilet, urinated on the radio, and came back to stand annoyed before Sara Felicidad, as though trying to stop the passage of Time; after a dense minute, he kissed her hands with trembling lips.

"My swan, our child will be born within seven months, and we have no merchandise and not a single peso saved. I've decided to go and earn money in the mines! Right now, I'll go and board the bus that's leaving for Antofagasta! From there I'll take the train to Chuquicamata! I will send you money, and I'll return once you've given birth. I promise!"

Sara Felicidad emitted not a single note. She closed Ukraine House and ran behind Jaime like a white shadow. Wherever her man went, she would go—period! . . . My father, without turning his head, hearing the light footsteps of those big white feet behind him, smiled in satisfaction. His wife had understood the lesson: better a husband in the hand than a thousand flying Jesus Christs!

TWO

THE EMPRESS
OF CHUQUICAMATA

O N THE TRAIN PLATFORM, as he ate nuts his wife cracked
between her molars, Jaime was still smiling. Of course, he
knew full well that the man everyone called the Hook was
a vulture disguised as a dove; but he knew that some people
get a break when they're born and others are born broken, to
him, who always spat upward and was sure he wouldn't be hit
in the face, the aforementioned character seemed inoffensive.
Sara Felicidad, on the other hand, sadly observed the herd of
hooked sheep who, with mouths stinking of wine, stumbled
into the cargo wagons waiting for them. The Hook, with the
help of a lot of lip service and alcohol extravagantly splashed
around, had separated them from their miserable farms, their
forests, from the rain and fog of the south, and brought them
northward by ship to Antofagasta, and from there, they were
crammed into trucks and driven to the station—men, women,
and scrawny children, all drunk, weighted down with mattresses,
chairs, sleeping bags, caged cats. There was no part of that fraud
not designed to obfuscate: the wide smile, the cocked hat, his
gold tooth, patent leather shoes, thick wristwatch, the wad of
bills in his pants pocket, his thundering voice.

"The Grugenstein Company awaits you with open arms, friends! Here: have another bottle per head and half an empanada! We will travel nonstop in our express convoy, all day and nearly all night. You will see how lovely these lands are, and lovelier than the land, the mine. There, the women wear silk and look like princesses. The men fill barrels with the dollars they earn, because their salaries, in spite of the light work, are better than the ones in California during the gold rush. Those Yankee bosses are the best! They'll even welcome you with a band!"

Sara Felicidad realized that inside the Hook was hidden a resentful man, a dupe who duped others so he wouldn't be the only one to suffer. With a deep arpeggio she pointed to the scar from a knife slash that marked the charlatan's face.

"Someone has given him what he deserves for his lies!"

"You're wrong, my dearest one, not all men are tin-pot Messiahs! This gentleman is excessive, agreed, his smile is insincere, also agreed, but he tells the truth: Chuquicamata holds millions and millions of tons of copper, and its miners are the richest in Chile. He has to act like that because when it comes to the *huasos* from the south, to get them to leave their rainy lands and come to the desert to do the work that's good for them, you have to impress them. A hook's job is to dazzle, to enthuse, to use siren songs to extract the jobless from their rat traps. Just like lies, the truth needs charlatans, because if they don't extol it, no one notices it!"

†

They were about to get into the cargo wagons where, huddled in a mass on the floor, future miners were draining their bottles, when the Hook took them by the elbows and murmured with lascivious complicity:

"Friends, these flea-traps are for the dark-skinned, the *blackies* as my bosses say. Whites go in the first car. That's all there is to it!"

In the spacious car with leather-covered seats, with her feet up on the backrest ahead of her, there was only one passenger, asleep. She was a girl with curly red hair, freckled skin, white canvas boots, riding pants, a khaki shirt, and thick eyeglasses. . . . Sara Felicidad, gentle as she was, sang a tune of deep notes.

"See, Jaime? Injustice is vast! All this empty space makes me sad. There are mothers nursing children. They, at the very least . . ."

Jaime, excising from his mind the idea that if you give a bum an inch he'll take a mile, went to the door intending to offer the luxurious car to the women, but no matter how he struggled with the latch, it wouldn't open. The Hook made a sign to the engineer, listened contentedly to the whistle that announced departure, and, with a mocking face and an indecent gesture, waved goodbye to the train. Sara Felicidad emitted a fluted wail and pressed her cheek against Jaime's head. Jaime buried his nose between her enormous breasts.

"Those poor souls are heartier than mules. Don't worry, my swan. You'll see how delightful our trip will be. You're going to love it, I promise."

†

At seven in the morning the sun was already punishing the sterile earth, inducing an asphyxiating heat. The metal worm, whistling, shaking, coughing, started off to skirt the hills and pass through the Carmen Salt Flat, then climbed with agonizing slowness across the Eastern Range and moved deeper into the Atacama Desert. The air became nearly unbreathable. All around them they saw sand and more sand, scattered with rocks beaten by the tireless whip of the wind. There was no tree in sight that could offer the green of its foliage, no stunted weed or living animal. No birds flew in the torrid sky, no streams wound their way, no smoke rose from any ranch. Only dust, crags, loose stones and gravel, and, here and there in the distance, a ditch full of round pebbles, silent testament to long-ago waterways. Over the whole vista, one could feel the thirsty waiting for a rain that would never come.

Hot blasts buffeted the cars, dragging clouds of dust that filtered in through the vents and covered the floor and the seats with an auburn layer, invading eyes, ears, noses, permeating clothes, infiltrating the insides of their bodies, irritating, suffocating. Jaime lowered the window for a second to launch a gob of muddied spit toward the horizon.

"You were right, Sara Felicidad! If these are the beautiful lands the Hook promised, he's a liar!"

Sara Felicidad rested her blue eyes on Jaime with an expression that warned of a nascent rebellion. Sensible as he was, Jaime had also let himself be hoodwinked. Now they were tied: a Jesus Christ on one side, a Hook on the other. His airs of the superior male were now unbearable! She was going to have to knock him down off that pedestal. . . . Luckily, the redheaded girl came over to them fanning herself with her explorer's hat and dissipated the tension. After two curtsies she gave free rein to her tongue, disguising a marked American accent:

"Excuse my indiscretion. I heard what the gentleman said, and if you'll allow me, I'd like to reply. It is true that the Hook lied, because to him these desert sands are indeed ugly, aggressive, deadly; but to me, a geologist, this is one of the most beautiful regions of the world. Those expanses that seem parched are really enormous deposits of copper. Just scratch around a bit and you'll find all kinds: variegated, indigo, arsenical, panaceic, selenic, sulfuric, vanadatado, frothy. And there, in those ranges of low hills, if you pay attention, you'll see the green of the brocatinta and the atacamita blend with the intense blue of the chalcantina. Nuances that combine with the yellow and red stains from iron, and among them you discover the sky-blue kroehnkite and the greenish-white coquimbite.... Don't be shocked when I tell you that these regions are not dry. Copper is the solid water that irrigates their insides!"

†

The girl's admiration for those shrouds of sand was contagious in its intensity. Jaime and Sara Felicidad carried it tattooed in their genes that one's relationship with land was essentially painful: it was always desired but never possessed. And if they felt good living in the north of Chile, it was because among those dunes, beaches, and unwelcoming rocks, they ran no risk of falling in love with a garden from which sooner or later they would be expelled. To discover beauty in the desert was to turn poverty into wealth. They realized that this desolate expanse that forbade any roots could well be the homeland of their nomad souls.... The sun was already setting, the wind was dying down, the sand was still like a lake of blood. With the last crepuscular light, the opaque outlines of the rocks and mountains stood out clearly against the steel-gray sky that changed its shading from one instant to the next, from sea green and purple to livid black. The myriad stars began to spill their intense light. With no clouds, no vapor emanations, not even the slightest fog, nothing existed between the sky and the sand but a thin atmospheric layer whose transparent and lucid rarefaction increased the splendor of the nighttime jewels.... Smiling with the same beatitude as the redhead, Jaime and Sara Felicidad found themselves suddenly immersed in a wonderful world.

†

As the minutes went by, the ground lost the heat that had accumulated under the torrid inclemency of the diurnal star, while gently, and then with rage, a cold wind began to blow that was as biting as the dust that had preceded it. It filtered into the train car and drove its icy needles into their bones. My future parents, benumbed, began to shiver. Sara Felicidad, shrugging her shoulders in resignation (she knew very well that every land, sooner or later, responded to her love with aggression), opened a small bundle and took out the four hard-boiled eggs that calmed her and Jaime's hunger every night. The redheaded girl, also shivering, directed an angelic smile at them. Immediately, my mother peeled an egg, sprinkled it with salt, and offered it to her. My father did the same. The girl protested, moved:

"Now I have two and you have one each!"

"It's better for you to have more than us, miss. I couldn't bear, under these circumstances, to feed myself better than my wife, and she, I am sure, could not bear to out-eat me either. . . . Moreover, the most basic courtesy obliges us not to leave you with an empty stomach. And do not propose to split an egg into three, because given its shape it is impossible to divide it into three equal parts! And if they were not equal we'd be committing. . ."

The girl interrupted him, bursting into laughter.

"A sin? How wonderful! It's like listening to a passage from the Talmud!"

She ran to the back of the car, opened a cardboard box that was traveling in the shadows, and extracted a blanket made of fine wool. She also took out two sausages, some apples, black bread, smoked salmon, cans of sardines, a thermos of hot coffee, and a bottle of whiskey.

"You two *are* Jewish, right?"

Jaime, annoyed as always at being what he was until death, grumbled:

"Jewish-Chilean, miss!"

The redhead, happy, clapped her hands. Then, turning serious, she declared:

"I cannot call you compatriots because we have no homeland, but allow me to consider you my friends. You shared with me the little that you have; now, please, share in my abundance as well. The mine's superintendents think I have the appetite of an ogre. . . ."

"But, why . . ." replied Jaime with his mouth watering, "do you receive so many gifts?"

"Because Chuquicamata is mine! I'm Rubi Grugenstein, the granddaughter of Fritz Grugenstein, the man who bought the copper mine in 1905. . . ."

Jaime whispered into Sara Felicidad's white ear:

"Things travel in threes! First the swindler, then a fraud, and now a mythomaniac. But by now we are cured of fear, my swan. Rather than reject her, we will play along. Her provisions seem first rate!"

Jaime flashed a smile as false as a doll's.

"If my companion and I, humble miners, can be of any service to you, you have only to give the order!"

"Oh, my friends! From the moment I saw you, I knew that you are honest and good Jews! You deserve to be more than laborers! I don't know anyone in the mine and Fritz advised me to trust no one. I want you to help me undertake the immense task that awaits me. I will get you salaries as private secretaries. Will you accept?"

Jaime, caressing the sausages and the black bread, blubbered, "But of course, miss, count on us one thousand percent!" Sara Felicidad blushed in shame.

†

The cold, ever more intense, obliged them to empty the bottle of whiskey and huddle beneath the blanket. Jaime, cautious—an erection can arise from even the most sainted pelvis—placed his wife between him and the redhead. The two women were asleep before long, but he, restless from the females' emanations, didn't shut his eyes for hours. . . . The contours of the Loa appeared, a ditch putting on the airs of a river, and soon the train began to cut through the middle of Calama, that hamlet disguised as a great city but unfit to house a thousand souls. Half of its homes were shacks converted into brothels. Jaime didn't wake his wife or the mythomaniac as his eyes, irritated from sleeplessness, received the impact of hundreds of blinking red lights. Strumming guitars! Dancing, stomping feet! Couples rubbing together shamelessly, suffocating smells of bitter wine, beer, urine, the clicking of dice, steel balls scraping the numbers on old roulette wheels, coughs, shouts, breaking bottles, crying children, stone-faced women kneeling in the doorways of bars awaiting their men, clay virgins and lit candles on diminutive graves along the tracks! . . . With no barriers, the train moved down the middle of the street at a snail's pace, letting out continuous whistles to shoo away the inebriated miners who stopped in front of it, fists clenched, challenging it to a one-on-one battle. The poisonous drink made them feel invincible. The locomotive, gaining ground inch by inch, pushed them until they fell to one side to snore in the dust while a pack of ragged children stole their clothes. Groups of prostitutes ran alongside the cars, inside which the new miners crowded together to look out, flicking their tongues with vertiginous speed. Behind them came gelled ruffians yelling at the top of their lungs to extol the virtues of the mouths, anuses, and vaginas of their girls.

"It must be payday," murmured Jaime. "I know these poor men—they work like animals all week long and in a single night run through their entire salary! They don't know how to save because they live without a tomorrow: if they can't overcome, why bother fighting? Better to surrender it all to wine, drugs, gambling, and whores!"

When the train crossed the limits of that one-horse town, from the darkness emerged a company of disabled miners who, wielding the stumps of their arms and legs, their deformed faces, and dented skulls, ran or dragged themselves alongside the train, pleading for cigarettes, bread, drink.

The locomotive gave a final whistle and launched full-speed toward its final destination. Far off, intermittently, the black hulk of a mountain was illuminated. Chuquicamata! The immense smoke-stacks of its foundry threw up mouthfuls of thick smoke and fiery tongues of blue, green, garnet. The buildings of the metal shop and other facilities spilled light from every window. The whole image looked like a swarm of giant fireflies. Fascinated by the spectacle, Jaime woke the two women. The redhead began to crow:

"Oh, it's the enchanted palace I've dreamed of since I was a girl! There a golden prince lived, waiting for his silver princess! There are peacocks spreading crystal fans, spheres of light that taste like honey, riverbeds over which spin tiny comets, one-eyed cats with diamonds in their sockets, orchids that can imitate the songs of birds, and sainted hearts that float in the air and give off splendid rays!"

"Not only is she a mythomaniac, she's also slow in the head," Jaime whispered to Sara Felicidad. She, captive to a strange premonition, replied with a funereal chord as her nose began to bleed. They were eight thousand nine hundred feet above sea level.

†

Abruptly, some three miles from the mine, the train tracks came to an end and the train stopped in the middle of the desert. Dawn began to break and the hills, red as the clouds, seemed like a tribe of millenary giants traveling through time to reach the promised instant, when the universe dissolves in the original moment. (That point of origin was the Rabbi's goal. When I asked him to describe it, he replied: "Impossible! That secret brooks no spectator; it is the first thought of God—blessed be his name—which no one can understand or conceive of; it is the elusive, limpid Inner Air that contains, in the form of loving will, the essences, the causes, the core, the things that were and those that will be. It is the bellybutton where all is created and all is consumed. To go there is to return to yourself, to lose your personal roots, ideas, feelings, desires, your memory. It is to drown in the primordial manifestation and become the void—that is, hope.") Trailing wakes of violet dust, four trucks pulled up, then two cars and a bus full of police. Enrique Jaramillo, an officer with a face pocked by scars, a blunt nose, jumpy eyes, and a mustache that hid his mouth, barked orders to organize the unloading of the southerners. When the cops opened the doors of the train cars, a smell of excrement and vomit wiped out the salty perfume of arsenic. The people staggered out, craning their necks to see over the policemen's caps and catch a glimpse of the promised brass band. They caught only the deaf melody of rifle butts, and Jaramillo's voice furiously intoning:

"You stinking yokels! You were hooked because you wanted to be! Here you won't spend the day scratching your balls! You'll be required to work eight hours straight, no little breaks for wine or empanadas, and you'll piss and shit right where you are, at the foot of the mine! Anyone who steals or makes any political noise will get this gun of mine up his ass! Don't get the idea you'll start out making twenty pesos; never mind what the Hook said, the salary is seven pesos! And if you don't like it, get going now, on foot! No one's going to take you back for free! And starting now, get it through your thick skulls that you didn't come here to sow wheat or any other plant: you'll have to be mechanics, oil gears, put your shoulders to the electric shovel, break rocks and stones, straighten out any crooked teeth on the crane that loads the conveyor belt, and, if you're not faggots, drive the locomotives! Know that my guard dogs have orders to kill any communists who try to stir things up in the barnyard! My words may be harsh, but hunger is harsher! Who's going? Who's staying? Choose now, motherfuckers!"

They had fallen into the trap: it would be suicide to try to travel one hundred and eighty desert miles on foot. With bovine resignation, the workers piled into the trucks. The officer and his men returned to the bus, and with the four overloaded vehicles following them, they moved off toward the camp.... The redhead, seeking support in the arms of Jaime and Sara Felicidad, observed the whole scene with the anguished face of one whose dream is becoming a nightmare. The violet wake expanded, covering everything. There followed a silence so intense it was like a wail. Jaime murmured:

"Sons of the damned bitch who fornicated with Ibáñez! Thanks to that dictator, any cretin in a uniform thinks he's master of the world! I will not let them treat us like this! My wife and I will return on foot, even if the desert consumes our bones! Without dignity, life is not worth living! And you, little girl, trade in that blanket and all the supplies you have left for a train ticket: you won't fool anyone here. They'll exploit you body and soul until you end up a whore in a Calama cabaret. If you like, I'll go with you to the station."

Sara Felicidad placed a protective arm around the girl, but she, shaking her head, pulled away, walked a few steps ahead and defiantly planted herself in the road with her feet wide apart and her hands on her hips. . . . When the dust raised by the bus and the four trucks returned to the ground, the doors of the two cars opened. First to get out, wrapped in a meticulous cashmere suit, was a blonde American man, short-waisted, long-legged, with hairy hands and a lower jaw that took up half his face. Attached to his left elbow and carrying a fox terrier, there followed a dark girl, short in stature, wearing a long dress; she was plump, full-mouthed, with dyed yellow hair, ringed fingers, and a diamond medallion hiding the deep furrow between her inflated breasts. With thick alcoholic breath, the gringo introduced himself as Robert Pinkel, superintendent, and his companion as Loretta Selkirk de Pinkel, his wife.

Loretta Selkirk de Pinkel! Jaime bit his lips to keep from bursting out laughing. The woman was none other than Perricholi, a stripper he'd seen perform in the bar The Lying Parrot in Iquique! She came onstage dressed like a decent woman, but undulated lasciviously to the rhythm of an eastern melody. When the drunks started to shout "Fur! Fur!" the fox terrier came out and began to fornicate with her leg. Offended, the woman kicked the lewd animal away from her, launching him offstage. The dog burst back onstage growling, then bit her dress and yanked it off with one tug, leaving her in her underwear. Then she started dancing like a snake in heat. The animal returned to the fray, pulling off her bra, her garter belt, her drawers, he got between her legs and pursued her relentlessly with his tongue. The female writhed in pleasure, groaning so salaciously that even those depraved spectators turned red in shame. Finally, on hands and knees, she let the animal possess her. The audience, excited, waving bills, lined up to take the dog's place. The night Jaime had seen Perricholi's performance, one hundred and ten had visited her, barking and growling.

†

From the second car emerged Jacobo Rentzel, general manager, Bronx Jew, dressed all in black like a rabbi. He was followed by Óscar Hidalgo, copper inspector, a Chilean with a limp, a sugary smile, dyed-blond hair, false American accent, and lizard eyes. . . . They all approached the redhead, bobbing their heads and bowing repeatedly.

"Welcome to Chuquicamata, patroness! It is a great honor for the granddaughter of Fritz Grugenstein himself to come work with us! We will do the impossible to make your stay here pleasant, Miss Rubi!"

What's that? So she wasn't a delusional mythomaniac? They'd traveled with the granddaughter of one of the world's richest men? Jaime almost drooled in surprise. Sara Felicidad recovered her oboe voice.

"You see? There are many miracle threads in the weave of reality. . . ."

Rubi, very seriously and holding back her disgust, introduced my father and mother as her private secretaries. Then she said to Rentzel:

"You sir, Jacobo, who seem to observe our religion, do you consider the treatment of those workers humane?"

The general manager replied in a nasal voice:

"We are here to achieve the maximum copper production at the minimum cost. The rest is not our problem. Lieutenant Jaramillo has a deep understanding of the idiosyncrasies of the Chilean blackies, who are far from saints. We are absolutely certain that his methods are appropriate: if you don't tighten the reins on a disobedient horse, it'll tear up the ranch with its kicks! I beg you, miss, with all due respect, refrain from judgment until later and for now, come with us to the mine. In a few minutes we're going to blow up a hill."

"Blow up a hill? Isn't the mine a cavern?"

"Not at all, Miss Grugenstein! Our Company's system is not to make holes, but to dynamite hills!"

†

While Pinkel's car, stinking of whiskey, carried them toward the explosion, and the cruel morning sun dried the nighttime dew, Rubi brought Jaime's head close to Sara Felicidad's and murmured very softly in their ears, so the superintendent and his proud slattern wouldn't hear her:

"It's criminal to destroy a hill. . . . How can they not realize that? The hills are ancient, sacred. They were the first to emerge from the chaos when the infinite spirit blew over the primordial waters, driving them to accumulate in one place so that dry land would be uncovered. They were born before plants or animals. Witnesses to the creation of the world, they are here to remind us of the moment when life began to separate itself from the muck, to pass from shapeless magma to consciousness. They teach us about immutability in the face of catastrophe, about the persistence of being despite the nothing that stalks us. They invite us to lift ourselves up toward our goal: infinite space. Only in their peaks can we comprehend the divine that carries us and transfigures us, and thus understand eternity. What sacrilege to tear them down!"

†

So, not only was she not a mythomaniac, she wasn't dumb, either. Jaime went from one surprise to another. The way the girl exalted the landscape that to him had only seemed dead made him aware that, because he was the son of nomads, he had always fought for the realization of man and abstracted the terrain: it was like trying to get quality wine from earthless grapes growing in the air. . . .

They stopped in front of a magnificent mountain that under the beating sun seemed surrounded by a multicolored aura. The redhead's belly shuddered as if that promontory martyr were a child that filled her insides. Workers were finishing the task of drilling a vertical hole from the peak to the center of its base and a horizontal tunnel along the ground, opening on the side facing the sun and meeting the other orifice inside. Through the horizontal excavation, little cars moved along rails carrying the dynamite that would be used in the explosion. In the union of the two galleries, five walls formed a star. There, a swarm of somber men laboriously piled up the enormous quantity of explosives.

Rubi, accompanied by some sad arpeggios from Sara Felicidad, murmured:

"They are betraying the ancient dreams of humanity! Instead of ascending to populate the cosmos, out of greed they transform their lofty destiny into a fallen star!"

An electrical current sparked the immolation. The hill collapsed as if a powerful hidden hand pushed it from its base. And like a fruit that implodes on itself when it ripens, it opened up from its root. There was no sound, but the ground shook with an earthquake. From the open crack rose a tongue of dust that, unmoving, took the shape of an immense crucified lamb in the air. What had been a colossus now lay in ruin, rubble, viscera of bloodied earth that the long transport convoys would have to swallow.

"Now, miss, you'll see the giant shovels attack!" said Jacobo Rentzel.

"Made entirely in the United States!" added the cripple Hidalgo proudly, intensifying his American accent.

†

Ten tremendous locomotives advanced on rails, with steam engines, smokestacks, and gas tanks. On the upper level groaned the scoop, a maw made of steel set with long, sharp teeth; it moved forward, turned left and right, dug into the remains of the hill, each time swallowing almost two tons of copper spoils.

The slave gang tending each contraption was made up of a machinist, a stoker, and eight workers who moved ahead to soften the earth with large, sharp spikes, pull down the crags that had been left half-fallen, break up clods, and prepare for the explosion of layers of hard material, perforating them with drill bits activated by compressed air.

"Our shovels devour hills twenty-four hours a day. Three eight-hour shifts, one after the other, with the workers taking turns. The mine never rests, never sleeps. . . ."

Rubi was feeling ill, and with my parents beside her, she ran to sit down again in Pinkel's car, where the dark woman was caressing her dog, the windows rolled up to protect her from the dust. Rubi turned green, and though she covered her mouth with her freckled hands, she vomited a nauseating stream all over the fox terrier. Loretta's sycophantic smile turned into a vile grimace:

"Motherfucker, how disgusting! Bob, give me your shirt."

Obediently, the gringo took off his shirt. His torso bared, a pistol stuck into the waistband of his pants, he gulped liquid from a flat bottle that he pulled from his back pocket. While Jaime took a shoe and fanned the Grugenstein girl, whose apologies were racked by deep sobs, Sara Felicidad pressed her to her breast. Thanks to a knee from the superintendent, the coarse woman recovered her fabricated refinement, trilled "It's nothing, boss-lady, don't you worry!" and used the shirt to clean the vomit hardening on the canine fur. Then, she took a voluminous bottle of perfume from a leather case—Amour Amour by Patou—and drenched her beloved animal. The narcissus mixed with red currant, bergamot, jasmine, rose, and carnation became a bayonet. Jaime felt his nostrils being violated, sliced open, corroded, like they were going to explode. He opened the car door and got out anxiously to breathe in the dusty air. His wife and the redhead followed him. The dog leapt as though stung by a scorpion, ran toward the shovels with his tongue hanging out, and was lost amid the swarming workers. The woman flew toward the work site, shrieking:

"Romeo, come here! You fucking hayseeds, stop the machines! You'd better not crush him!"

Jacobo Rentzel rushed toward the shovels, blowing a whistle. The cripple Hidalgo followed behind him, still using a handkerchief to whip off the layer of red dust that his rabbi's suit attracted like flies to honey. The behemoths went still and the workers formed a jumbled circle of hot-blooded silhouettes around the animal. Screeching one last "Romeo!" the harpy elbowed her way through the crowd. She found her mutt digging desperately in a clod of earth. The feet of a mummy appeared! In a few seconds, the workers, blowing tubes of compressed air, uncovered an Indian of a bronzed race in a perfect state of conservation.

Mister Pinkel scratched his head and laid out his calculations:

"It's a miner buried in a landslide while he was working. The dry earth has conserved him like this. It's over four hundred years old, but it's not a real mummy. . . ."

Back in his mistress's arms, the dog shook his hide to rid himself of that smell that was so un-dog-like. She, to protect her eyes from the corrosive drops, let him go. Romeo, his maroon appendage on shameless display, ran to the Indian and began to hump one of its legs with rapid thrusts. . . .

The miners burst out laughing. The irate woman interrupted his lewd endeavor by kicking him through the air. After rolling over the gravel, he growled and launched himself at his mistress to bite the edge of her dress and pull on it with the intention of removing it. Hundreds of red shadows began to whistle the eastern melody that accompanied Perricholi's number. Not knowing what to do, she hugged the fox terrier and cried helplessly:

"Bob! . . ."

Robert Pinkel brandished his pistol in the air and spun around, taking aim at his blackies, who buried their mockery under a dense silence. After yelling a violent "Shit!" he unloaded all the bullets into the mummy, exploding first its head and then the rest of its body.

"Break time is over! Get the shovels working and take this garbage out of here!"

While the diggers started shoveling again, leaving not a crumb of the Indian behind, the American put an arm around his beloved, who was dripping eyeliner-colored tears onto the fox terrier's head, and led her toward the car. Rubi blocked their way.

"Mister Pinkel, stop the machines and leave me here alone! Get everyone out of here, and come back in two hours!"

"Miss Grugenstein! You want the mine to stop working? But how could you think of such a thing!"

"I *can* think of it, because this all belongs to me! Leave now, I don't want to hear another word!"

The hundreds of miners and their big shovels, the American and his libertine, the Jew and his sycophant, all wrapped in a thick layer of dust, moved off until they were out of sight.

Where had that girl, who seemed like an eccentric and inept gringa, found such strength? All on her own she'd been able to stop the mine for the first time in twenty years. Two motionless hours! Millions of pesos lost! For what? Jaime went back to his first theory:

"Millionaire she may be, but we're dealing with an idiot here! If she wants to stay here and let the sun burn her to a crisp, let her! We're going to the camp!"

My mother ignored him: she opened the umbrella the superintendent had lent her, and, shielding Rubi from the sun, she followed the girl as she began to wander around the gigantic amphitheater. Soon, assaulted by the burning rays, my father caught up with them to beg for a bit of shade. Without the swarm of workers on the giant steps of that destroyed mountain, the wind raised little red clouds that looked like desolate spectators waiting for a show that would never be staged.

"Look at this scene: what was once a mountain range is now sacked, pulverized, demolished! No tall peaks where mystery nests—now it's a ridiculous valley! When my grandfather sent me here, I expected something else. He has talked to me about copper with such admiration that I believed, naively, that our Company respected it. It's not about reaching the maximum production at a minimum cost! The metal is where it is because it fulfills a cosmic function. To deplete a mine is to strip the planet of its skeleton. But the employees are as blind as their master! Today they saw a king and they treated him like a beggar. That Indian was better conserved than an Egyptian mummy. In these lands there once existed a superior civilization: they knew that human beings don't bring their riches with them when they die, so they dressed the monarch in a humble cloth and buried him without jewels. They didn't give him a stone pyramid, but rather something even more sublime: a mountain of copper. And that barbarian, to save his whore from humiliation, shot bullets into that valuable relic and

43

ruined it! Madness! Even worse: on seeing this crime, none of the workers rebelled! They didn't consider the fact that this noble mummy embodies the ideal of their race! The misery and alcohol has made them lose their will! The hero no longer exists because his people have ceased to be! Still, nothing proves the truth of my vision. Is it possible that the sacred is a dream, that existence has no creator or meaning, that the unearthed man really is a miner, as miserable as those who uncovered him, and my faith just one more instance of insanity? If it is, I'd rather die! I need proof, a sign, something!"

†

Sara Felicidad was sorry she didn't have the words to tell that girl, so intelligent: "To think is to create and to create is to believe. Do not allow doubt into your soul, do not desert the reality you believe in, instill it; you can do it, this world is yours! Kneel down: if you pray with all your guts, illusion will become reality!" Jaime wanted to translate his wife's musical notes, but he didn't have time, because an intense buzzing sound cut off his words.

Skimming the sand, a golden beetle flew around the trio and landed on a dark stone. It started to push at a crack in a rock as if it wanted to enter. In that dry cauldron, the golden insect's appearance seemed like a supernatural occurrence. Where did it come from? How many miles had it traveled? What was it looking for? Food? And why inside a rock? Ruby murmured:

"It's living gold, metal that rose from the dense crust and flew. Is it the sign I've been waiting for?"

The beetle went on pushing at the stone. Sara Felicidad approached it. Emitting a chord of surprise, she picked up the false rock and ran to show it to Rubi. The golden animal was scrabbling in an ear! The mechanical shovels thought they'd devoured every fragment of the mummy, but they'd missed one!

My mother, with extreme delicacy, detached the beetle and launched it into the sky. It started to buzz around them, as if asking for a gift. The Grugenstein girl stuck her little finger into the narrow auditory canal the beetle had tried fruitlessly to enter. She extracted a little black stone carved in the shape of a drop. Her face shone.

"Like I said, he wasn't a simple miner crushed by an avalanche, he was the mummy of a king! The priests buried him, stripping him of his attributes of earthly power, but, as a distinctive sign of his royalty, they put in his ear this meteorite fragment, metaphor for the divine word that falls from the heavens and must return to them. Thus the spirit of the king, enclosed in petrified flesh, must return to his celestial homeland."

She gave the black drop to the beetle, which caught it in its legs and, lifting it higher and higher, disappeared in the shining sky. . . . The two women embraced. Amid that infernal heat, a shiver went up Jaime's spine. His metaphysical edifice, built on "real reality," creaked and threatened to collapse. He shook his head. "It was a dumb Indian crushed by an avalanche," he thought. "Some rocks must have gotten not only in his ears but also in his mouth, his eyes, his nose and the lower hole. Women want to be amazed by everything." Satisfied, he smiled.

†

As soon as the two hours had passed, the train brought back the crowd of workers. The sacking of the mountains immediately started up again. This time only one car came, driven by the cripple Hidalgo. In a precarious English, he said:

"My bosses have stayed to prepare the welcome party. They wait for us. You will see how beautiful is the camp, patroness!

45

Its lovely buildings are unique in the world. We have a hospital, a dance hall, a church, a school, and a military barracks for three hundred men. You will feel very much at home. And, of course, so will your personal secretaries."

With the foot of his shorter leg he made a figure eight in the sand and looked with cynical lust at Sara Felicidad, calculating the amount of pleasure all that flesh could give him. She hunched over as much as she could, trying to hide behind Jaime. That creep of an employee, with his mouth soaked in whiskey, arrogantly flaunting his dyed blond hair and imitating his bosses' brutal gestures, ashamed and contemptuous of his own Spanish language, made her sick.

Rubi's reply made her happy:

"I won't go with you, Mister Hidalgo. I'm less interested in official receptions than in direct contact with the workers' reality, with no suck-ups around. Introduce me to the miners."

†

Like a general reviewing soldiers, the queen of Chuquicamata looked the workers over one by one. Finally, she stopped before a man of a toasted brown color, with short, bowed legs, a narrow torso, muscular arms, and hair gone prematurely white.

"What's your name?"

"Eulogio Gutiérrez, Madame."

"How long have you worked in the mine?"

"In this solitude the time just disappears! Could be two years, could be four, I don't know. . . ."

"You have honest eyes. I want you to show me the camp. I want to see it as you do. We'll go in the train that carries the ore. . . ."

"The trip through the hills is hard, ma'am. The wagons for us, the miners, are open platforms with steel benches, and it will be very uncomfortable for you. Your whole body will hurt, you will swallow dust, the mosquitoes will bite you. . . ."

"That's my problem, not yours! Let's go!"

†

Jaime admired the girl's decision. Refusing to look through the eyes of her exploitative partners and see the truth of gold, she would know reality through the eyes of the exploited—the truth of bread. Still, he dolefully caressed Sara Felicidad's belly. He could bear the discomfort, but she was pregnant.

"Miss Rubi, can my wife go in the car? Her condition will not allow—"

A sustained *do*, followed by a brusque, flat *me*, cut off his words. Sara Felicidad was not about to get in the car alone with the lustful cripple or be separated from her man, and she ran to a wagon and lay down on one of the steel benches.

The cripple Hidalgo, bowing every which way he could, tugged at one of his boss's sleeves, led her to the car, and, whispering grimly, said:

"Don't believe in appearances, Miss Grugenstein; you can't trust Chileans. Before letting that man go with you, let me consult the red list."

He took a sweaty notebook from his pocket and paged through it to find the letter G.

"Just as I suspected! Here it is: Eulogio Gutiérrez. Not much is known about him. Seems that in the nitrate town at María Helena his wife and three sons were blown to bits by a dynamite explosion. He never talks about it, and he behaves like an exemplary worker, which is serious: his income matches his expenses, he has no debts, doesn't drink to excess, isn't a gambler, he's never been caught stealing, and he also knows how to read. He's sure to be a rabble-rouser! The first mistake he makes, he'll be beaten till his bones break!"

"But, how can you be so sure of that? Maybe he's just a good man . . ."

"Impossible, miss! The blackies aren't like that, they're full of vice. . . . The spy service makes very few mistakes. . . ."

"Spy service?"

"First-rate! We monitor the workers' private lives very closely. We know whether they sleep in their rooms; when they get drunk; who their regular companions are; what they talk about; what brothels they frequent in Calama; what illnesses they carry (there is a lot of syphilis in these parts). . . . Wherever they go, they have someone following behind them in a perfect disguise. . . . You can be proud of your company, Miss Grugenstein, there is no other that maintains such a severe surveillance service. Just say the word, and I can recommend one of our men, very reliable. . . ."

"Mr. Hidalgo, I'll keep what you have told me very much in mind, but I will stick with my decision: my personal secretaries and Eulogio Gutiérrez will be the ones to accompany me."

†

Like two silver snakes, the tracks went up, dipped down, and returned majestically to the heights of those mountain peaks tangled with bumps and knolls. The route for the narrow shortcut had been opened using sticks of dynamite. The broken rocks lay like dead animals; the fortitude of the hills looked humbled by the explosives' brutal cleaving. In the gorges shone a thousand vengeful eyes, points of crystallized rock, which reflected the sun's rays and transformed them into long daggers. One moved through there squinting one's eyes, covering the mouth and nose with a hand because the grit raised by the loaded cars wounded the nostrils, making them bleed. With the other arm one had to clutch the back of the steel bench; at every curve the car threatened to overturn. Eulogio dug into the mineral cargo and extracted a petrified snail.

"Look, ma'am, sometimes you find fossils in the hills! This whole region was underwater. . . . As you can see, if we let time run its course, what is below always makes its way to the top."

Rubi, unoffended by the worker's mordant smile, took four lemons from her backpack and handed them out. They sucked at them avidly; the acidic juice seemed sweet to them. Eulogio rubbed his face, hands, and clothes with the pulp.

"Do as I do. The smell of the lemon keeps the horseflies away. Soon we will go through the area where they're swarming, and their stingers can pierce clothing."

†

The flies arrived like a dun-colored cloud, emitting a steady drone that drowned out the train's muffled chugging. They formed a living fog that hid the tracks from view.

"Make an effort, masters, and try to see through the bugs. Observe the rocks. Can you see? They are all carved. Warriors, puma-men, snakes in condors' claws, hares devouring the moon, priest heads crowned by another head, as if the one below were controlled by a superior spirit! Before the Incas, the Paracas lived here. They had a method to soften the rock: they molded their sculptures by hand, obeying the rock's wishes. They believed that a spirit nested in each stone, and, thanks to the smoke of certain mushrooms, they were able to see it. They didn't sculpt to invent a new shape, but rather to guide the material's external appearance toward its inner reality. They brought out into the light what the rock carried within it. . . . Well, I'd better shut up: you, who come from a culture born in the cities, will think what I am telling you is delirium. . . ."

Jaime smiled, sarcastic.

"Or a pretty lie. Children see faces and bodies in the clouds, in stains, in the rocks. . . ."

But the redhead said, with sincere respect:

"Don Eulogio, what you are saying fits with what I surmised when I saw the mummy: a superior civilization lived here. This place is sacred."

A little before reaching the plant, the train stopped. Using a parallel branch, the locomotive went to the end of the convoy, and the cars began to be pushed instead of pulled. There was a bridge waiting for them, three hundred meters long and twelve high, whose many pillars were settled into deep concrete bases. They advanced along its narrow spine without a screw trembling, though each car with its load weighed seventy tons.

Two colossal machines, as high as the bridge, opened their hungry maws. The pieces of mountain were dumped into them and crushed to bits.

"These are the mills, ma'am."

Practically dancing, agile and silent men wearing masks affixed the car they were going to unload onto a dumper platform. As the mineral was emptied into the tremendous jaws, there rose a cloud of fine dust so dense that for moments at a time they couldn't see their hands. The workers stopped working and waited for the dry fog to dissipate.

"The task of the mills is complex, ma'am. Their action is split into several sectors, which are linked by conveyor belts, and they gradually reduce the rock to flour. . . ."

"I want us to see that process!"

"As you like, boss, but you'll all have to wear masks. . . ."

†

They were given little rubber trumpets filled with cotton soaked in water to cover part of their noses and mouths. Sara Felicidad returned the protective apparatus, and, without singing, she spoke normally for the first time:

"I cannot follow you. It would hurt my child. I'll wait for you here. . . ."

Jaime lost control of his jaw. With his mouth open and the look of a lost puppy, he stared at that stranger. A white giant who emitted musical notes instead of speaking was a regular part of his dreams, but a white giant who spoke like any other woman was a terrifying reality. He chose to follow Rubi. Maybe when they came out of the mill, the normal abnormality would have returned, and Sara Felicidad would once again be the musical angel of his dreams.

†

(After the tragic events gestating at that very moment had transpired, Jaime, now used to his wife's flat speech, was calm enough to listen to what she was feeling as she faced the crushers:

"Until that moment I had lived stuck to you as if your skin were mine; I lived like a ship adrift in the infinite ocean, saved from going astray by the north star that was you. I wanted your brightness to be not only my guide but also my goal. You lit the way and I, dark and rocked by the waves at the lowest level, needed to reach your heights, believing them, nevertheless, to be unreachable. In a world of caged beasts you were the only human being, and my eyes saw only you; and my ears, in the din of hollow voices, listened only to you; and my other senses, finding neither place nor answer, flowers rooted in death, only opened thanks to the insemination of your caresses. . . . The unconscious organism that moved in my belly was like a fish guzzling lymph in the shadowy sphere of an underwater grotto, at the edge of the visible, far from me.

Suddenly, without the slightest wriggling that would have warned me, before those two colossal monsters that unheedingly committed the infamy of devouring the earth, the spirit of my son came into being. For my consciousness, it was a cataclysm: everything I had thought I was broke into pieces, a hurricane carried off the pieces, and in a single second it changed me from lover to mother. What was it? How can I explain it to you so you'll understand? You are a man, doomed to see your life from within your life; you are, somehow, always central. I am a woman, and I see not only the life around me, but also, as though by miracle, I become a vessel and I understand the life of that which I am not, inside of me. I'm not talking about the fetus in its first months, when its vital drive is focused on reproducing cells and forming organs, a viscous animal growing like one more viscera, at times even taking on the characteristics of a tumor.... I'm talking about an instant when, in the impalpable wall that separates us from mystery, a door opens and a burning impulse brings over from a dimension impossible to imagine a complete human being, a soul in the totality of its time—that is, ancient—with a memory that reaches back to the explosion of the point that became a universe, and a yearning for the future that reaches toward the instant the cosmos will cease to expand and start to swallow itself; and moreover, the memory of the infinite number of times the process has repeated; and further still, the supreme instant when the individual drop separates from the divine ocean and is launched on the path of countless deaths and resurrections; that total consciousness suddenly made a nest in my belly, received the organic shape that would be its coffin during the fleeting spark called a human life, and in that instant, knowing that matter entails forgetting, it deposited in the current of my blood words that my brain absorbed like thirsty sand: 'Mother of mine: you must know that I am a universal demand, that my total need for your care is the only thing I can give you, because I have come to devour you. Not only do I need your milk, I also want to digest your soul. The man who engendered me, his mission now complete, must move into the shadows; that is, he must be my shadow. You must dedicate yourself entirely to me. You will give me calcium from your bones, the meat of your flesh, the vitality of your blood; you will let your brain soften so that I, like a hungry squab, can make a nest in its center and gobble up its lobes; you will direct your hopes toward me, and I will be the Supreme Father now become a cannibal son; there will be nothing more ideal for you than my development, nor any other pleasure but my growth. I will be your power, your internal lover; like a miraculous blanket your essence will swathe my body. That is why you will have to descend from the Eden of dreams and drag your heavy feet over the base world, the one that demands density as its essential passport. You will lose your song, you will let the walls of articulated language harden you so that you can be my refuge, the granite mother that all the mills of the world could not reduce to dust. I need to believe in surety, leave the shadow and inhabit the tangible, trust in the world that you have prepared for me. Please, don't let me down! . . .' The wish to give him the best of myself, if necessary to give him the breath that kept me alive, carried off the last traces of my personality like an irresistible flood. I became a generic mother, a molecule of the cosmic female, she who with her eight feet weaves all of incarnation; my fertilized and creative body became part of the landscape, it stretched out over the earth until it surrounded the planet; I was the figurehead on the prow of all humanity, wanting to give birth to my child in a perfect society. But when I saw those two hulking mills implanted in the sacred desert like two fatty masses of steel, I realized into what a tragic bath I was about to submerge the being I carried inside me. I felt responsible. Responsible and guilty. Guilty for all the damage that man inflicts on the Earth. If I'd been able to, I would have aborted right there. But my absolute master, his memory now lost, was asking all of my cells for help. He demanded to live. And for that, I, a weak woman, had to change the world, starting with closing the maws of that mine. Do you understand my anguish, Jaime?")

†

Rubi, led by Eulogio and followed by my father, observed the different phases of the crushing process. The workers had stopped covering their faces with the rubber trumpets, and instead used handkerchiefs that could hardly keep out the strong smell from the wet dust. After five minutes, Rubi and Jaime understood this change: the powder in the air, when it mixed with the mask's wet cotton, turned into mud that obstructed breathing.

"Gentlefolk, you who have just entered are already coughing and sneezing. All these workers, who absorb the grit all the day long, are condemned to die within a few years, their lungs destroyed. . . ."

The endless conveyor belt delivered its load to various tanks, each with a capacity of two hundred sixty-five thousand pounds. Once full, powerful pumps poured in streams of sulfuric acid, until the flour was covered and turned into a solution that was carried to the cells where, by means of an electric current, the copper was separated and deposited on sheets of the same metal that made up the center of each deposit.

"Sometimes, when the foremen rush production, the batteries blow up. Columns of lethal smoke invade the space. The workers, as they die, struggle like flies. . . . The worst is that there are children working here. During my time at Chuquicamata I've seen one thousand four hundred little ones buried. And I won't tell you the number of adults who've given their lives for a laughable daily wage of seven pesos! Every day, six cadavers are thrown into the pit."

"Unbelievable!"

"That it is, patroness! The mine keeps no records or anything of the sort. We are people with no legal existence. The Company digs a giant hole in the desert, and with no ceremony, they toss in the deceased. When that pit is full, they dig another one."

"But does no one complain, does no one fight for their rights?"

"Madame, this is not Chile. It is, begging your pardon, Grugenland. The gringos make the law. The workers keep quiet because at the slightest protest they hear the order *Out of camp*, and they're dispatched outside of the camp's radius within an hour. The expelled man is left with his scant luggage at the train station. If he has no resources with which to transport himself, as happens much of the time, he will walk to Calama where he'll beg for charity, and, it is utterly certain, end up trapped in vice. . . ."

†

The sheets thickened by electrolytic copper were placed onto cars pulled by small locomotives that transported them to the smelter. Eulogio invited Rubi and Jaime to get into one of the little trains. They came to a hot air convection oven, a mass of steel covered in black grease that could hold two hundred tons of liquid copper. Amid crackling and long wheezes, it vomited an acrid smoke.

"Cover your noses well, this vapor contains chlorine! This is where the liquid copper is transformed into two-hundred-pound bars that go straight from the mold to the train cars, which carry them to the Antofagasta port so they can be brought by ships to the United States."

"I understand," said Rubi, her face red with shame. "The copper loses its original shape and changes from a hill into a load of bars, like coffins. It all goes abroad, not a drop of these riches stays in Chile. My grandfather's bottomless treasure chests swallow the country's solid blood."

"We lose not only blood, patroness, but also flesh. Night and day the mine dumps a stream of thirteen gallons of sulfuric acid per second into the surrounding lands. The impermeable layers of the earth keep that residue from filtering through, and when it reaches the Calama oasis intact, it is carried along by the Loa river, polluting the water around the salt mines and killing the crops throughout the valley. The foremen drink water bottled at pure sources; we, who have no money for that luxury, calm our thirst gulping freshwater mixed with salty, which causes tumors in our stomachs. Add to this the acidic smoke we breathe in, the poor diet forced on us by low wages, the unhealthy conditions of the camps, alcoholism, corruption of minors, cocaine abuse, syphilis and gonorrhea, illegal abortions, the brothels and foremen, the constant accidents because the Company does not provide protection, and the beatings from the police at the slightest protest! All to make you rich, boss—we have lost not only our blood and our flesh, but also our souls!"

†

Rubi sat down next to the thick tube endlessly spewing a tongue of mud and acid. She curved her spine, dropped her head between her knees, brought her elbows to her waist, crossed her hands, and, curled into a ball, meditated. An hour passed. My parents and Eulogio Gutiérrez waited, poorly protected from the sun by the shade of a pillar, for the girl to come out of her trance. Another hour passed. Without knowing why, Jaime placed Benjamín's notebook between Rubi's fingers. Unfazed, as if it were a butterfly that had landed in her hands, she opened it, and very slowly, with a small thread of a voice, she began to read. . . . Little by little she spoke more loudly, and when she reached the last phrase that had been cut off, "[The poet] cuts to the essential, the center of the world, and from there . . ." she continued declaiming, with her gaze fixed on the pages as if deciphering a poem written in invisible ink:

". . . and from there expands in all ten directions to find his deep meaning wherever it lies. He always lets circumstances decide, because he knows he is the one who creates them. He seizes a thousand things by surrendering himself to them, but when he walks here he is already walking on other planes. Removed from the fantasy of separation, he is the same before and the same after, he is the secret song enclosed in every rock. Space is his infinite body and Time is what happens to him. Dissolved in consciousness, now become Creator, the universe appears to him as an only child. He looks at all beings and things with the love of a father, and his tenderness for fleeting existence is intense. Nothing begins, nothing ends, nothing is born, and nothing dies. He knows that on throwing a stone into the most remote place, he will see it one day land in the palm of his hand. Crewman of sleep, he does not fear waking. He is not an arrogant fish who on leaping from the water fancies himself lord of the heavens. He recognizes that he is only a minuscule gear in the oceanic apparatus, and he lovingly accedes to the sacrifice of his illusory figure so that the light-filled heart will open to him in a rose of fire. Of his thought only perfume remains—for words, before music, were scent—and of his steps, only the raw rhythm of the absent image. He knows that beneath the industrial world's cement lurks the tremendous rattling breath of the enraged Earth!"

Jaime could not keep listening as sobs that came from his childhood wracked his chest. Like a tower toppled by a bolt of lightning, his "real reality" suddenly collapsed. There were ideals capable of vanquishing death. In some unknown dimension, the dead went on living. And certain privileged brains could establish a bridge. Rubi was not the creator of that text; it was his own brother who was describing the free man. Finally he understood what the poet had tried to say! More important than the political act—always oriented toward a future finality—was the poetic act, where cause and effect came simultaneously, converting hope into pure present action. That unfinished poem, a treasure extracted from the bottom of the sea, had to be continued by all people, not just with words but with actions. . . .

Rubi closed the notebook, put it away in a chest pocket, and then silently stood up. She seemed to have shed an old skin to become a mature woman, decisive and implacable. She looked intensely at the miner, took his hands and caressed the calluses on his palms for a long time.

"Don Eulogio, you are a lonely man. . . . Your instinct obliges you to visit the whores of Calama once a month. Do not deny it, it's written on the red list. . . . I want you to look at me right now, without false respect, as a man looks at a woman! My body is beautiful and, I am sure, you will find its volumes agreeable. I propose that you stop working and come live with me. I will be yours with a precise objective: let your race conquer my womb! Once I am pregnant, I will say goodbye to you. Do you accept my proposal?"

The man, in spite of the granite tension that the miners' facial muscles took on, made a proud grimace of refusal; then he turned red, stared into the green eyes of the woman who dared propose a sexual relationship in such haughty terms, and felt a desire to bury a knife in that cold heart. But the honest spirit keeping those eyes open wide and unblinking captivated him definitively.

"I do not feel humiliated, patroness, and I respectfully accept the agreement, because I understand that what we will do is a political act."

"Poetic!" Jaime corrected him.

"Eulogio, I am no longer your patroness, I am your lover. Call me Rubi!"

THREE

THE FATE OF THE WORLD

T HE LUXURIOUS CENTRAL CAMP was full of paper banners. The police choral society, with exaggerated slowness,
massacred the United States' national anthem. The windows
of the spacious houses boasted flowerpots with bougainvillea,
the only flower that could withstand the dry climate. On a wide
strip of calico, a WELCOME festooned the group of imposing
offices, while the steel church that had been fabricated by Eiffel
hoisted its tower high, flaunting a silk flag with a blue square
full of stars and thirteen red and white stripes. The employees,
mostly Yankees apart from some English, Italians, and Slavs,
accompanied by their swollen-headed indigenous servants, stood
beneath the plaza's tall palms submerged in solemn silence. In
the first row, beside the Spanish priest who brandished a banner
of the Virgen del Carmen, wobbled Robert Pinkel, inebriated
as usual, sporting an impeccable tuxedo, and Loretta Selkirk
de Pinkel who, between dodging her husband's stomping feet
and Romeo's tantrums, kept the plunging neckline of her ball
gown at mid-breast with admirable skill. Beside them, Jacobo
Rentzel nervously crinkled the paper with his official welcome
speech, while the cripple Hidalgo continuously whipped his
back with a silk scarf, simultaneously giving haughty orders to
the Chinese waiters to cover the punch bowls with cardboard

before the aguardiente mixed with orange juice filled up with flies and dust. Enrique Jaramillo barked an order: his three hundred cops clicked their heels and raised their rifles. The owner of the mines was arriving!

Sara Felicidad, more of a white shadow than ever, now making no effort to disguise her great height, tall and defiant, walked behind Jaime; and Jaime, tense and trembling with hatred, walked behind Eulogio; Eulogio, with an aspect between mocking and fierce, kept close to Rubi's side. . . . They were covered head to toe in dust. After the mills, they had visited the grocery stores and tasted the poisonous wine sold there, seen for themselves the abusive prices that squeezed the workers who were forced to buy their food in those stores because of the voucher payment system the Company imposed on them. They had seen the camp of Pueblo Hundido—sunken village—a hodgepodge of houses corroded by salt, where entire families lived crowded in like rats in a fog of bedbugs and lice. They examined those large barracks used to house single men, called "ships," whose ugliness was disguised with the quaint names of Chilean steamships: *Teno*, *Cachapoal*, *Aconcagua*, etc. In cramped, dark, foul-smelling rooms, with putrid latrines, up to fourteen individuals were housed in a chaos of fetid promiscuity. They inspected Ciudad Perdida— the lost city—miserable constructions made of gunnysacks and corrugated iron, inside which crowded bestial people, engaged in drunken binges, brawls, rapes, and crime. Finally, Eulogio showed them the clandestine brothels where young women, in rooms divided by calico partitions, on blankets spread out on the dirt floor, gave themselves to quick coitus with no more hygiene than a bucket of salty water and a dirty towel. With a bitter smile, daring to call the patroness by her first name, he said:

"And all of this misery, Rubi, happens beside a road where the cars carrying the foremen and foreign functionaries rush past, never stopping."

†

Sara Felicidad felt that this world was a viper devouring its tail. The child she was carrying in her belly could not be born in it. She, Jaime, Eulogio, and Rubi had to stop the voracity of that suicide industry. But how? She searched for an answer in Jaime's eyes. As he approached the festooned camp, Jaime's hatred transformed all that prosperity into moral pestilence. However, Chuquicamata was only a symptom of a profound worldwide sickness. No political movement could stop that gangrene. Since he didn't believe in God, he prayed to Karl Marx: "Oh bearded one, make it so my brother's spirit does not abandon this good woman and continues to speak through her mouth. Perhaps a poet can halt our dreadful fall!" Eulogio, for his part, deeply modest, did not worry about the fate of the world. He considered himself able to achieve only local changes, and on seeing the miners' inertia he decided to dedicate his energy not to showing them the infinite road before them, but rather to teaching them to take a step. Grugenstein, on the other hand, felt herself able to transform everything: the mine was a point connected to the entire planet; pressing a button there could make the world leap. To her, neither violence nor words were useful. Somehow she would have to convert her greatest obstacle, her grandfather, into a devastating weapon in her service.

†

The parish priest, beating a copper baton on the shaft of his banner, directed the chorus of girls and boys who were dressed for their first communion, each holding a wax candle, and intoned, "Blessed be your purity." Rubi, as she approached the plaza, threw her backpack to one side of the road, then her explorer's helmet, and then all of her clothes, including her glasses. On her lower belly, the red pubis emerging from freckled skin looked like fire.

†

No one made a gesture, asked a question, voiced a reproach. They stood paralyzed, as if time had stopped. The children's singing dissolved into the buzz of flies, and the wind turned the cardboard lids on the punch bowls into giant sparrows.

Elegantly, holding her worker's arm, Rubi walked as if she were wearing a dress with a long train. She reached the plaza, shredded the sweaty paper where Rentzel had written his words of praise, dodged Robert Pinkel—as she passed, his amazement added to his drunkenness made him collapse—climbed onto a bench, and from there haughtily observed the Reception Committee, while the priest, hiding his banner of the Virgen del Carmen under his robe, ran to lock himself in the metal church. Then she said in Spanish:

"*No he venido para parecer, sino para ser*. I have not come to seem, but to be. What I have seen in Chuquicamata has expelled me from childhood. We have acted like rapacious beasts. Even if we pay our debt, it will be difficult to convince these lands to forgive us. First, we must descend from our pedestal. Thanks to Don Eulogio, the blood of the Chilean people will enter my flesh, the flesh of a foreign conqueror. I shall gestate. I want no one to bother me. I reject the luxurious chambers you have prepared for me. For the moment, accompanied by my common-law husband and my two assistants, I will live locked in a machinery workshop, where I will turn one of these sinister ingots that our mills vomit out into the sculpture of a goddess. That is all for now! At ease!"

The police, musicians, bosses, office workers, and kept women murmured among themselves the word "crazy" several times. But, obedient—the power of money is law—and pretending to see the naked queen clothed, they returned to their labors, forcing themselves to believe that Chuquicamata was still the same Chuquicamata. All of them, very quickly, seemed to forget that capricious undesirable.

†

Rubi, who had decided to live in a state of nudity, never left her sculpture studio. Indefatigable, sleepless, hour after hour she caressed the two hundred pounds of an ingot, trying to soften it with the heat of her hands. "The Paracas had no alchemical secrets. They loved the metal, and that sentiment was so deep that matter surrendered to it. I have to empty myself in the attempt, until my love opens the coffin my grandfather made from the copper, so that from within it, the sacred shape can emerge. Then I will know that my ignorant complicity has been forgiven."

†

Discreet as always, most of the time crouched in the shadows, Eulogio constantly watched the body of the woman who—without the slightest shame, on her knees with her buttocks higher than her neck, obsessively caressing the metal surface—displayed dark crannies from which, he imagined, surged intense floral effluvia. . . . Jaime, too, had to make a great effort to hide under his shirt the impertinent swelling beneath his fly; he could not get the unclothed redhead out of his brain. Of course, that befuddlement had nothing to do with the utter love that joined him to Sara Felicidad. But the erection that his wife's enormous white body provoked in him was nothing like the one produced by the arrogant spirit, the stippled flesh, and the dense aroma of the Grugenstein girl. It was like having two phalluses: one calm, tender, protective, and another like a bar of red-hot iron that wanted not only to possess, but also to leave a mark, so that the woman would have his signature on her flesh and be always his and no one else's. He envied Eulogio's mission; he would have liked to be the donor, to plummet like a meteorite into her viscera and ejaculate into her soul, enter in her like a dead man into the crypt and there, in that intimate paradise, ferment until he filled her completely, proudly swelling her breasts and belly. . . . Fearing his wife would read his thoughts—not that he was guilty, only he was convinced that a female, monogamous by nature, would never understand a man's polygamous essence—he dissimulated: he sat on a washbasin full of cold water and wet his head every ten minutes while he played canasta with Sara Felicidad. He fumed when she threw the cards down offhandedly, attentive only to the creature she carried in her belly. That his wife did not notice the impossible desire corroding his marrow sunk him into a disturbing feeling of solitude. A strange being had infiltrated his palace and was usurping his throne. At times, with no apparent reason, he threw down his cards and roared a violent "Traitor!" and went off to the store to return with a cart full of provisions. Neither Sara Felicidad, engrossed in her gestation, nor Eulogio, converted into the shadow of his betrothed's shadow, nor Rubi, feverishly massaging the copper ingot, seemed to notice his comings and goings.

After caressing the metal mass for twelve weeks, sleeping only five minutes every two hours, Rubi collapsed one night in a cataleptic state. That was when the miner, slow as an iguana, emerged from the shadows as naked as she. His dark, hairless skin had the same texture as the copper's surface. While Jaime, using Sara Felicidad as a pillow in the narrow bed, was anxiously dreaming that he was Miss Ukraine and, dressed as a woman, was sunk in the marine cemetery alongside Benjamín, Eulogio, with gentle gestures, opened the virgin's legs little by little and observed for a long time the door that between two smooth lips was an amber line emanating ambrosial fragrances, and then, reverently, he rested the head of his member, black as ebony, inside her. While he blew a warm breath over the sleeping face so she wouldn't wake up, he pushed, millimeter by millimeter, until the hymen opened in four petals without the slightest ripping, letting the entire member be absorbed by the damp walls, so that it could reach the uterus and deposit there, with no thrusting, the offering of a large liquid pearl.

With his eyes fixed on the motionless woman, the man withdrew, slowly backing up, and was swallowed by the shadows once again. . . . A little while later Rubi moved her fingers and toes. She felt a pleasant tingling all over her skin. Now awake, full of a bodily pleasure that she had never felt before, she looked at her thighs. She saw a thread of blood run out of her sex. She took in a breath of air and let out a long sigh. She was no longer a girl. . . . With sensual movements she stretched, yawned, and threw a grateful look toward the two embers that shone in the darkness—Eulogio's loving eyes. Then she went back to massaging the ingot, mute, hour after hour, not resting, not sleeping. . . . Every time she collapsed, exhausted, into her deep lethargy, the miner emerged from the shadows, raised those long freckled legs, and, on his knees as though before an altar, deposited in the chalice his seminal offering. . . .

Jaime woke from a nightmare, opened his eyes, and caught the miner mid-task. He pretended to be asleep. When Rubi went back to work, he crawled over to her and got her attention, asking her to forgive him for causing her displeasure when he described what had seemed to him a cunning and hypocritical violation. Rubi replied:

"I've known since the very first time that Eulogio has decided to inseminate me while I sleep. With admirable honesty he has sacrificed the pride it would give him to bring me sensual pleasure, and he has confined himself, as we laid out in our verbal contract, to be only a stud. It is a kindness I will be grateful for until I die."

Jaime bit his lips and returned to his bed, climbed onto Sara Felicidad's body and stuck his head between those mammaries that were growing ever more voluminous, and gathering all the strength of his will, he began to dissolve his hopeless love in the acid of his disappointment. Soon, frenzied, with a dozen thrusts of his hips, he obtained from his giant the pleasure that returned him to the "real reality." Unnecessary crown, let it rust!

A month later, the Grugenstein girl realized she was expecting. . . . When her menstrual flow ceased, it seemed to her she had won the forgiveness of the ancient inhabitants of those lands. The wound the conquerors inflicted had scarred over. The vanquished race now occupied the throne again, and from the center of her womb it was reestablishing union with the Earth's solid blood. Feeling it inside her, the copper was hers, finally. . . . She approached the ingot, rested her burning hands on the burnished surface, and little by little, with light caresses and intense love, she shaped it. The metal obeyed the energy of her passion and became a soft mass that took on the forms her fingers impressed on it, offering no resistance. The woman, sacrificing her will, in a trance, obeyed an ancient force that she felt as it emerged from the depths of the Earth and moved through the soles of her feet, invading every one of her cells, and surged out through the palms of her hands. Little by little, there appeared a goddess wearing a mask of a bird and brandishing a stalk of corn.

†

Sara Felicidad did not find it strange; quite the contrary, she smiled with relief: the vision of the miracle confirmed the magical, immaterial weave, pure consciousness, with which the cloth of the world was knit. But Jaime, opening and closing his mouth like a dying fish at the edge of the water, was witnessing the collapse of his rational fortress. Matter depended on the spirit! He had the feeling that his mind was jumping from a horizontal line to a vertical one. That finger-softened copper, on revealing an inner shape and passing from vulgar ingot to work of art, granted him a wisdom that in other circumstances would have taken thousands of years to achieve. What was the origin of such a change? What force issued from the contact of hands with metal? It was clear that flesh and copper were united in the force of love. Then, reality was only that which came from the heart? All of life, by nature, was a miracle, except for that which went badly? If devotion, loving concentration, could invert physical laws, then those laws were really thoughts, levels superior to the spirit that obeyed neither matter nor time. A pure being could cancel out the past in the present, thus liberating the future. Rubi, who had so much, wanted to give to those who had so little. And her greatest gift was not money, but the miracle she would work in all minds as she joined with God. . . . Inside my father, the Rabbi, catching the concept of God for the first time in that stubborn brain, murmured "Blessed be" and felt his host freed from a nightmare: real reality was not that dense inferno with no escape where for so many years he had wandered, refusing his own light.

That same night, a drunken foreman's carelessness caused a charge to explode unexpectedly and an arm of fire to reach out through a tunnel that contained hundreds of tons of explosives. Groups of workers were thrown to the ground with dementing force. Others were driven into the gallery's sides like human nails. A mountain of rubble thundered down to bury the remaining groups. More charges exploded. The moans, shrieks of pain, and anguished death rattles were drowned out by that colossal shaking. Eardrums shattered like glasses; broken heads flew, exploded bellies hurled garnet jellyfish. An oily noise made it impossible to distinguish the source of any sound. Everything stayed in shadow for long centuries. From the crumpled rocks surged crimson wakes that crawled like snakes of light through the confusion. Amid cataclysmic shaking, gray, dense, sinuous vapors advanced greedily to suffocate the survivors, whose agonizing cries rose from the shadowy crevices. In the ocean of smoke, terrified, maddened groups of survivors crawled to huddle together. Little by little, after filling the intimate hollows, the connecting galleries, and the roof of the cavern, the great clouds began to fade. Amid a long silence interrupted by the wails of some dying man, a milky light appeared, stained by the greenish gray and red of those asphyxiated or dismembered bodies. . . . Strident whistles sounded. From everywhere, groups of women, children, and men who worked other shifts emerged. Avid for news, they approached the US camp, where they were stopped by the police, who contemptuously showed them a blank chalkboard.

"We still don't know if there are dead! Return to your work!"

Desperate voices burst out, wails of protest, muffled insults, while the guards pointed their rifles at the crowd. Four ambulances went past, leaving trails of dust that the nascent dawn turned luminous. Names began to appear on the chalkboard. There were so many that, for lack of room, they ended up writing them on the walls. One woman, shrieking, made her way through the mob and went to stare fixedly at the lines of chalk. They needed three soldiers to take her away. She fell to the ground like a bundle of rags and began to convulse.

†

With his pupils dilated, Jacobo Rentzel blew into the workshop like a whirlwind.

"Miss Grugenstein, there have been hundreds of deaths! But do not worry, there are many blackies left! Production will not stop for a second!"

"And what do you plan to do for the bereaved, Mr. Manager?"

"Don't worry about that, either, miss: we will have a lottery to choose ten winners, who will be compensated with one thousand pesos each. They'll have to be content with that; better a little for a few than nothing for anyone. . . ."

"Jacobo Rentzel, bring this order immediately to the supervisor: I want tomorrow to be a day of mourning! No worker will work, but we will pay their wages! After burying the dead, with all the honors, the inhabitants of the mine both Chilean and foreign will meet with me and this copper goddess beside the monster of the first mill! I will make an important statement and a dangerous sacrifice!"

†

Jaime thought the Grugenstein girl was exaggerating. What truly serious thing could befall the owner of Chuquicamata? She was going to indulge herself and exhibit her sculpture: how dangerous was that? He soon changed his mind. He never imagined that the idol would cause such a tumult. For those Chileans, in whose souls the Incan myths and Catholic catechism had mingled since they were little, the image that had appeared in the copper was a miraculous emblem. Six rough men, some with scars from knife fights, others with missing fingers, came at eight in the morning. They placed the goddess on a rectangle of boards adorned with paper flowers made from cigarette boxes, and they lifted her onto their shoulders. They set out with her very slowly, taking small

rhythmic steps along the road to the cemetery. They were gradually joined by a silent cortege of men, women, and children, all
dressed in black, who carried on their backs boxes in which they
had placed the pieces of flesh they'd recovered from the accident.
This crowd, as it spread out over the auburn plain, took the shape
of an immense crow. A shaft of the sun's light reflected off the
idol and gave the bird a golden plume. Rubi, naked as always but
wrapped in a Chilean flag, marched ahead of the idol's platform.
Discreet, now become a shadow, Eulogio Gutiérrez walked close
upon her heels. Ignoring his surroundings, he kept his eyes fixed
on the future mother's tense neck. That drill-like gaze was born
of a passion that had flooded him like a giant wave, flattening his
defenses, washing away the last crumb of his past. An impossible
love that wanted to flow from his mouth in words of adoration,
but that he contained by clamping his jaws shut until his teeth
nearly broke. . . . Jaime, lagging behind in the bird's tail, walked
under the umbrella that Sara Felicidad, now quite paunchy, held
to protect him from the sun. He had felt obliged to curse the
childish ceremonies, the useless gods, the ridiculous belief in the
afterlife, but now he began to absorb the collective silence, and,
as he perceived in the pain the impotence of rage, he sped up his
steps, ran, crossed through the black ocean, and when he reached
Rubi, he broke the silence with a raspy, thunderous, continuous
cry, a mixture of colossal suffering and protest. Now the crow had
a voice, and it cawed to make its deep wound known!

The mountains multiplied my father's howl, and from peak to
peak they relayed it to the caves. There, the foreign employees
and their concubines reluctantly waited. To silence the piercing
lament, Officer Maturana ordered his police orchestra to begin
the funeral march. The Spanish priest prepared the incense and
the aspergillum and sprinkled holy water. The hillsides began

to turn black. The enormous living shadow moved down them until it surrounded the ignoble hole they called a cemetery. The three hundred police fired several salutes. The priest, in a voice slow and sharp, declaimed in Latin. The tarred wooden boxes began to be lowered into the hole. Jaime went on with his lament, not because he wanted to, but because he was possessed by the collective spirit that had accepted him as its throat, and he could not cease to assert the pain they all shared. The improvised caskets filled the pit to its brim. In a few minutes, an electric shovel covered the area with large stones. At the highest point they cemented a cross made from a shovel and pickax. Only then could Jaime fall silent. Rubi, without giving any order, headed toward the mill. Immediately, the workers carrying the goddess followed her. And behind them, like an army of ants, all the mine's personnel.

Far behind, the general manager, the superintendent, the cop Jaramillo, and the cripple Hidalgo exchanged bitter grumblings:

"She's got bats in her belfry! To bury a few blackies she'll waste millions of pesos! She gives those bumpkins too much importance! What's she going to say to them? They could give a shit about words. Money is the only thing they want, so they can spend it on drink and whores. Stupid, shameless woman, she thinks she's a great artist! She thinks she'll seduce them with her bare ass and her copper puppet! We have to send a telegram to Mr. Grugenstein so he'll send a shrink to come and get her!"

†

The workers placed the goddess on the turning platform that raised the mineral-loaded cars up to the mill's pulverizing maw. Rubi got onto it as well, and with a grave gesture she let fall the flag that enveloped her. Within the pampa's silence—a new silence, for it was the first time in twenty years that the thunderous mill had been muzzled—was embedded an ancient silence, that of the conquered workers. For all of them, any emotion had to open its way through an armored heart as hard as the rocks they daily split. As it rose, the platform granted a new dimension to the bodies it held, as if the idol were the robe for nakedness, and nakedness were the idol's secret interior. . . . Only then, crowded along the bridge and at the foot of the immense machine, making the two women—she of copper and she of flesh—into one, did they start falling to their knees. . . . In the background, on a plateau reheated by the noontime sun's vertical rays, seated in collapsible chairs as if they were in the balcony of an immense theater, the foreign employees watched that populist fervor and flashed mocking smiles that abruptly dissolved when, with unexpected strength, Rubi picked up the two hundred pounds of her statue and placed it beside the muted monster. In that total absence of sound, the slightest step, the least movement of cloth, the buzz of a fly, sounded like a gunshot. From on high the redhead did not raise her voice, and still every word she uttered was clearly heard by the four thousand workers.

"Noble miners, my friends, before you I will speak to the child I carry in my womb! Because the sperm that engendered it is the elixir of these lands, flesh of your flesh, and to speak to him is to speak to all of you! My child: who am I to seize your attention? I seem to be the owner of these fabulous viscera, but in reality I am no more than the servant of that which manifested through my hands, and is the essence of copper. Sacred metal extracted with pain, shaped with pain, and used to increase the pain of the world, making it complicit in a voraciousness that, spurning the treasure of eternal life, aspires to the ephemeral power of money! You and I, both of us Fritz Grugenstein's heirs, are, here and now, principally culpable for this ignominious sacking! We had not realized that the desert is not a cadaver but rather a gestating spirit, not a sterile expanse but a fertile center where human conscious ness must flourish. For each ingot we extracted, we should have planted a tree, to convert the seeming desolation into a region of forests able to attract clouds, rain, animal life, human communities that would cultivate these generous lands with wisdom and joy. You, who drink my Jewish blood turned to poison by centuries of unholy repudiation; you, who grow from the semen of a humiliated class, unable to shake off the moral torpor into which misery has pushed them; you, mestizo, who from before you are born are likewise guilty of exploitative riches and of resigned poverty, you will help me make this stop! If you do not, four thousand heads of vanquished cattle, unable to seize what belongs to them, will continue going to the slaughterhouse! The battle we will launch is monumental! In order to conquer my grandfather's rapaciousness, which obliges us to fill the bellies of those countless ships that sail for the United States, and to return Chuquicamata to its rightful owner, the Chilean people, we will have to extract him from the mental shell that separates him from reality and submerge him in pain, so he will learn of the destruction he sows by experiencing it in his own soul! Understand, my son, you are the only possi-bility for the Grugensteins' survival! My grandfather has pinned all his hopes of world domination on you. You are his ambitious continuation. We will have to shred his heart, pulverize his future, make his profits useless to him, so that, with claws but without prey, he himself destroys the machine of power that the bankers operate with his money! Forgive me, my son, forgive me infinite times over: for this to change, I must sacrifice you!"

†

Eulogio Gutiérrez, the only one who knew about his lover's plan, heard the words "sacrifice you" and pulled the lever that set the mill to working. The jaws clanged their steel teeth. Amid the thunder, Rubi, raising the goddess high once again, leapt with it into the ferocious beast's maw. In a few seconds they were turned into golden dust.

†

Bewilderment paralyzed the crowd. Eulogio, taking advantage of the stupor, stopped the machine, came out of the cockpit, and climbed the scaffolding to reach the roof. There, he began to shout:

"Compañeros, this divine woman has given her life so that you will awaken! Let her sacrifice not be in vain! Let us go on strike! Let us form a union to demand salaries that will give us a tolerable standard of living! Let there be a weekly rest of twenty-four hours! Let child labor in arduous jobs be abolished, let the Work Accidents Law be complied with, let overtime be paid for night and Sunday shifts, let us have healthy quarters, medical services, libraries, schools for our children! Let us hold stock in the company because the copper is ours! Let us—!"

Robert Pinkel howled to Enrique Jaramillo:

"Shut that communist's mouth!"

The growing murmur of the miners, who little by little were beginning to react, was silenced by the policemen's weapons. The frenzied wolf pack turned the black stain green as the cops made their way kicking and striking to reach the mill, climb onto it, and began to beat the leader. Eulogio, smiling as they broke his bones, knew he was dying more for his beloved than for his people.

†

The cripple Hidalgo ran as well as he could toward the central tower, where he turned on the siren that indicated a shift change. The superintendent, as he emptied his flask of whiskey, shouted:

"Quickly now, return to work! Right now, as you are, dressed in mourning! Anyone who doesn't take the train in the next five minutes will be beaten and kicked out of the mine, dammit!"

†

The policemen shoved the workers with the butts of their rifles to get them to pile into the trains that were setting off, one after another, toward the hills. More than one laggard had the dust knocked off his back with a spear handle. The survival instinct, fear, and the doglike reflex to obey silenced the protests and turned the miners into mute beetles. The women, timidly making the sign of the cross, ran to seek refuge in their sordid rooms. . . . Robert Pinkel breathed in relief: the blackies, with their tame nature, could tolerate any kind of oppression. . . .

†

Jacobo Rentzel, meanwhile, first with a shovel and then with a spatula, was trying to gather every bit of the bloody flour, storing it in a steel barrel. A thousand-year-old instinct made him respect the mortal remains. Unable to stop himself, he murmured in Yiddish, crying:

"*Aineh villen leben un kennen nit, un andere denen leben un villen nit* (Some wish to live well and cannot, while others can live well and wish not to)."

†

Sara Felicidad dropped to sit on the hot sand and murmured, between hoarse sighs:

"Oh, Jaime. . . . What a terrifying and heroic sacrifice! We must never forget Rubi! We must help her continue her work! But how? Four thousand people watched Don Eulogio be murdered, and not one was capable of protesting. Are we the ones who must teach them to throw off the yoke?"

"Sara Felicidad, since you've been pregnant you have worried not only about the health of the being you carry, but also about the entire world! Please, be content with giving birth well! We cannot offer newcomers the Paradise that, according to the sacred fairy tale, Adam and Eve lost! The situation here, after Rubi's suicide, is going to be dangerous. In addition to cops, they will bring in soldiers and fill the camps with spies. . . . We've saved enough money to pay for your delivery. We'd better go back to Tocopilla."

FOUR

THE EMPEROR'S HEAD

SARA FELICIDAD began to feel the first contractions. The midwife predicted a difficult birth within the next forty-eight hours. Since there was no hospital in Tocopilla, deliveries took place behind the church in an improvised clinic built of corrugated metal. . . . They closed Ukraine House and went to sleep in that suffocating place. At three in the morning, my mother woke up crying, worried about the fate of the world. In dreams, Rubi Grugenstein, while she fell with agonizing slowness toward the crushing machine, had told her:

"It will not be me that Fritz's arms receive, but rather a coffin filled with a paste of bone and copper. Then he will see his illusions collapse, his last name will become a sterile hump, his claws will find only emptiness as prey, his neck will lose its pride, he will enter solitude like a ghostly ship. A deluge of hatred will flood his soul. He will want to take revenge on the system, on history, on humanity. He will start to withdraw all his money from the banks. Taking advantage of the economists' confusion, he will sow panic in the markets. He will strip the future of its shining colors, he will change the announcements of benefits and capital increases into a sinister tragedy. He will launch a cruel accounting in the stock market, chimerical kingdom where gamblers savor their triumphs of unreal roots. Without the support of his money, the universe, driven by the irrational forces of the desire for power, will devour itself. Fritz Grugenstein, driving Wall Street into bankruptcy, will shatter the American dream into a thousand pieces and start a crisis that will sink the planet into misery. Arrogant citizens, from one day to the next, will go from golden ostentation to bitter joblessness. Everyday currency, which disguises its copper body with a layer of nickel, will be devalued, transformed forever into a capricious, fluctuating entity. The invincible dollar, stable as a mountain, will become the toilet down which all the Earth's pain is flushed. Never again will anything be certain: uncertain ideals, uncertain borders, uncertain justice, uncertain jobs, uncertain family, uncertain future; humanity will be sunk into the same uncertainty in which my ancestors were forced to live for centuries. . . ."

†

My father tried to calm Sara Felicidad:

"Rubi was an artist with an excessive imagination. A single man cannot bring down the global economy. Individual actions are useless. Sleep calmly, my swan, nothing will happen!"

But when the trembling voice of a policeman on the radio announced that on that Wednesday, October 23, an earthquake in the New York markets had begun—vertical falls in prices, desperate liquidations alternating with spasmodic recoveries; the villainy of agents who shamelessly sold assets they did not really possess at low prices, stocks acquired on credit with insufficient funds, the bankers impotent and unable to help the buyers, who, in the midst of the panic, saw their chimerical fortunes vanish—Jaime finally believed Rubi Grugenstein's predictions.

While Sara Felicidad suffered painful contractions, he separated her legs, sunk his nose deep into her vulva, and, tenser than a bar of steel, let out a long, powerful exhalation, driving the

Caucasian out so he would enter my body through the burning vaginal canal. . . . I have already said that I cannot state definitively that this character is real. Even today, after enjoying his company for many years, I still doubt. Could he be a hallucination that my grandfather transmitted to my father, and he to me? In the end, with all of these reservations about the case, this is how the Rabbi described the difficulties of my birth:

†

"Pleased to no longer be living in Jaime, a man who detested me, and to have another opportunity to incarnate myself, I moved into your little body, which was struggling at that moment, victim of your fraternal twin sister's kicks as she tried to make room to turn and be born correctly. . . . I thought that I could help you, but I had hardly curled myself around your pineal gland when I realized that your developing brain could not comprehend my presence until it was completely formed. Seven years of silence lay ahead of me.

"Sara Felicidad, feeling herself unable to give you and your sister the earthly paradise you deserved, was overcome by guilty pain and began to fight against the bones of her hips, trying to keep you from separating, to keep you both inside her belly where she could protect you your whole lives. . . . In place of the contractions that should have acted on the feet and pelvis of her twins, starting in the depths and carrying them forward in a sinusoidal wave, there was instead a wave of muscular movements to carry them back up to press their heads against the uterine base. . . . You two, kicking angrily, propelled yourselves through the tunnel in a V shape, trying to move into the uterine canal that refused to dilate. The amniotic fluid, which at that point should have been situated behind your bodies, went into your noses and mouths, invading your lungs, tracheas, and stomachs. . . . In spite of all that, anxious to be born, you managed to move forward, but without the help of the contractions, unable to carry out the necessary rotation, you hit against the protuberance of the sacrum. . . . Sara Felicidad was injected with a strong anesthetic that crossed the placental barrier and drugged you. Unable to have normal reactions that would facilitate the birth, you gave yourselves to chaos. With your breathing weakened and without muscular energy, you were kneaded by the unsynchronized shudderings as though in a compressor. The liquid filled with foam and began to suffocate you. Raquel Lea thrashed desperately against the pelvis several times, and finally, scraping against the rough surface of the sacrum, she managed to get through and bring you, Alejandro, with her, holding onto her ankles. . . .

"When her head was about to emerge from the canal, Raquel Lea's feet were tangled in your embrace, and she couldn't use them to push herself out. Stuck there, paralyzed by the drug, you started to lack oxygen. A pair of forceps grasped your sister's soft skull and in just one yank—because you didn't let go—brought you both into the world at last. . . . You were hung head down so you would vomit the liquid you'd swallowed, the umbilical cord was cut early, you were wrapped in scratchy towels and carried to another room, a hundred thousand miles from your mother's, and there, in a cold metal cradle, you were left isolated during the first hours of your lives.

"Raquel Lea's heart was twice as large as normal, and beat so strongly that it could be heard throughout the clinic. You, my Alejandro, on the other hand, always smiling, breathed slowly and scarcely moved. Later, the nurses found out with astonishment that you had a small heart, no bigger than a pigeon's."

†

At fourteen months, Raquel Lea was already speaking nonstop. Teetering, finding her balance, she ran from one piece of furniture to another, murmuring enigmatic phrases: "Do you hear the barking of the air buried among the nettles, beneath which the rocks ferment their solid memory? Do you let loose what your eyes refuse, like melancholic fog, wishing to leave marks on the hard rock? Your shadow's soft feet walk around my roughest path!" From the moment she woke until she fell asleep, and sometimes also while she slept, she never stopped spilling out that river, which, transforming into a poem, moved through the days, the weeks, the months; it threatened to last years. "Forward I seek myself in the places I have not been. . . . I know that the steps we left behind await us still. . . . In the hostile inauguration of the mornings, the storm brings a scent of seagulls. . . ." Jaime, first intrigued and then exasperated by so much gibberish, put earplugs made of breadcrumbs in his ears. Sara Felicidad, on the other hand, was enraptured as she listened to what seemed to her messages from a magical dimension; but, out of deference to my father's inveterate rationality, she sealed my sister's mouth with a pacifier spread with honey, which Raquel Lea sucked until the sweetness was gone, then spit it out to go on orating. "Subject my dreams to other dreams. Open my bones between your yellow hands. Sink your wings into my shadow. . . ."

Meanwhile—poor me!—I was incapable of uttering a syllable, much less of walking. In my tender gums four incisors had grown in painfully, two above and two below, and along with my long nose, they gave me the air of a rodent. Like a furtive animal I slid on all fours under beds, chairs, and tables. Sometimes I spent an entire day in the depths of a closet I had found open in my wanderings. I liked to bite the hems of my mother's dresses, so impregnated with her exquisite pine scent, to tear long strips of cloth and suck them until forming balls soaked in saliva. (Thus I turned her wedding dress into a pyramid of spheres.) When Sara Felicidad arrived home from the store, she sat in the rocking chair and, without looking for me, amid the shadows of the burgeoning night, she uncovered one breast that shone as much as the moon, and she hummed a silvered thread that came to tie itself to my ears: "Alejandrito." I crawled out, climbing her long legs like a snail, gave my mouth to the robust nipple and swallowed that white snake that made my tongue explode, making it into a starry sky. It undulated down my throat, driving the walls of my esophagus mad, to finally coil in the depths of my loving stomach and grow, grow, push my skin toward the horizon and further still, until the end of the universe. "Mother, you are everything, I am nothing; the more I eat you, the more you kill me!" Erased, sated, characterless but joyful, I slept in her arms, a little stone protected by a mountain. . . . Nevertheless, fourteen months before, the entire world had collapsed. Although Colonel Ibáñez did everything possible to hide the crisis, muzzling the newspapers and the radio, decreeing arrest and solitary confinement for anyone who spread alarmist news, and declaring that never had the Public Treasury been in a better state, little by little cruel reality infiltrated that false paradise. Slowly but steadily, unemployment increased. Through the clean and well-paved streets of the towns wandered packs of starving dogs that searched the garbage bins for a bone to gnaw. Apart from the global depression, the European invention of synthetic saltpeter, which was much cheaper, dealt a mortal blow to external trade. The US banks stopped lending money: Chile, a nation whose economy depended on a single product, was not a good debtor. The saltpeter companies, drowning in their reserves, began to close. . . . Great crowds of ragged people—starving miners with their women, children, and lice—struck out for the far-off capital. The parishes, aided by municipal authorities, organized communal pots of thin soup that the tattered masses formed long lines to collect in empty tin cans. But there was terror as well as commiseration. Fantastic rumors rode from one tongue to the next: "The mangy lowlifes have converted to Communism and are preparing a nighttime uprising, they'll take us by surprise and cut off our heads! To get revenge for their misfortunes they'll throw lice on our children and infect them with typhus!" The result: the miners were forced to stay out of the streets and to sleep crowded together in the foothills of the mountains. Unfortunately, the lice could walk miles, and from those insalubrious encampments, perhaps seeking more wholesome blood (for that of the workers was pure water by then), they headed for the town and provoked the much-feared plague. In a panic, the army, bayonets drawn, pushed the jobless as far away as possible toward the coast. With its variety of shellfish and algae, the ocean took care of feeding them. . . . That solved the problem of hunger, but not of thirst.

Jaime exchanged fifty pairs of stockings for a water cart pulled by three donkeys. (In those years, most of the houses in Tocopilla didn't have potable water. Beat-up trucks brought it in barrels from the Mamiña springs and sold it to private companies, who resold it to houses, carrying it in wagons.) He called his bony asses Faith, Hope, and Charity, and he took upon his own shoulders the arduous task of distributing the vital liquid to the pariahs for free, even if he had to invest the last bit of clothing in the store to do it. The cripple Gamboa deigned to visit him. He entered Ukraine House with the sole of his high-heeled shoe ringing out against the cement.

"Look, Don Jaime: your effort and generosity are quite laudable, since to calm the thirst of so many gullets you'll have to sacrifice all you have and more, going deeper and deeper into debt. Fuck, by my own damned foot, I'm telling you: you deserve an ovation with a giant's hands! But—and it's a 'but' bigger than Don Pancho Hill, which from the beginning of time has protected our town from evil winds—those comings and goings between here and there can lend themselves to the transport of sneaky lice, and, as we all know, they have poisonous snouts. How many besides you yourself will be bitten and fall, struck dead by the epidemic? One could say it's just your problem, for at the end of the day each body is private property, and no one has the right to stick a finger into anyone else's intimate cavities, clean or dirty as they may be. However, given how contagious this bug is, you are placing in danger your better half, your little ones, your neighbors, and, no less tragically, your three donkeys. Let them drink salty water, Don Jaime! Those lowlifes are hardy, tougher than any Christian, and they adapt to everything. And he who doesn't adapt, as the wise man says, for his weakness he should break and leave room for stronger ones—"

"Shut up, you treacherous cripple! Be grateful that the witch who pulled you from your whore mother's cunt didn't have those slimy beliefs, because with the shriveled foot you drag along she could have cut you into pieces and thrown you to the dogs for being 'weak!' Understand, *compañero,* that the individual is an illusion. We are always, in every circumstance and every moment, a flock. If they are thirsty, you and I are thirsty. As the men we are, we must assume that responsibility. . . ." Jaime replied.

"Have I understood well? Are you saying that if I have a deformed foot, you should also limp? With great pleasure, I cede my stride to you!"

Jaime, exasperated, pushed the cripple out of his way, got into his wagon, and with three vigorous "giddy ups!" he had Faith, Hope, and Charity take off at a trot. My mother, sensing what was

going to happen, said goodbye, shedding two threads of tears. . . .
She wasn't wrong: after he distributed the water, entering that
forest of bodies with layers of grime so deep that, like tattoos, they
held fast even after bathing in the ocean—all of them shoving
toward the ladle, stepping on the donkeys, elbowing children in
the head, bawling "Me first!"—my father had been bitten by lice,
and he returned trembling with fever.

The neighbors were frightened when they saw him coming
down the street with his face reddened by eruptions that looked
like measles, babbling incoherent words like a drunk, and they
ran straight to the police station. Sara Felicidad rushed to get him
down from the wagon and into the store, and to close the metal
shutter behind them. The soldiers came, doused the vehicle and
the donkeys in gasoline, and lit them on fire. The animals, wrapped
in flames, fled for the hills in a zigzag, and when they reached the
peak they collapsed, now become black carrion. . . . The cripple
Gamboa hit the shutter with his big shoe:

"Look, ma'am, you are causing problems of a public nature.
You do no good by locking yourself in there. You're going to catch
it. That fucking epidemic doesn't forgive. We will stand guard
here night and day; don't think you can escape. If you don't turn
yourselves in you'll die in there, making Ukraine House a center of
infection, which will oblige us to burn down the whole building.
Better to die in the hospital! And so you'll see that we are good, we
have already reserved for your little ones, who are now at Cristina's,
a place in the orphanage in Iquique."

Sara Felicidad's only reply was to add three chains to the shutter's inner lock. They had recently bought an unopened chest,
perhaps stolen, from some Swedish sailors, and it turned out to
contain all kinds of canned food and fruit juices. They could hold
out during a siege of months. What's more, Cristina, in spite of

her mystical madness, was an excellent wet nurse. Certainly, her eccentric look made her the butt of all of Tocopilla's jokes: the rubber gloves she never removed from her hands, and how on the instep of her satin, flesh-colored shoes, she had sewn a circle of red sequins that symbolized the wounds left by the nails that pierced the palms and feet of the Lord; also, on the tight shower cap she never took from her head, she had glued a crown of little red crystals shaped like drops. Nevertheless, she cared for children with a devotion akin to saintliness. Knowing that my sister and I were in good hands, my mother threw herself body and soul into healing Jaime. . . . Unafraid of the typhus, she sprinkled rice powder over the skin eruptions to ease the atrocious burning, licked his forehead continuously, and placed on his belly towels soaked in cold water. She embraced Jaime, absorbing the painful convulsions provoked by the high fever into her enormous body. The sick man saw thousands of demonic faces on the undulating walls, and he saw a rain of sand fall from the ceiling, every grain creaking insidiously. He wanted to break through the steel shutter and run burning through the streets, setting the town ablaze with a tail of flames. Sara Felicidad, squeezing him in her arms, held him and let him throw his fits, until he was exhausted and hung limp, feeling himself to be a piece of dead meat harassed by swarms of flies. . . . My mother laid him on the counter and spent hours shooing away imaginary bugs with a Spanish fan and praying. She had long since stopped asking for things for herself; all of her prayers begged for Jaime's health, and she did not think for a second about how that recovery would lead to her own emotional benefit. A secret instinct told her that wresting her husband from the abyss of death, giving him new life, would oblige him to create a new world for himself, where perhaps she would lack importance. Believing in the omnipresent consciousness she called God, she was convinced that she formed, along with every living thing, part of Him. Not being separate from the Lord, she considered her healing power to be limitless, as long as she abandoned the illusion of an individual "I" and became the channel for that absolute presence, concentrating on the work and forgetting its fruit. She couldn't fail! Transcending her body and her memory, she transcended all limitation. With infinite gratitude she let the light enter her, and she waited for the healing to happen. Belonging entirely to God, she also belonged entirely to her patient. . . . She blessed the typhus because it gave Jaime the wisdom that, for the lack of roots in a true homeland, he did not possess. The blessed fever was granting him unity. If he survived, he would never again be separate from the world.

In his delirium, my father began to stretch out. First he was ten feet tall, then a hundred and then a thousand, ten thousand, a hundred thousand, more. He ended up with a height of two thousand seven hundred miles, extending the length of Chile end to end. In his head he felt the vast dry expanses, hiding under the burning crust a colossal energy in the shape of a temple. In his feet throbbed ice, a white mother, frigid and deep, seemingly a tomb but actually a sacred reserve of every vital seed. Sand and snow, two extremes hiding the hope for a cosmic awareness beneath their mortal surfaces. . . . He felt the paved roads as long wounds on his back, his belly filled with vineyards and fields, his legs with damp forests, the ocean lashed against his right side, now become beach, and his left side filled with mountains. Then came the animals and finally human beings, digging, drilling, blowing up his hills, poisoning his fish, wiping out his eagles, building in his valleys purulent cities, sapping his energy. I am not an idea, I am not a flag, I'm not a history of conquering wars! I am a being that in every rock, every drop, every clod of earth, is pure love! Children of mine, unite north with south, sand with snow, create the circle of knowledge: fertilize me! Make of me the garden of delight! And Jaime was filled with trees, from foot to head: cinnamon, palms, pataguas, araucaria, oak, larch. And millions of birds came and chirped: meadowlarks, goldfinches, diuca finches, thrushes. And the waters of the ocean, clean again, were turned silver by the shining scales of millions of fish: albacore, conger eel, sea bass, clingfish. And people began to live on great floating balloons, and an earthquake made the demolished mountains grow again, and the Andes recovered their wildlife and gave birth to friendly condors the size of whales, and an immense multicolored cloud spoke to them with great affection, introducing itself as God and promising never to abandon them again, never again, never again. . . . Letting out a jubilant cry, Jaime recovered his senses, completely cured! He didn't remember anything, but, with absolute conviction, he said:

"Sara Felicidad, the country cannot go on living the lie of a tyrant! I have to go to Santiago to kill him! I will put a bullet in his head!"

†

One cool dawn, when Ukraine House's shutter finally opened, the drowsy police thought they were still dreaming when they saw the Jodorowskys emerge in perfect health. First they pointed their rifles at them, then they applauded and cried out excitedly. That couple offered hope: the plague, thanks to them, was no longer fatal. . . . Cristina arrived throwing fistfuls of hosts into the air, to hand over my sister and I with our diapers covered in prayer cards and camphor tablets. I, who until that moment had never stopped smiling, began to cry and throw a tantrum. When my mother had been absent I felt her presence, but now, when I saw her there, the forty days I'd been without her fell onto my soul like a black anchor. Raquel Lea, imperturbable, went on declaiming:

"In the sad brilliance of the obvious the stars are not named.... Memory gathers only dead facts from the floor, like ripe fruit.... In the infinite desert we celebrate the feast of a tear."

Jaime suggested to Sara Felicidad that, because she was going to be left alone and shut up in the store almost all day, she leave my sister, such a restless child, with her grandparents in Iquique, and keep only me, because I was so upset. My mother exclaimed:

"It seems the typhus has given you amnesia! You've forgotten the fuss that our wedding ceremony caused!"

✝

At first, the wedding had seemed like all Jewish weddings. Sara Felicidad in a wedding dress and flats, Jaime in a tuxedo and triple-soled shoes (at the family's urging, to even out the embarrassing inequality of their height), they waited patiently in a banquet hall under a velvet awning for the rabbi to finish warbling his Hebrew prayers. Then they exchanged the rings, but instead of drinking wine from a glass that the groom would then break with a stomp of his foot, they gave themselves over to a personal ceremony. Sara Felicidad gathered up her long skirts to show, without underwear, a wide pubis with silky golden hair; she lay on her back and spread her legs. Jaime modestly extracted his sex and launched a thin yellow stream toward the adored vulva—to the terrified relatives, the urination seemed to last centuries—then he lowered his pants and lay down on his back too. The bride, squatting, launched a potent, thick, hot stream, inundating his penis and testicles with the golden nectar. "You are mine and I am yours!" "And you are mine and I am yours!" They kissed, trying to decant their souls into each other. On seeing them thus, dripping urine, the rabbi, relatives, and guests, who until then were statues frozen by that unthinkable act, turned around and fled that tainted place. They had to get away from that pair of crazies as soon as possible. . . .

†

"How do you expect my parents to receive me after our—to them—unforgivable scandal?"

"Humph! They call nature a scandal! No animal considers any territory its own if it has not urinated on it first!"

†

Contrary to what the authors of my days feared, Raquel Lea's grandparents received her with open arms, sobbing hoarsely. But her poetic garrulousness continued: "Here we are all become clowns . . . slapping ourselves on our rotten cheeks. . . . Crying twenty-foot tears . . . under our dog-like masks!" The old couple almost fainted. "Look at her, poor thing, her parents' madness has made her speak hysterically! We will start to fill her mouth with sweet rice: that way, chewing and growing fat, she will learn to keep quiet!" Rice or no rice, my sister went on reciting. "Without roots in the train of Time, expelled from all its cars, beset by the shame of others, we transport the sublime secret between races that do not wish to know . . ." To get her to stop, they forced her to keep her pacifier in her mouth day and night until she turned ten years old.

†

Jaime was calm now that his daughter was safe in Iquique and his wife was stuck in Ukraine House nursing me, and he had time, before going to Santiago to blow the lid off the tyrant's brains, to enter the Municipal Library for the first time, overcoming his hatred for books. He began to study there for hours, reading the biography of Carlos Ibáñez del Campo. The topic was hot, and documents abounded. All censored, of course. . . . Jaime, faced with such a potent enemy, wanted to learn about his most intimate life, find his weaknesses, discover the sensitive man beneath the invulnerable outer shell. For that, he had to learn to read between the lines: no historian or journalist, out of fear of repercussions, beatings, jail, deportation, would dare reveal a defect of the leader. They described him as a noble gentleman, simple and dignified, hiding the fact that he spoke little, gave stuttering speeches, and was incapable of understanding anything written, or of writing a line himself. Jaime felt a shiver run down his spine. Ibáñez's stubborn and disbelieving character was, in a way, similar to his own. The same rejection of the written word and the same difficulty, on a different scale, with speaking in public. Both distrusted any kind of intellectual or aesthetic pleasure, both mockingly rejected metaphysical problems, refused to treat their anxieties with the aspirin of religion, were interested only in the physical, period. Jaime, proudly, did not consider that to be proof of stupidity or of lack of wisdom. The tyrant went straight to the essential, and the essential was never in a book, sacred as it may be. However, to have reached the position of president of the Republic after starting out a simple cavalry lieutenant, he had to have found a teacher at some point. But who? His father, perhaps? Don Francisco Ibáñez was descended from a long line of moneyed landowners who were capable of living over a hundred years. Tall, distinguished, imposing, with perfect manners and the courtesy of a great lord, but poor—the fields of his small estate in Linares, worked intensely, produced very little—and with enormous pride. Faithless, so unbelieving he could not pray an Our Father, his precarious situation could never change. He could not accept asking for divine help, nor did he tolerate parental aid. Believing himself to be solely responsible for his lean reality, he sunk into a stubborn silence and made desperation his companion; trying to mask his poverty with a strict life, he sacrificed his family's vital happiness. A bad businessman, his dignity kept him from arguing over the vulgar paragraphs of a contract, and he gradually lost his possessions, sinking his home deeper and deeper into want. From working so hard to hide his shameful penury from his moneyed relations, his character grew bitter and he spoke little, almost not at all, to his wife, María Nieves—who overcame the cold prison of her name by multiplying prayers in a suffocating private chapel—or his children: Carlos, a boy who never learned to smile, and Nieves, the cold half of her maternal name, who went straight from the melancholic family setting to the habit of the Sisters of Charity in the Andes hospital. And distant Nieves burying herself in the mountain snows.

Jaime had known very well what it meant to have a present father with an absent soul, confusing duty with pride, poverty with failure, out of his own lack of self-worth, refusing to give his children tenderness, manly caresses, and above all the guiding word that encourages, that builds the bridge between family and world. Until he found Sara Felicidad, he had lived with a lack of affection, longing for sweet words (that from his wife were music) that would make him discover love for himself. No, Don Francisco could not be his son's teacher! The first thing a father must teach is the celebratory value of the moment, the laughter that sweetens the rind of life. Carlos Ibáñez, for the same reasons that drove his sister to become a nun, decided to don a uniform and enter the Military Academy. Those who are forbidden from being themselves are given uniforms, those who instead of affection have received demands for order, an order that tries to exorcise the chaos of

existence and obliges one to behave in life as if dead. His mother
was religious and subservient. His sister entered religious life, he
himself submitted, both chose economic hardship as a principle
of reality. The future president of Chile, as a poor military man,
lived half a century with a Spartan sobriety that defined his table,
his clothing, his entertainment. He was withdrawn, silent, he had
no friends, did not engage in parties, affairs, or games of chance;
he almost never opened his mouth or smiled, guided as he was
by severe concepts of discipline, personal sacrifice, willingness
to work, and military honor, which took the place of paternal
guidance. However, being hard on oneself, making obedience
one's credo, does not necessarily grant power. Who transmitted
the gift of command, the charisma of dominance, and made him
into a leader? It was a mystery! Jaime gave up and decided to look
for other elements so he could better understand his enemy's
personality.... Perhaps love ...

In 1903, the Chilean Army, trained by Prussians, maintained
close ties with General Tomás Regalado, *caudillo* of the republic
of El Salvador, who had decided to found a military academy.
Regalado knew that the Chilean army was the most prestigious
in Latin America, and he asked for officers to be sent to govern
the brand-new school. Among those sent was Carlos Ibáñez, a
humble cavalry instructor, who lived first in the Salvadoran capital
and then in San Miguel, a provincial city that spread out its bore-
dom at the foot of the Chaparrastique volcano. Jaime tried to put
himself in the skin of his future victim. Immediately, he was suffocated by the tropical heat, he felt his senses overcome by the
insidious perfume of the coffee flower, he was depressed by the
maddening monotony of the narrow valleys covered by that same
plant, among sterile mountains and sleeping volcanos threatening
to awaken, and the despotic omnipresence of a mafia of fourteen

families, descendants of Spanish adventurers who in previous centuries had been able, with blood and fire, to snatch the lands from the natives. Now sunk in misery, they depended entirely on the three months of the coffee harvest. Carlos Ibáñez was a youth of twenty-six when he was relegated to the volcano's shadow. He used words only to give orders, for, in a landscape very different from his native land, among aristocratic cadets and an army of suffering mestizos who still carried impressed in their flesh the humiliation of their native mothers raped by their foreign masters, with whom could he truly communicate? Like the volcano, he hid his rage deep inside; lonely volcano, lonely man, both capable of one day making the entire earth tremble. In less than three years, he had disciplined his army. In the process, he had to teach them to break a horde of horses. Where did he learn to do it? It became clear to Jaime that it was on the small farm of his childhood. There, on that sad land, unable to break his father's muteness or his mother's pious iciness, he could only get close to his horse. If he'd had any emotional relationship during his childhood, it was equine. And to break the horse, he had to understand it, integrate his own character with the animal's. Thus formed, with the competitive mind of a quadruped, without a purpose, shouting and kicking, possessed of a pride as great as his father's, he overcame the provincial tedium and trained a cavalry worthy of the world's greatest armies. Wasted time? Useless effort? In July of 1906, Guatemala declared war on El Salvador. The arrogant Regalado invaded the neighboring country and faced down his rivals in Jícaro, where, after three days of bloody struggle, he lost his life. Other battles followed, until an armistice was agreed. But the six thousand Guatemalans were dragged forward by another arrogant general and invaded El Salvador, attacking the enemy contingent. Right at the center was the regiment Ibáñez had trained. Disobeying a stern instruction from the Chilean government not to interfere in that war, at the head of his equestrian forces he clashed with the enemy in a primitive and gory battle. The soldiers abandoned their muskets that fired only one shot, and they fought with slashing machetes. Jaime, putting himself in Ibáñez's place, rode a filly that had been broken to the point of blind obedience, directing her without reins, driving his spurs into her sides. Now become a centaur, he sliced off arms and legs, he decapitated torsos, he hacked open bellies, stomped masses of guts. Slashing ferociously, the gray of his uniform covered in hot red, his troops behind him, he opened a triumphant tunnel through the flesh of the enemy army.... Cadets and mestizos, haughtily astride their horses and wearing the exalted look bestowed by legal murder, trotted victoriously through San Salvador's streets amid the delirious enthusiasm of their inhabitants. At the head of the parade, Ibáñez, now a popular hero, was as powerful as his steed. Beast and man were one. With secret envy, my father imagined his enemy letting out triumphant whinnies amid the hurrahs and applause of the crowd.... He also imagined the moment when Rosa Quiroz Ávila, an aristocratic orphan who lived with her grandmother, came out onto her balcony. When she saw the champion moving impassively through the crowd, erect atop his mount and exuding an intoxicating aroma of human and equine sweat, her sixteen-year-old heart, open in two deep wounds from the early deaths of her father and her mother, was inflamed. The invisible fire that rose from her nubile breast went to sweetly burn the warrior's eyes. Ibáñez's dark irises greedily absorbed the intense blue of Rosa's. And the man who had pitilessly spilled a river of blood grew tender at the shining red of the thick hair framing that angelic face. That look was enough to unite them until death separated them. ... Soon after, one Sunday morning, he went to wait for her by the church door. Without a word, considering themselves engaged, they took each other's hands. Her grandmother, alarmed, pulled the girl away to hide her on a distant estate beside an extinguished volcano. Hero he may have been, but that foreign officer, poor, socially opaque, did not deserve to join an exalted Salvadoran family! Ibáñez did not give up: without sleeping, he rode for entire days to reach his beloved, even if they slammed the door in his face. Tense astride his horse like an equestrian statue, he sat motionless for hours, sometimes under torrential rain, knowing he was breathing the same air she inhaled. Rosa, locked in her bedroom, let out cries that seemed both birdlike and feline. Ibáñez, exasperated by that family's contempt, turned his horse around, backed up to the house, and had it kick in the doors. First the outer one, then the hall, and finally the bedroom. Seeing her granddaughter perched happily on the animal's hindquarters and holding fervently onto the Chilean, the grandmother began to howl and beg for help. None of the peons dared interfere. The couple, in an all-out gallop, fled to the military barracks in San Miguel, and in a small room next to the horse stables, began to sate their inexhaustible desire. To avoid scandal, the family organized a quick marriage. Ibáñez, who had just turned thirty, honest and proud as he was, would not agree to become a dark part of the brilliant clan—the last names Quiroz and Ávila were boasted by judges, doctors, financiers, senators, university rectors, presidents and vice-presidents of the republic—and he requested a transfer. A year later he returned to Chile accompanied by his wife and a little girl, baptized Rosa like her mother. Very soon they would have a second child, named Carlos like his father. . . . Jaime, moved very much in spite of himself, recognized the romantic intensity of that passion. It was written in the tyrant's destiny: since he was born, Carlos carried the four letters of Rosa in the middle of his name.

The two of them, so thirsty for affection, enclosed themselves in a love that admitted no one else. Considering their children intruders, they refused them individuality, making them into a reflection of the couple: Carlos and Rosa planned to repeat themselves in Carlitos and Rosita. Just as for them, neither father nor mother had seen their essences, they did not see the essence of their children. . . . Believing themselves to be only two, in spite of the hard, narrow beds they slept on, they made every night a paradise, giving themselves without complaint to military discomfort. Pilgrims of cities and regiments, making use of the dwellings assigned to officers or renting modest houses close to the barracks, they perched like migratory birds in innumerable and fleeting homes, never building a true nest. . . . That flexible body, as it pressed against the rigid warrior, inundating it with the scents of a finely bred animal, transformed the rough beds into magical ships and the crude bedrooms into palaces. . . . But uprooting a plant, healthy and acquiescent as it may be, in the long run leads to its extinction. After Carlitos was born, seemingly exhausted by the birth and doubtless also by nostalgia for the warm climes of her homeland, the young Salvadoran of marine eyes, igneous hair, and a pubis orange like acacia honey, contracted the same pulmonary illness that had finished off her parents. After countless months of languid decline, sad that she could no longer kiss her man, she died in the small clinic at the Police Academy, which Carlos Ibáñez directed at the time, and where he had transferred her so he could visit her as often as his work allowed. . . . Widowed, sullen, taciturn, he continued his Spartan and errant barracks existence for nine more years. He slowly ascended through the ranks; he was entrusted with the police prefecture of Iquique, then the directorship of the Cavalry School. He gained the public's trust, he was War Minister, Minister of the Interior, Vice-President and, on 21 July of 1927, after being elected president of the Republic, he took control. He wasted no time in marrying, in a pompous ceremony, Graciela Letelier, seventeen years old, also the daughter of an aristocratic family. . . . Jaime jumped: he had realized something very important. The man who married that girl was not a man, but a president. The man was still enclosed in the mortuary bedroom of Rosa Quiroz Ávila, a room that Ibáñez had locked and kept everything as it was when his wife was alive, so he could return frequently, allowing no one else to enter. How could he forget that innocent woman who had abandoned an opulent life, sacrificing luxury, social triumph, the exuberance of the tropical climate, to sink into penury and submission? All to prove her love to him, who had not received love from anyone, not even his mother. Jaime knew what it was to desire a girl with red hair and blue eyes: Rubi Grugenstein had bewitched him with her thin body, her smooth and firm curves, her intoxicating smells, her polished skin whose every pore gave off a heat that brought inexhaustible pleasure to the hands that caressed it. Such a woman, so delicate, so full in soul, vibrant with love, could only take possession of the rough soldier's heart forever. He never forgot her, never let the wound scar over, never accepted her absence. He, who was not a believer, turned her into a saint. He locked himself up in the death chamber to pray for her, spilling uncontainable tears: "I must overcome death: someday, in this world or another, I will see you again!" If the Salvadoran aristocracy had not held him in contempt, Rosa would not have had to move to another country, and would still be alive. Graciela Letelier was a pale copy of his first and only love. Same age, same social class, same wealth. Same contempt felt by the oligarchical family for his person, but the same overwhelming admiration for his position. Graciela, a fervent catholic of traditional lineage, her umbilical cord wound tightly around her, married the president of the Republic, not out of passion but out of duty—satisfying the vanity of Doña Margarita, her mother—and out of ambition—satisfying the political aspirations of Don Ricardo, her father. A big church, a priest wearing a robe from the sixteenth century embroidered in gold and silver, hundreds of white lilies, an orchestra with sixty musicians, a wedding cake six and a half feet tall, the bridesmaids and their male escorts, members of the oligarchy all, most of them close relations. Ibáñez, on the other hand, as if his progenitors didn't exist, was accompanied only by a few military friends. Once the ceremony was over, the couple went to live on an extensive estate (when Jaime learned this he smiled, delighted, realizing his deductions were on the right track) that the brand-new husband had bought with the sixty thousand gold pesos from the inheritance Rosa Quiroz left him, and that he had kept in a savings account until then, never wanting to spend a single cent. Carlos Ibáñez, faithful to his deceased wife, gave her the spacious house and sunny garden she had always wanted, and he even had the yard planted with a large fig tree, the kind she had always preferred for its aromatic shade. For her part, Graciela never stopped granting her parents absolute first place in her emotional life, giving respect instead of affection to her husband, who came third. Second place was taken up by the first two children she rushed to give birth to: they were baptized Ricardo, like her father, and Margarita, like her mother. Though he tried to avoid being belittled by the aristocratic family's fortune by visiting them as little as possible, Ibáñez had to suffer his in-laws' invasion in his own home. The children, through the repetition of their names, had become reflections of the Letelier family. Loving his dead wife inconsolably and hating the oligarchical class, the president, now as in his childhood, had moneyed relatives but was scorned by them; again, his only tender relationship was with his horse, Grenadier, black with a white spot on his forehead.

"That's it! I have it! I know how to get close to him!" my father exclaimed. He put on a pair of baggy pants over tight underwear, and he hid between his thigh and testicles a small revolver bought from Tina, the one-armed whore, who had gotten it from a drunk stoker in payment for letting him lick her stump. He had decided to turn that gun, no less deadly for its size, into his second sex. "No damned soldier's manliness will let him pat me down there. I'll carry a sleeping snake in my intimate shadow, and I'll only let it bite when the tyrant is alone with me, defenseless and trusting."

Jaime didn't have a precise plan, but, seeing what he'd seen, experiencing what he'd experienced, he no longer denied the miraculous possibilities of reality. He understood that everything was linked by invisible ties, woven by an infinite consciousness that was all-powerful and willing to obey, if only one had the audacity to proclaim himself its master and issue it ironclad orders. Then it would grant everything necessary to carry out a plan, caring nothing for good or evil. What counted in the plan was not the hero's moral character, but rather the strength of his will. And he had that strength, he was sure, at least as much as the damned horse-trainer did. What was going to tip the scales in his favor, apart from his cunning, was a miracle.

Neither Sara Felicidad nor Jaime had wanted to pronounce the word goodbye. They knew the separation could be forever or for many years, but the arrow had been shot and they could no longer change its course, much less return it to the bow. My father, holding back tears, introduced his sex into my mother's mouth, and after some delicate rocking, deposited on her tongue a stream of sperm that took the shape of a cup, its bottom toward her lips and the bowl toward her throat, as though spilling hope, the essence of life, into the depths of her body. My mother swallowed the white chalice, and through the sweet spice of the semen she moaned a musical phrase that followed the beat of my father's footsteps as he walked off toward the pier. There, he would board the ship that would carry him, sailing laboriously against the Humboldt current, to the port of Valparaíso. When Jaime disappeared from her sight, Sara Felicidad's body shrank as if the bones of her spine collapsed one into the other. Transformed now into a small señora, she went to sit behind the counter, her life now become the hope for a miracle.

Meanwhile, in a small private cabin on the ship, a miracle was waiting for Jaime. When the ship began to dance violently, someone traveling hidden under his bunk began to vomit. My father pulled him from the shadow by his foot. A chubby, green-faced boy emerged and looked at him with wide black eyes, like a dizzy frog.

"Compañero, we oppressed have a duty to help each other. I'm a stowaway, it's true, but I am justified by the mission that history has given me. If you try to turn me in, as much as it pains me, I will be forced to erase you from this world, innocent as you may be."

With nervous movements he extracted a revolver from his breast pocket and pointed it at my father's mouth.

"It's a Smith and Wesson nine millimeter. It can open a hole in your head the size of a fist. This trip will last three days: I will keep you locked up here in this cabin. Neither you nor I will eat. The water from the bathroom will be our only nourishment. If you decide to behave, when we reach Valparaíso I will leave you here, bound and gagged. If you rebel, then I will use the pillow as a silencer—"

He couldn't finish his sentence because Jaime, leaping like a furious cat, grabbed him by the arm, kicked him between the legs, smashed his fingers against the wall to make him let go of the gun, which he threw, in a sprawling flight, into the toilet. The boy sat right down, whining like a child. My father extracted the five long, thick cartridges from the cylinder, and then returned the weapon to the boy.

"What's your name?"

"Luis Ramírez, sir."

"Where did you get that revolver?"

"It was my father's. He was a journalist for the *Mercurio de Antofagasta*. He cited Bakunin in an article—'Abolition of the tutelary state and the financial monopoly: this is the negative goal of the financial revolution . . .' and Ibáñez accused him of being an anarchist and sent him to a military camp, where he died from an intestinal infection they wouldn't treat."

"I understand. The tyrant provoked your father's death, and now you . . ."

"Now I'm going to kill the tyrant! It's only fair, right?"

†

It seemed that the invisible weave that held up Jaime's present was squeezing together to become a single thread—or a thick rope—to wrap him up and drag him toward the vortex of the cyclone of his destiny. Luis Ramírez was in a way like the absurd rabbit who guided Alice, without seeming to want to. As soon as he lowered his pants to show him the pistol he carried sunk in the shadow of his thigh, telling him the story of Benjamín's drowning and the genocide of Chuquicamata, the boy understood that fate had placed the two assassins in the same cabin. Agreeing with Ecclesiastes ("Two are better than one"), he conceded to exchange information. Jaime's was of no use to him. For him, the tyrant was a symbolic shape, an evil doll activated by the demonic magic of history, and in no way a human being. His strategy was not about finding psychological weak spots or wasting time making the tyrant understand why he was being erased from the present; rather, he planned to crush him when his guards weren't looking, like a stinking pest.

"No," Jaime told him patiently. "You will never make it to the mountain that way: it's protected by countless barriers. The only way is for it to come to you and offer itself to you in full confidence, without defenses or defenders. To achieve this, you cannot aim at the body, you must aim for the soul!"

The chubby boy smiled stupidly without understanding the words. His information, however, was first rate: on such a day, at such and such time, the president, his wife, their military and civil police—their personal hit men—would visit the livestock show at Quinta Normal. Among so many fillies and shire horses (the only thing the soldier was interested in), cows, pigs, and the rest of the livestock, in an atmosphere reeking of dung, full of those swollen quadrupeds neighing, bleating, and mooing, rough huasos brushing their hides and a throng of pale families crowded in and applauding sweetly as if that shitpile were paradise lost, it would be difficult to protect the tyrant one hundred percent. Luis planned to wait in a corner of the livestock show, hide the revolver in the marsupial pouch of a dog disguised as a kangaroo (because there was a contest of dog costumes), and let loose a rain of bullets point blank, unceremoniously sacrificing his own life in order to rip out the tyrant's by the roots. Jaime, faced with such delirium and bile, said nothing, but thought: "When the Chinese say that if you save someone from suicide you must feed him for the rest of your life, we must understand that each person's fate is their own. If this madman has decided to give his existence to eliminate my enemy, I must accept that fate is offering him to me as a weapon. My duty is to support him in his madness, buy him the dog, the felt for the kangaroo disguise, pay for his meals and hotel until the day of the event. Then, once the crime is committed, I'll wash my hands and return, safe and sound, to where my beloved awaits. I'm certain it's the god Sara Felicidad believes in who is protecting me now. I can't forget that night when, as I gave her a monumental orgasm, my wife, so as not to wake the neighbors with her cries, sank her mouth into the pillow, leaving a saliva stain in the shape of a heart. . . ."

They spent a month shut away in the Mapocho Hotel, eating only canned mussels and quince. With demented patience, Luis Ramírez dangled a thick German sausage just out of reach of a mangy Saint Bernard bought on the cheap at the municipal dog pound, determined to teach him stand on his two hind legs. Jaime, overcoming his disgust, took the dog's measurements and fabricated the kangaroo suit. The long, fat tail stuffed with burlap turned the cur into a more stable tripod. At Quinta Normal, the policemen burst out laughing and didn't think to look in the marsupial pouch. The contest judges, indignant, refused to reward such a monster, preferring to give the golden bone to a Pekinese dressed as Marie Antoinette. Ramírez, pretending to be offended, sat down beside his immense kangaroo between two corrals of milk cows, and he waited. Jaime, from afar, paler than a dead man, his tongue now a heart, hid behind the chicken coop. After a little while, a growing murmur announced the presidential committee's arrival. Carlos Ibáñez del Campo, dressed in an impeccable military uniform crossed by a tricolor sash—insignia of supreme authority—tall, straight, robust, bony, his low shoulders offering firm support for the epaulets, his face strikingly white, in which shone two intense blue eyes framed by short, jet-black hair and a thick black mustache. Like the leader of a herd of elephants, he would not let anyone walk in front of him.

All of his companions—soldiers, police, ministers, ecclesiastics, even his wife—followed behind him. Jaime could not help but feel terror at seeing the mythical mass, whose lack of expression gave him the look of a marble mask as he walked with a velvety, regular stride; his arms, disdaining motion, hung frozen at his sides and culminated in long and beautiful hands. Something emanated from that body, a kind of dense atmosphere, an invisible egg white that invaded the minds of the citizens, imposing respect, affirming his dictatorial power. Now my father understood why the wildest horses, in the colonel's presence, were paralyzed in terror. . . . With a duplicitous kick, Ramírez shook the Saint Bernard from his torpor and made him stand up. He extracted the revolver from the belly pouch and ran toward the president, aiming the gun at him. Jaime's mind entered another dimension of time where seconds were eternal. Everything began to slide past with extreme slowness. Ibáñez looked at his aggressor without the slightest expression changing the stateliness of his face. He confronted death like a wax statue. And in his cold immobility, before my father's entranced eyes, he was cloaked in nobility. Ramírez, on the other hand, his face contorted, streaming sweat, trembling like an epileptic, made Jaime ashamed for his lack of dignity. Ramírez let out a fevered cry and pulled the trigger of his Smith and Wesson, but the bullet didn't fire. Jaime returned to normal time, and, with a couple of quick leaps, he stood in front of Ibáñez, opening his arms in a cross.

"Don't shoot! This is not the death Don Carlos deserves!"

"There is only one death!" shouted the boy, beside himself. And, aiming at my father's forehead, he pulled the trigger a second time. And for the second time, the bullet didn't fire.

Jaime leapt toward him, took him by the arm and turned him. Ramírez fired for the third time. The bullet discharged and exploded the head of a 650-pound champion cow; after disgorging a greenish stream from her anus, she collapsed onto her caretaker, smashing his ribs. A tremendous strength born of madness turned Ramírez into a raving lunatic. While Doña Graciela Letelier walked elegantly toward the exit, unconcerned for her husband's fate, soldiers and military and civil police tried to tame the possessed man. The kangaroo dog, with no apparent master, destroyed his long tail and began to devour chickens. The huasos, brandishing rakes, cried for the frustrated assassin to be lynched. Jaime tumbled with him to the ground, receiving some of the kicks that rained down on the guilty man. He thought his final hour had come, but an authoritative shout that made the windows in the ceiling shake silenced and paralyzed humans and animals alike.

"Do not kill him! He is only a poor madman! Take him to the madhouse and let the visit continue!"

The dominating power of the president's voice was so immense that, in an instant, the cow, the crushed man, the chicken-eater, and Ramírez had all disappeared. A Viennese waltz played and the public followed the committee from corral to corral, as if nothing had happened. Jaime, groaning, got up and shook the dust from his suit. With a slight but precise movement of his right hand, Ibáñez ordered him to approach.

"I congratulate you, sir: you not acted not only as a brave man, but also as a model citizen! You put your life in danger to save the life of your head of state! If the gun hadn't jammed, that crazy man would have blown your brains out! You deserve a reward!"

"Your Excellency, sir, I want neither honor nor money. I only ask one thing: since I love horses, my dream is to become a groom and serve you. I would care for your animal like my own son!"

"Your request is timely: Don Aquiles, Grenadier's old care-taker, wants to retire. I will send you immediately to the Linares estate so that he can prepare you, and in a couple of months I'll come and see how you do. If my horse looks happy, I will hire you permanently."

Just like that, like a pawn moved by gods in a cosmic game of chess, Jaime had achieved his two main goals: win Ibáñez's trust and become the caretaker of his favorite horse. That is, the only being with whom the tyrant abandoned his cold carapace and displayed a vulnerable heart. . . . Still, Jaime did not feel proud of his victory, because in truth he did not understand it. He gave himself rational explanations to justify his illogical risk: if Ibáñez had fallen under the chubby boy's bullets, he wouldn't have really died, because the man walking through the animal exhibit was not a man but an image fabricated to impress the masses, a hollow, soulless shape. And it was precisely there, in his soul, that the bullet had to enter. That true soldier was not afraid to die, and he was willing to sacrifice his life for a heroic cause. Assassinating him during an official act, dressed as military man and president, was to offer him a gift, to open the doors of history to him with honor. No! The crime had to happen intimately, with the caudillo dressed in civilian clothes and shedding human tears. My father also told himself: "It's useless to eliminate a symbol, because symbols are replaceable; scarcely does one colonel disappear than another one comes to occupy the vacant place. I must eliminate a man not in uniform, because he is unique, and his loss irreparable." These reasons were valid, but they did not explain why he had stood in front of the tyrant with his arms open like Christ on the cross, giving himself to the bullet with a feeling so strange that when he thought of it, his throat closed up and his face turned red. Better to bury it all in the irrational swamp, and continue with his plan without looking back. His plays were masterly: if he went on like that, very soon he would achieve a checkmate.

Don Aquiles, a little old man with a face crisscrossed by deep wrinkles, his smile that of a toothless child, gave him his first lesson.

"Look here, friend: if you aren't humble, you'll ruin the horse. Recognize that you are not his master, that you are here to obey him and never demand anything the noble beast cannot give. Remember that as tame as he may seem, even if he does not show intelligence, he possesses a long memory and he has his pride: if you offend him today, he might bite you tomorrow. Have a great respect for him: don't make any sudden movements when you're around him, and if you begin a gesture, finish it without getting ahead of yourself. Speak to him in a serene and monotonous voice until the sound comes to form part of his world. Look at him with honor and affection, directly in the eyes. If he backs away, you back away as well. If he approaches, then you approach. Forget yourself, learn how to sense when he wants to be alone, when he's hungry, when he's asking for mares, when he has finished grazing and wants to return to the corral. Try to understand his language, never force him, be always calm and don't try to tame him or give him orders; rather, try to insinuate actions and encourage him. The horse's soul is generous and thirsty for affection. But if some cruel nobody offends him with bad treatment, it will ruin that beautiful soul. Rewards and punishment, the carrot and the whip, are reserved for Don Carlos, who knows how to impose his authority without brutality. You, rising devotedly each morning at daybreak, should take care of Grenadier's health and well-being, leaving no inch of his body untouched, un-rubbed and un-caressed. The good priests dedicate all the hours of their lives to God: you should be no different from them, only in place of God, the horse."

On the Linares farm, trying to rid his brain of the thousand fragrances of Sara Felicidad's paradisiacal body, Jaime concentrated on absorbing Don Aquiles' teachings down to the smallest detail.

The old man was eaten away by rheumatism and arthritis and moved with difficulty, but he and Grenadier understood each other to perfection. He knew how to discern the horse's mood from the position of his ears, the tremor of his nostrils or the intensity of his huffs. He caught the slightest change in his eyes, in the tone of his whinny, the position of his tail. From the taste of his sweat he could say if something had frightened the animal, or if he was tired, or if he needed to change the balance of his food. Moreover, observing the varying shine of his hide, he could predict the weather.

"Today Grenadier woke up with his back opaque: though the morning is sunny, after midday there will be torrential rain."

He was never wrong.

Two months passed. The old man said:

"Don Carlos will come tomorrow, but tonight, I'm going back to my origin. Don't worry, friend, you know everything now, and the horse won't notice I am gone. Bring a shovel." Walking painfully (his joints almost didn't work at all), Don Aquiles, by the light of a candle and followed by Jaime, crossed the pasture until he reached a leafy willow. "Since I have no one, this tree will weep for me." He indicated to Jaime where he should dig the hole. The clouds dissolved; a concert of frogs, following the rhythm of the digging shovel, celebrated the full moon's shine. When the hole was finished the old man took off his clothes. His dry flesh seemed silvered in the clear night. "You do the same, friend. Give me your clothes and put mine on. Never take off this straw hat. That way Grenadier won't realize that I left and he'll give you the same affection he gives me. Tomorrow at dawn rub yourself with oats, spit on his snout, and give him a carrot. Everything else will happen on its own." Rolling up my father's clothes like a pillow, he lay down in the pit. "Now I'm going to give up my soul. It wants to go home. I was only passing through here. Cover me with a lot of dirt and tomorrow have the horse stamp on it. Tell the president that I left to see my family and I won't be back. With you here, he won't take long to forget me. The powerful have a thousand more important things in their heads than remembering a poor old man. Thanks for everything, friend, and let's see if some years down the road you don't come lie down beside me." Smiling, the old man looked toward the starry sky, took in a long breath of fresh air, and with a sudden exhalation, blew out the candle and died. . . . Jaime covered him with the sweet earth, and amid the delirious croaking of the toads, wearing the mended pants and shirt and a rough poncho that smelled of equine sweat, plus the straw hat licked by countless rains, he set off back to the stable, where a hard mattress and two army blankets awaited him. . . . To free himself of Sara Felicidad, who appeared to him waving a garnet tongue a foot long, he began to masturbate; but the calluses that covered his hands, though he soaked them in saliva, made his rubbing into torture. Moreover, the pistol incrusted in his thigh gave off such a disturbing stench that his vigorous desire softened until it was suffocated in a leaden sleep.

†

At three in the afternoon the bulletproof car arrived: an enormous Ford painted khaki. Two muscled soldiers with machine guns and mushroom helmets got out. Then the driver, another uniformed Hercules, and finally Carlos Ibáñez del Campo, dressed as a colonel. Jaime's knees gave out, he lowered his head and began to tremble. The president said in a friendly voice:

"How are things, Don Aquiles? Is my horse behaving?"

"The horse is in excellent health, Don Carlos. But I am not Don Aquiles."

The henchmen immediately pointed their machine guns at my father. He took off his hat.

"Remember, sir . . . Quinta Normal . . . the attack , , , you rewarded me with this job . . ."

"Oh, yes, of course! You're the one who risked your life for me! How could I forget you? Well, bring Grenadier to me. We'll see how you've managed."

The white spot on the horse's forehead shone like a star, his hooves were brushed and coated with a thin layer of oil, his mane thinned and braided, the areas where sweat built up clipped, the saddle lay nice and straight on his back, settled over the ribs and not the spine, the bit rested in the corners of his mouth without deforming them; the quadruped showed his happiness by trotting with his head and tail raised. He stopped in front of his master and demanded attention by lightly bumping his head against his chest. Ibáñez's face lost its rigidity and broke into a mute laugh that showed two lines of teeth almost as large as the horse's.

"You look good, Grenadier! Let me see you up close!"

The colonel checked the color of his eyes and of the membrane in his mouth, making sure there were no wounds from a tooth rubbing too roughly. He palpated the legs without finding any swelling, examined the shoes to see if they were missing nails, took a watch from his pocket and timed the movement of the horse's sides to be sure that the animal had sixteen respirations per minute; he placed his fingertips on the artery that went along the lower jaw, and after measuring the heartbeats, he exclaimed:

"Bravo, Aquiles, my horse has never been better cared for! You can stay here your whole life! Here!" And he handed a roll of bills to Jaime. My father, his face red, refused to take it.

"You can send supplies once a week as usual, sir, that's all I ask for. I don't need money. I work because I love it."

The president put his money away. He sighed in satisfaction.

"Your disinterest moves me, Aquiles. I will send supplies twice a week."

Jaime fell to the ground and kissed one of the caudillo's boots, thinking: "One more master move, and the emperor will lose his head."

"Get up, Don Aquiles, and go prepare a ration of oats, beet sugar, corn, barley, and bran! I'm going to trot and gallop for an hour, and then I'll give the animal to you so you can feed and water him. . . ."

†

Jaime walked toward the stable smiling. "The man is stupid. He can't even tell the difference between Don Aquiles and me. He reacts just like the horse. Because I'm wearing the old man's clothes, he thinks I'm him. And the smell of the oats I rubbed on myself inclines him to like me. Maybe if I put a carrot in his mouth, he'll love me to the end!" He began to laugh, and looked back toward the pasture to scorn the pitiful soldier. He could not.

The sunlight, partially veiled by a herd of clouds, wrapped horse and man in a golden skin. Dazzling vision of a centaur whose matter, converted into spirit, into gold, was dancing a dance that melded beauty with efficiency. Angel-animal, triumphant artist, forgetting war and ambitions to power, Ibáñez maneuvered intricate steps at a trot, a canter, a gallop, changing lead, pirouetting, rearing up on hind legs, backing up, jumping; the man's aim was purely aesthetic. Between rider and steed there was no tension, no resistance, hand and fists were light, the powerful hindquarters reacted to the slightest call, the cadence was rhythmic, harmonious, and suddenly there was active immobility. That golden animal was focused as a hungry beast stalking its prey, a vibration moving all through his body, and he fused with a rider whose entire awareness was on his center of gravity; he concentrated there the strength of his kidneys and the vitality of his being, ready to move at the slightest cue with lightning speed and with the dense harmony of a lake.

Jaime, openmouthed, observed the centaur's dance. It seemed to him that the thrushes and the turtledoves froze in the air, enchanted by the sight; that the leaves of the trees, in spite of the riled wind, ceased to tremble; that the earth became a living hide and purred as it welcomed the impact of the four shining hooves like caresses. . . . He furiously shook his head: "Though the tyrant dresses in silk, a tyrant he remains! None of this weakness or childish admiration! Art is extraneous to morality! Though that perfect rider creates beauty, it does not wash the blood from his hands!"

†

Carlos Ibáñez del Campo began to come to the farm every weekend, always accompanied by his mushroom-headed bodyguards. After doing some marvelous exercises with Grenadier, he would have them take from the car a common soldier's pack, and, while he helped Jaime brush the animal, he would share some delicious seafood empanadas and a bottle of wine, taking long sips from the bottle's mouth. The alcohol loosened his tongue. His monologues always started the same way:

"Look, Don Aquiles, you represent the people of Chile, and as such, it is your duty to learn about the philosophy of the one who governs you. . . ."

Then, these ceremonial words recited, he would expound on one of his credos, all of them one hundred percent inspired by equine psychology.

†

"A domesticated horse whinnies very little, but when he does it means he feels that his everyday world has been disturbed. That is, the animal, accustomed to his good stable and his assured ration of grain, does not wish to recover his freedom or change his habits. People are the same way: if they have daily bread, a roof over their heads, and cheap wine, in no way will they desire progress. We must keep them content and maintain them in that small world. A modest but secure salary prevents revolutions."

And:

"The horse's ancestral instincts make it take every unusual sound to mean an enemy is present. . . . The people are just as faint-hearted. That's precisely why the government must tie the hands of the media vultures who live to sow uncertainty. The more catastrophe there is, the more newspapers are sold. The herd must be soothed! Although the national and international river is rough, the State must not let upsetting information get out. No sudden noises: better a calm lie than a true hurricane."

And:

"A wise rider gets as far away as possible from the grooms so the steed understands that their presence has no power, and the orders come only from the master. . . . The secret to dominating the people is to show them that you, the president, are the one who gives orders, annulling all other powers like Congress or the Lower House."

And:

"To make sure one is obeyed and at the same time loved by the horse, the master has to know very well how to mete out the whip with the carrot. The carrot is simple; it is a single thing. Pain is complex, and all kinds must be used: whips, reigns, spurs, blows on the bony parts of the body, and intense beatings. To be effective, the carrot must be given as soon as the horse carries out the desired action, and the punishment in the very moment of disobedience. . . . Any good government traces a line of conduct for the citizen that their own interest will keep them from crossing: this obedience will be supported by economic incentives, honors, prizes. On the other hand, if they stray from the correct path, they must be reprimanded with arrests, torture, deportation, firing squads. The citizens only behave well when they live between hope and fear."

And:

"To break a horse you need only to decrease the field of its possible choices, make it renounce its own being to exist only for the master's will. . . . The president's attitude regarding his people must be compared to the firm but affectionate authority of a father who cares for his obedient children's health, guiding them down the right path, establishing his authority as in implacable law. It is just, then, that he run the disobedient children from his house."

†

They conversed in the stables like that many times. Still, Jaime always had the impression that the tyrant was not talking to him, but to Grenadier. He caressed the animal, sliding his long hands—too fine for a soldier—over the animal's flanks with an intense love. When he felt the horse was cold and threw a blanket over his back, his brusqueness, his severe attitude, dissolved and gave way to profound affection, a child's tenderness. Jaime realized that the change was not the effect of the drink, but rather sprang from deep roots. In his whole life, the soldier's only faithful friend and confidant had been that horse. . . . One night, my father woke up with his hair standing on end; he was possessed by a thought that terrified him: if the dictator saw the Chilean people as horses, that meant he loved them from the very depths of his being. His excesses, his persecutions, his crimes, were not, then, the result of an evil soul; instead, though they were built on incorrect principles, they came from the most intense goodness. "Nooooo! Out of my head, treacherous ideas! He is not a father, not a son, he isn't a good man, he's a disgusting pig, a bloodthirsty beast, a paranoid cretin, an egomaniacal monster, a piece of shit colonel!"

†

The longed-for moment arrived. Finally, the veterinarian of the nearby town announced he was going to take a couple of weeks' vacation. The January heat was only bearable at the beach. . . . At dawn, Jaime took Grenadier to a distant corner or the estate, a small plot of land hidden in the forest where he had planted bushes of a certain yellow flower that were as delicious to horses as they were poisonous. While the animal greedily devoured those golden buttons, Jaime, on his knees, begged his forgiveness:

"Friend, I know you are worth as much as a human being, that you don't deserve the death I am giving you, but your mission is great, sacred, and your sacrifice exalted. The ancients did not sacrifice ill or defective animals on their altars, no! They offered up the most beautiful specimens to the Lord. Christ on the cross foretold your sacrifice: he is the beautiful man who gave his body not only to God, but also to humanity. So you will be: thanks to your martyrdom, the people of Chile will shake off the dictatorial yoke. Though unknown to any, you will be a sainted hero in the universal memory. I'm sorry a thousand times over, noble beast!"

†

He ran two hundred yards so he would be out of breath, and he called Ibáñez's personal phone.

"My colonel: Grenadier is very ill, he seems to be dying, and the veterinarian is on vacation! I don't know what to do, boss!"

An hour later, the president arrived at the wheel of the khaki Ford, a coat thrown on over his pajamas. With Jaime behind him he ran toward the stables, where he found a bloodcurdling scene. All of the animal's muscles were contracted, and he was alternately jumping, rearing up, falling onto his side, stamping his feet, rolling, standing up, and beating his head against the walls until his teeth broke; his eyes were bloodshot and his breath whistling—he was clearly in the throes of unbearable suffering.

Shouting vicious curses against God, Ibáñez ran to a chest and took out a first aid kit, readied a syringe and approached Grenadier, making an immense effort to switch from rage to sweetness.

"Shhhhhhhh! Shhhhhh! Easy there, friend! I'm here! This will take the pain right away! My lovely, my dear, please, hold still!"

Jaime was feeling ever guiltier for the tremendous suffering he was causing the horse, and when he heard the voice full with sadness with which that man, always so stony-faced, tried to calm the animal, he felt a tightness in his chest and his eyes filled with tears. . . . Grenadier looked at his master, opened his bloodied mouth, let out a feeble neigh, and gradually went still. The colonel rushed desperately to inject him with the medicine then pressed his fingers to the artery along his jaw and counted his heartbeats. When they went from accelerated to slow and then to total silence, Carlos Ibáñez burst into sobs. Weeping like a child, on his knees, he embraced his horse and begged in a breaking voice:

"Please, don't die! . . ."

My father, seeing him collapsed on top of the animal like that, took the opportunity to extract the foul-smelling pistol and take aim at his enemy's neck. Checkmate! He made an effort to pull his mouth into the shape of a smile, and tried to pull the trigger.

He couldn't do it—his entire hand clenched up. He took the gun in his left hand and aimed again. It clenched up too! He could not murder a man whom, very much in spite of himself, he admired. He couldn't murder a man to whom he had an incomprehensible debt: in his heart he was grateful for something, something that was mixed with an unbearable shame; but shame of what? It produced a short circuit in his mind and he was left an idiot, his two hands paralyzed.

The dictator turned his head and looked at him, then slowly got up and took the pistol, murmuring:

"Thank you, Don Aquiles." And he put the animal out of his misery. Then he fell to his knees, let out a hoarse cry, shook his body like a dog emerging from the water, threw the gun far away from him, and exclaimed: "We will douse the stables and the houses with gasoline! I want it all to burn!"

Late that night, after the flames had turned the buildings into a pile of rubble, Ibáñez gave my father a tight hug, a hug that he could not return because the paralysis had reached his elbows.

"Don Aquiles, you have been a faithful servant: take this money and go. I'm sure you have relatives who will receive you well. Tomorrow, I will put the farm up for sale. And don't try to see me again, because your presence will only bring me painful memories. Goodbye, friend!"

With energetic steps, his brusqueness recovered, he got into the Ford, and without looking back he set off, leaving a cloud of dust behind him. Jaime stayed standing in the middle of the road in the fog of dust, watching as the bills escaped from his dead hands and fluttered around him, chased by dragonflies. When the sound of the motor could no longer be heard and the dust cloud had cleared, he wasn't Jaime anymore. He had lost his memory.

✝

At first he thought someone was shooting a machine gun at him. Then he realized it was hail lashing against a corrugated iron roof. He was lying down and covered with potato sacks, newspapers, and corroded blankets. From the dirt floor where the thin mattress lay, a penetrating smell of urine emanated. The walls of the room were made of sheets of corroded tin, cardboard, and gray wood. Beside him, a woman was snoring. In that windowless shadow it was difficult to make out her face. He tried to get up. When he put down his hands, he realized they didn't react, but were hardened like claws. He brought them up to his eyes: he saw they were painted in three colors, blue, white, and red. On the blue part there was a five-pointed star. . . . His eyes gradually got used to the darkness; he pushed back the earth-coated hair that invaded his face and scratched the beard that covered his cheeks as well as he could, feeling little creatures crawling about in it. The woman moaned, pressed up against him and covered his sex with a small and soft hand. Then she went on snoring. Like a photographic negative revealed in an acid bath, he started to distinguish her features. Thin, short, straight, rancid hair; a round face; ocular globes overfilling their bleary eyelids, a mouth lacking many teeth, withered breasts, ribs visible under the skin, and, on her freckled back, a hump. . . . Something moved in a corner. A rat, maybe? The shape crawled closer to him. The body stood up and raised its arms, determined to use them as cudgels. The thing let out a human-sounding babble and climbed up on the mattress. It was a boy—five years old?—with a stomach swollen by malnutrition, thick lips and an abnormally small head. He attached himself to the hunchback's breast and began, drooling, to lick it. Jaime shrieked, shook off the flaccid arms, and went running out, half-naked under a tattered soldier's coat.

He realized he was in Santiago. The shantytown was built between the train tracks and the Mapocho river—an anemic current the color of milky coffee. Hundreds of shacks made of refuse; a purulent village sunk in the mud, dissolving like a black sugar cube under the persistent rain. A pack of dogs followed him, all of them scarred by the bald spots of mange. Desperate, he sat down under a squalid tree on an old tire that had been painted white for children to play on. The dogs stopped barking and came to lick him, pressing up against his body in search of heat. The little woman, holding a bottle of red wine in her hands, came running out with fast, short steps. Her globular eyes, gray as the roof of clouds threatening to fall onto her head, pierced him with a tragic gaze. With the voice of a beaten child, she asked:

"Salvador, my pretty puppy, are you all right? What's wrong? Are you feeling bad again? Have a drink!"

"Ma'am, my name is not Salvador, it's Jaime! Tell me what I'm doing here!"

The hunchback fell facedown in the mud, sobbing pitifully.

"So . . . you've recovered . . . your memory. . . . The dream has ended. . . ."

With his crippled hands, my father tried to pick the woman up. She sat up, leaving her legs in the mud.

"Seven years ago I found you wandering the streets, half-dead from hunger, and I brought you to live with me. Since I had never had a lover, I abused you. I gave birth to Mono, your mongoloid son. Mea culpa: for the nine months of my pregnancy, I was always drunk. I suspected that one day you would come back to yourself. Wishing the moment would never come, but knowing that no one escapes fate, I wrote you a letter. I suppose you know how to read. Here!"

†

It had stopped raining. The fog let through the first rays of a tobacco-colored sun. The hunchback rummaged around in her bra and took out a piece of ordinary paper wrapped in card stock.

"Read it now, take your time, go as slowly as you can, so you'll get to know me and understand. Meanwhile, I'll go to the shelter and feed Mono. When you finish, come say goodbye. I swear you won't have any problems. I hate making trouble for people!"

The hunchback, curving her monstrous spine even more, moved off down the deserted alley. . . . The neighbors, drunk and jobless and expecting nothing from the new day, woke up as late as possible. . . . Jaime opened the outer paper and began, with some difficulty, to decipher the compact and nervous letters.

My name is Antonia. I was born in Santiago. I am the daughter of Abel Lagos. He was a military policeman for many years, until one day, in 1929, he felt himself become a different man: he let his hair and beard grow long, and he said that since it needed no master, his head was free to cast forth hair and thoughts. They kicked him out. As soon as he was no longer a military man, he joined an anarchist group called Sol de Mayo, and he became its leader. . . . In 1930 the group tried to ambush and kill the chief of the secret police, Ventura Maturana. He was a lawyer with a cool head, tall and elegant, who had gone to Germany to study legal medicine, profiling, and, especially, new methods of torture, such as electrical shocks to the testicles, the abrading of nipples, the rupturing of eardrums, injected drugs, and other refinements. They managed to throw a bomb into his car, but in a diabolical miracle, the fucker didn't explode. The anarchists had to scatter and flee. . . . Very early the next day, I woke up to the sound of crude insults, gunshots, screams of pain, and police car sirens. A great anxiety made me get out of bed. As though I were dreaming, I ran through the streets toward the commotion. In the kiosk in the plaza, Ñato Reyes and Big Corona, the group's deputies, lay riddled with bullets. Crazed, I ran toward my progenitor's house. (I must confess that I had an intense filial love for him that amounted to devotion. Although I saw him very little, and he gave me beatings instead of caresses, his existence gave my childhood an axis around which to organize my life.)

I knock at the door. He opens. He is very nervous. He doesn't want to let me in. I ask him what's happening. He yells that I shouldn't be there. I pay him no mind and go in. I find his house converted into a bunker: tables, chairs, and mattresses covering the windows; guns, ammunition, and dynamite everywhere. My heart beats anxiously. Though I don't understand what is happening, I know my duty is to be with him! For three days I don't move from his side: we sleep side by side, we tiptoe around, we eat cold food from cans, we go out into the street both armed, and I cover him, ready to give my life for his.

At midnight the telephone rings. I'm summoned to a meeting I had requested with the heads of the Communist Party. My idea was that with their help, we could get Abel out of Chile clandestinely. . . . I say goodbye to my father to go to the meeting, I tell him not to worry and that I'll be back soon, that I'm going to ask for help. He hugs me, and for the first time in his life he doesn't turn away, and he caresses my hump. I see tears in his eyes, and I think that the dangerous situation has made him into a senile man who is very afraid to die. I feel sorry for him, not realizing he is saying goodbye to me forever, and that his first caress is also his last.

The Communists knew how to get my father's address out of me. Then, saying that the upper leaders would only arrive the next day, they locked me in a room, telling me that that way, no one in the house would realize I was there. That is how they buy enough time to carry out their plan to snitch. I think they drugged my coffee, because I sleep like a rock all night long, on a desk. . . . They wake me up late in the morning, and after a tedious political explanation, they tell me they cannot and do not want to help the anarchists: given that the workers' movement must guide their actions in agreement with the norms of revolutionary syndicalism and proletarian internationalism promoted by The Communist Manifesto, *my request was absolutely "inappropriate."*

When I left that place in desperation, I read in the newspapers that an anarchist, after fleeing his house—a real arsenal that had been raided at dawn—had attacked the Civilian Police Headquarters, throwing grenades and killing ten civil policemen. The aggressor was cornered, and he went flying through the air when he detonated the dynamite cartridges he was wearing around his waist. Much of the place was reduced to rubble.

Unable to accept the truth, I went to the store owned by the woman who lived with my father. There she was, sitting straight-faced behind the counter with staring eyes. I asked her about Abel, and immediately several men fell on top of me. I struggled beneath a mountain of bodies until they subdued me. After checking my clothes, anus, and sex for explosives, they brought me to Police Headquarters. There were a large number of police, detectives, and journalists gathered around the smoking rubble. With cameras flashing, they made me look at bits of flesh one by one until I recognized my father in a piece of foot that stuck out of his shoe. I didn't have time to bury him because I was immediately thrown into a cell, which they brought me to with my eyes blindfolded. Many policemen looked in at me through the window, wanting to burn my face into their memories in case one day I tried to take revenge. From there I was transferred to the madhouse, where they kept me for weeks in a bath of cold water so I would give up my imaginary co-conspirators. Coughing almost to the point of vomiting out my guts, I was released with unconditional freedom due to lack of grounds, since the only thing tying me to the anarchist group was the fact that I was Methuselah's daughter. (They'd given him that nickname because all the members of Sol de Mayo were younger than him.)

When I emerged into the city, without friends, without a mother—she was lost in a dingy cabaret in the red-light district, working as a whore—my suffering truly began: I had the impression that my father was still alive and that if I looked for him long enough, I would find him. And so, uselessly scouring all the neighborhoods he had frequented, I fell into the deep pit of depression. . . . Why did my parents treat me with such contempt? Why, as soon as I was born, did they get divorced? Why did they leave me locked up in a neighbor lady's house and almost never see me? Did a hump keep one from being loved by one's parents? Why was I beaten so badly by that man I adored? Everything would be calm, then he'd stare at me, he'd start to sweat, and suddenly an unwarranted rage would explode. On one occasion, after taking me out for a walk with no apparent reason, he left me hanging from a tree branch by the foot. The firemen had to come and untie me. I was entirely purple and unable to walk for a month, and I was humiliated, because from that day on, the whole neighborhood called me The Hanger.

I combed the bars in the red-light district over and over, I was assaulted for an empty purse, I was chased by people who threw rotten fruit at me and threatened to rape me, but I kept going until I found my mother. Unconcerned with the butcher wearing clothes stained by cow's blood who had her in his arms, I asked her point blank why no one had ever touched me tenderly when I was little. She got nervous and looked at me without a word. I saw guilt in her eyes. I understood, finally. "He's not my father!" Her face filled with contempt. Amid sibylline laughter she confessed the reason for so much violence. Abel had been raped. When he was ten years old, his own father, a civil policeman, drunk, had punched him several times in the testicles, leaving him impotent forever, and then destroyed his anus. . . . It turned out that I was the daughter of an uncle, my mother's brother, who I'd always seen near her, groping her. . . .

I lost my axis, I lost my north star, I lost everything. Depression had me on the skids. With no one to help me, no job, no possibility of a companion, deformed as I am, I ended up sleeping in the grottos of Santa Lucía. On that hill in the middle of the city, I plied a miserable nighttime trade. Certain depraved men came to urinate, defecate, and masturbate onto my hump. That's how I survived for several months, until a police raid put an end to the business. I started to collect paper, empty bottles and cans, I searched for food in trash cans, I cleaned the bathrooms of bars in exchange for alcohol. I cultivated fleas and lice. I was no longer human. The Hanger didn't deserve to be treated any better than a street dog. The days disappeared, the eternal night swallowed me . . . until you arrived.

Your pants were destroyed and your behind exposed, you were pursued by flies, wandering skinny as a skeleton, unable to talk, waving your cramped hands. Cruel God had finally sent me company. I robbed a drunk soldier's coat and covered him with your rags. I gathered materials from the dump and built a shack in the shantytown. Kicking and biting, I made them respect us, and in that minimal territory we found peace. Don't think you were useless: when I painted your hands with the national flag and set you to begging, I received many patriotic gifts; your paralyzed hands came to symbolize the misery and unemployment that plagued the Chilean people. Thanks to that money, every day we could buy six liters of wine, a little bread, and a couple cans of sardines. In the nights you were my glory. Though you couldn't caress me, my affection gave me the energy of four hands to massage you, fondle you, worship your entire body. Lying on your back, motionless like a Christ, you let me impale myself on your member, fountain of my life, and ride you. For seven years, I lived with the knowledge that one day you would come out of your amnesia, and once you were yourself again, you wouldn't recognize me; I lived between the sublime pleasure of our union and the pain of knowing it to be ephemeral. . . . When you recover your memory you will vanish from my life, and my life will vanish. Without you everything loses meaning, even the wine will find no soul to inebriate, for I will be empty. . . . If you are reading this line of my letter, that means that Mono and I have left the road clear for you, and from the other world we are blessing you. . . . My love, may life be benevolent to you from now on, let the cruel God become good, let him lead you to your people and cure those hands that have been the jewels of my poor existence! Goodbye forever!

Your Antonia.

Jaime, with desperate clumsiness, clutched the thick paper against his chest, let out a hoarse cry and started to sway from side to side. Suddenly, a ragged old woman went by shouting:

"The Hanger hanged herself!"

Squalid beggars began to emerge from the shacks, men, women, children, dogs. They pointed and ran, frenzied. Jaime followed them. They came to a telephone pole. There, strangled by the same rope, hung the hunchback with her purple tongue hanging out, and the mongoloid child, smiling beatifically. My father threw himself against the pole, trying to shake it as if it were a tree that could let its fruit fall. He started to shriek wildly:

"Death to Ibáñez! He's to blame for this! Down with the murderous dictatorship! Enough with the military! I call for a general strike! Social revolution!"

The shabby onlookers giggled. A young man with a face scored by wrinkles offered him a drink of bitter wine:

"Compañero, listen to a dignified anarchist that the government turned into a flea-bitten drunk. I celebrate that you've recovered your speech, but your dented memory needs to incorporate a few facts: the economic crisis was unmanageable and forced Ibáñez to renounce power and flee to Argentina. Then began the dance of coups and counter-coups. For us, it was more years of repression, assassinations, flagellation, and lack of freedom. After the uprising at the Aviation School, Marmaduque Grove—a colonel, for a change—installed a socialist government that lost no time in failing, and was substituted by the only state we have always known: the state of siege. The civilians, naively, unanimously called for democratic elections, won by Arturo Alessandri, a treacherous demagogue. After conquering the votes of the people, he has used extraordinary faculties conferred on him by Congress, just like Ibáñez, against the left, against the opposing press, labor leaders, attempts to strike—against, purely and simply, the general interest of the country, to protect foreign imperialism. We came out of the cage only to break our snouts against a stone wall!"

†

The ambulance and police sirens sounded. The unemployed men ran to disappear into their shacks. Jaime started to walk along the train tracks. He was twelve hundred miles from Tocopilla. Somehow, he had to get there to find out if Sara Felicidad and his daughter Raquel Lea still existed. Oh, right, he almost forgot, he had a son, too! What was his name? Benjamín?

FIVE

THE BOOK OF THE PRIESTESS

M Y CHILDHOOD transpired not only without the presence of my sister and my father, but also without my mother. It's true she was always there, but she wasn't complete. When Jaime left he took Sara Felicidad with him, and in her place he left me a woman who borrowed years from the future to mask her youth under the look of a mature woman: she gathered her long, sensual hair into a severe bun; she shortened her gaze by nesting it behind nearsighted glasses, and, with an insect's skill, she folded up her skeleton until she seemed small. She transformed her joy at living into a paused philosophy, and that's how she survived: hidden within herself and converted into Doña Sara, with half of her soul awake in the quotidian world and the other half sunk in waiting, determined to sleep until her Jaime, bearer of the illuminating kiss, returned. For me, she was a teacher more than a mother, a legendary being capable of seeing in the most minimal occurrences the infinite grandeur of miracle. Before the Rabbi appeared to me—a memorable event that shattered my seven-year-old spirit—I was incapable of threading moments together: between one hour and the next yawned abysses, every day was eternal, a single effect hid all of its causes, the law that ruled the world was a senseless "Just because!" Bodies were like hotel rooms where each night another spirit came to dwell, and that reality dried out while we slept; by dawn another one had grown. . . . Of that period and of my mother I remember only fragments, island-events become short stories, loose pages of a book of flesh where, with painless cuts, the acts of a humble priestess are inscribed.

THE DARKNESS

As long as the light lasted I was tied to everything I saw, to all I heard, to smells, to the surfaces that were born on contact with my skin, and these sensations combined little by little, until at dusk, when the metal shutters of the stores were lowered in a riotous symphony, they formed an enormous ball that digested the edges of my body. I was the furniture, the old wooden floor, the squawking of the vultures, the fragrance of the sea, the walkways, the wall of hills, the seagulls that flew like arrows through the window to sink their beaks into the bread. Being everything, I stopped being me until, into that chaotic and impersonal sphere, my mother slid. . . . Doña Sara, distant and present, single heart of my deformed longings, in a voice so sweet that even today, sixty years later, I can't help but weep when I remember it, sang to me the delights of giving in to death. To please her, I closed my eyes. Thinking I was asleep, she blew out the candle and went to the back of the house, which stretched out more and more until it became a ship: the bed began to rock and the sea swallowed the sheets, the rugs, the curtains, the walls, the sky, the stars, the entire earth. And I— alone, deaf, and blind—as the sphere was erased, gradually reappeared inside the cell of my consciousness. The darkness had swallowed everything, and in its black belly, everything had become an enemy. That gigantic tarantula cornered me, paralyzed me, turned me into a scream:

"Mamaaaaaaaaa!"

She came running, took me in her arms, sunk me between her breasts that smelled of newly cut grass. I trembled, sweating rivers, my pigeon heart about to explode:

"The darkness came, Mama, it's there, swollen but not full—it still has to devour the two of us!"

"My son, do I love you?"

"Yes, Mama."

"How much?"

"From heaven to earth!"

"My boy, the one who loves you is not I: the love is not mine, it comes from the Creator, I only transmit it. And as He has made everything, He loves everyone, and everyone constantly transmits the totality of His Love! Alejandrito, the darkness loves you as much as I do, because it is the shadow of the absolute Lover—she took a box of shoe polish and covered my body with the black paste. You see? Now you are part of it, the shadow is your kingdom. If you're a hunter, you must disguise yourself to catch your prey, which is a victim only because fear separates it from Love. Go on, hunter, roam the house hidden in the darkness and stalk! I'll pretend to be afraid. Follow my track silently, until suddenly you surprise me and catch me."

That's what I did. I felt my way, then my eyes got used to the darkness and I began to see the objects converted into friendly shadows. I visited the depths of closets, the bellies of the tables, the backs of the furniture, the maw of a corner. Doña Sara moved about with bare feet, but the darkness, now part of my body, transmitted her steps to me. I savored her pretend fear until, unable to resist any longer, I leapt on her, pulled her to the floor and kissed her, staining her white face with my shoe polish. Then she also dissolved into the darkness, and I was never afraid of the night again.

INTOXICATION

The first package (which my mother insisted on calling a letter) arrived five years after they'd turned my sister over to my grand-parents' care. She had written each clumsy but beautiful letter of our address with a different colored marker. Inside the metal box we found no drawing, no words, only a wax apple, cut in half and reglued, in whose heart lay a glass eye. Sara Felicidad began to cry:

"Not only does she complain that the world my parents make for her is a flavorless imitation, she also feels that her gaze is dead."

My mother sent her in reply a violin whose strings were broken, along with a little heart-shaped box that contained five new strings. In the lining of the black case she embroidered: "The strings wear out, but music is eternal. . . ." It wasn't long before she received a new package that contained the now splintered violin accom-panied by a multicolored phrase: "For the deaf divinity, only its shadow is music."

Although she loved her daughter as much as me, my mother couldn't allow herself to bring her back. The money from sales was scarce, and unemployment afflicted seventy percent of the population. The families of unemployed workers lived crammed into shantytowns in three-walled shacks, so they could save on the fourth. Some afternoons, when not a cent had entered the till, my mother closed the store and brought me to the beach to feed me on sea urchins and limpets she extracted, diving, from the roots of rocks. When I saw her disappear under the salty magma and its foamy claws, an invisible but black hand squeezed my throat. During those long seconds when the shapeless beast swallowed my mother, the entire world became an empty sphere; the seagulls, the waves, the rocks, the hills, the sea, the sky—nothing, not a scrap of matter, had meaning any longer. Only the shadows, darker and more sordid, continued to exist, advancing toward me like a net of flat snakes. I didn't scream: the cry rose up in my throat and opened my mouth until its corners split, converted into a red bird trying to grow until it filled the space of the sky. Then Sara Felicidad emerged, her luminous presence turning that dead world into a living caress. The shadows, duplicitous, glued themselves to the hot ground and passed themselves off as cool carpets. I preferred a thousand times to devour my shellfish under the sun's severe rays than to sit in those black spots that could suddenly adhere to my body and dissolve it. My mother, though she didn't understand, accepted my terror and began to sing, very sweetly, very gently—strands of honey dripping from her mouth. I calmed down and the shadows did too; they turned feline and began to purr.

One day I was feeling brave, and without asking her permission, I escaped to the sea. The first thing I found on the beach was a large crab run aground. Since I was hungry, I ate it raw. An hour later my stomach began to hurt, and I reached Ukraine House with my body swollen and a one hundred and four-degree fever. Doña Sara called the doctor, who said the poisoning was severe and they would need to bring me to the hospital in Antofagasta, a port sixty miles away. We set off in a collective taxi. I was naked and wrapped in a wet sheet, sitting on my mother's lap. When my high temperature dried the white cloth, she poured a bottle of mineral water over it. There were seven other passengers besides the driver, all looking out at the arid hills or the flat sea, all still, mute, deaf. I was being threatened by a large gray dog that held my head between her jaws, and I wished those stone statues would move, shoo away the evil beast and then caress me and sing me lullabies until I fell asleep. But no, in spite of my cries they kept their noses pressed to the glass of their windows. Doña Sara folded a newspaper to make a fan, and she waved it sweetly before my face.

"Calm now, Alejandrito, we'll be there soon."

"Mama, I don't know where I am!"

"I don't know where I am either, but I know I'm here, beside you." Her reply calmed me for a few minutes. Then the gray she-dog threatened me again.

"Mama, I don't know where I'm going!"

"I don't know where I'm going either, but I know with whom I go: I'm going with you. Will you go with me?"

"Yes, Mama."

"Then, my child, we're doing better than our neighbors. They want to be far away, and don't even know they are here. And the driver, who knows where he's going, doesn't know who he's going with."

I laughed, I breathed easier; I was a little less hot. I looked out the window. Bigger and more ferocious, the gray dog was running alongside the taxi, biting at the tires!

"It wants to tip us over, Mama. We can never defeat it."

"It's true, we cannot defeat it or avoid its attacks, but we know how to resist it. If you flee, it chases you. If you give yourself, it disappears, because it is your refusal that creates it. Give it your body, give it your fever, give it your fear."

Trusting in Doña Sara, I let the animal come and I watched it eat me. Now the dog was swollen, the dog had a fever, the dog let out a continuous cry. I began to feel better. . . . When we reached the hospital they wouldn't admit me, because I wasn't sick anymore.

THE FUNERAL

Although synthetic saltpeter—which the Germans, extracting nitrogen from the air, began to manufacture during the blockade in

World War I   was conquering more and more markets, the companies in the north managed to draw out their death throes: they lowered production costs by paying their workers' salaries in tickets valid only in the mine's stores. Those men saved little or nothing—a loaf of bread was four hours of work—and the whores in Tocopilla, gathered in cabaret-hotels along Ramón Freire Street (named after the head of state who abolished slavery in 1823), half-dead from hunger, fought kicking and scratching over the sailors from the few cargo ships that docked in port. Enormous halls, where throngs of seamen and whores used to dance hot boleros to incite a more intimate grinding, were now haunted by two or three painted wraiths who, to squeeze a few bills from a sailor after inflicting on him the most insidious pisco, had to rock him like a dead weight. Brainless from alcohol, the drunk became easy prey for those scavenging females, who sometimes fought over him with blades. Sometimes the stabs missed their mark and landed instead in the customer's body. That's how one Swedish stoker's penis was cut off. . . . Squinty, a little blond girl with slanted eyes—the daughter of an unknown man and May Li, the Chinese whore—came to the beach giving little cries and skipping. I was playing with little lead soldiers under Doña Sara's parasol, while she took a siesta. Squinty opened a tin box that had once contained English biscuits, and, enraptured, she showed me the flaccid member cut off at its root.

"It's from a gringo sailor. He bled out and died. My mother and the other girls threw him in the ocean last night."

She gave us a nervous laugh. My little friend pretended to bend over to kiss it, then grabbed it and threw it at my face. I jumped like a startled cat and dodged it. It flew and landed right between Doña Sara's breasts. Squinty was scared, and she made a break for it. My mother woke up smiling, but her mouth contracted when she saw the pale creature in front of her face.

"Great heavens, what is this? A strange shellfish, or a real penis?" For long minutes my laughter wouldn't let me explain so mysterious a visit. When I could finally explain its origin, she deposited the remains in the little box, closed it, gave a somber sigh, and said: "Though they have a great destiny, human beings make it small by defying God's designs! What an absurd death: a being created to sail through the ether to the ends of the universe, turned into fish chow! Still, his sacred organ has survived him, and it is in our hands to give it the fertile destiny it deserves. Alejandrito: every day from the doorway of Ukraine House, we see the wall of dry hills rising up without a blade of grass lightening the sad color of their red dust. Poor things, there they are, abandoned like giant, masterless dogs! We're going to claim them as ours, we're going to take care of them! This severed member has come to give us the encouragement we needed to begin our act of insemination: we will go and bury it on the desolate peak of Don Pancho Hill. Then, in the same place, with the Mayor's approval, we will plant a pepper tree, the only tree that can survive in these dry lands and that can easily grow over thirty feet tall. We will work hard so we can pay the salary of a municipal employee, who will go every day for a year to nourish it with twenty-five gallons of water. After that it won't be necessary, because the roots will be strong and the great plant will live from the nighttime humidity. . . . It's true that the two of us alone cannot create a forest, but . . . You understand?"

"Yes, Mama, I understand: you can't change the world, but you can start the change!"

Many children went with us in solemn procession to climb to the top of the hill, where we buried the tin box. One month later, on that land that had been sterile for ages, we attended the planting of the first tree. Maybe, little by little, the inhabitants of Tocopilla would go on offering pepper trees until finally, with the passing years, the sad mountain wall would be colored green.

KITES

"Mama, you always talk to me about God. What's God?"

"I don't know what God is, my son, but I feel his presence."

"Where is he?"

"Here! If he's not here, he's nowhere."

"What is it you call 'here'?"

"All of this, the earth, the sky, you, me, others. 'Here' is also God: there is only God."

"Then he's alone! He must get really bored!"

"No, because he dresses up like us to play. We are God's game."

"Is the game also God?"

"Alejandrito, go play and you will be with God!"

"And if I stop playing, Mama?"

"Then the world will end!"

Doña Sara finished gluing a rectangle of tissue paper to bamboo sticks, then added a tail and a long string rolled around a metal bobbin.

"Here's your kite. There's a good wind blowing today, you can fly it easily."

Happy, I felt I was master of the celestial elements, a magician who could raise my bridge made of thread and paper up to the center of the cosmos, where God's immense eye would be obliged to reply to the two questions I was going to send up him: "Where is my father?" and "Why has he abandoned us?" In front of the pier stretched a vacant plot of land occupied by a tribe of pelicans, fat and pretentious and sashaying about with a sultan's airs, savoring the albacore guts the fishermen tossed out to them. They thought the food they received without effort was an homage befitted to their bodies' sublime beauty; they didn't realize the fishermen saw them as feathered garbage cans. Doña Sara had told me: "As soon as it is uttered, the word believes itself more important than the mouth. Distrust your vanity." The miserable birds deigned to leave me a few square yards of terrain, and, with intense pleasure, I raised my little comet. On the pier, the seafood sellers were using spikes to crack open dark spheres. While my silky square beat in the sky, I thought I heard an angelic choir intoned by those sea urchin tongues. On a piece of paper with a hole punched in the middle I wrote my two questions, passed it over the bobbin, and the wind helped it start to climb up the thread. But its trajectory was cut short. How short my party had been! A boy with long yellow ringlets, a little velvet suit with a lace collar, and patent leather shoes, flying a big British flag, shouted defiantly and crossed his string with mine. In a few seconds it was cut, and my kite and my messages were carried off on the wind. I realized he was maneuvering his bobbin wearing leather gloves. "Rotten boy, he's using cured string! He's put the string through carpenter's glue and passed it through ground glass!" I started to cry at such an unequal fight, and I ran to Ukraine House to ask my mother to give me a more robust string. . . . Doña Sara, smiling, dried my ears with her fragrant, starched apron, placed a candy in my mouth, and told me:

"In his game, God sets out battles for you to see if you can triumph without destroying your enemy, converting his attacks into riches. Don't try to fight him with the same conditions, don't respond to him with the same kind of weapon. Neither you nor I are so ferocious as to cure our good string. We have to attack him outside the cruel system with which he has adulterated the world. . . . My son: create alliances. The pelicans will help you.

They're greedy animals, so they defecate a lot. Put on overalls and roll in their excrement. Then, once you are smelling awful, when the elegant little gringo flies his national flag, put your body next to his. Press against him. The stench will disgust him, and to save his suit from the fecal matter, he'll run away and leave his double-crossing kite behind."

That's what I did. I came home euphoric. I hung the English flag like a trophy at the head of my bed, and then I turned myself over to Doña Sara's hands as she sank me into a perfumed bath and rubbed me until, in pure delight, I started to imitate the proud cawing of my pelicans.

LOVE POTION

When I turned five years old, the Rabbi, corroded by impatience but still not appearing directly so as not to burn my childish brain, dictated images to me in a sweet whisper in order to teach me to read. He started with the letters, one by one, interpreting their shape, their personality, and their function. I couldn't understand much; however, in the shadowy zone where one is an ancient being from the moment of birth, the message was received. The A, he told me, is the point of an arrow preparing to travel to infinity. The B is the Universal Mother, doubly pregnant, ready to give birth to us in flesh with the lower curve, and with the upper curve in spirit. The C is a half-moon, symbol of intuition, active, hungry for knowledge. The D is the other half of that moon, in repose, but only half full. The C and the D unite in the O, a complete star. The E is the body, vertical line, with its three horizontal manifestations: the desire of the sex, the feelings of the heart, and the mirages of the brain. . . . What he told me of the rest lies buried in my memory. However, I retain the act of love or of hate that the syllables signified. For example, in AB there is first the cosmic impulse, fecund, of the A, and then conception, the concrete birth of the B. Material becomes spirit. On the other hand, in BA, the desire to conceive, to go down—the density of B—is put in front of the divine longing to rise up, A, and the latter becomes a prisoner. The spirit becomes material. For the Rabbi, perfection lay in the phrase ABBA. What did it mean? Crazy Caucasian! After five years of life, how did he expect me to understand anything? However, the Rabbi's cryptic whispers turned letters forever into a sacramental theater, and soon, as Doña Sara led me through the newly inaugurated Municipal Library, I grabbed the first book that my short stature allowed and I started to read fluently, without a single mistake, from *The Hunchback* by Paul Féval. My mother almost fainted, but on seeing me reciting the lines as if I were in a trance, she sat down beside me and listened to me for three hours. Then she said:

"You read marvelously! But do you understand what you read?"

"Of course, Mama, this book tells your story!"

"My story?"

"Enrique de Lagardere is a beautiful man who transforms his body to disguise himself as something he isn't, hiding his inner light, his love. Before my father left, you were Sara Felicidad, an enormous white angel who sang instead of speaking. Now you are discreet Doña Sara. I'm impatient for my father to return, so your body will lengthen and you can show the world what you are."

My mother hid her tears, took me in her arms, and went back to the store. There we found the sign painter, who was changing the name of Ukraine House. From now on it would be called Faith Corner. . . . Business was bad. In the past, the men had been drawn there by their desire to see a giant of sculptural proportions who waited on them with her opera singer's voice. But now, the spectacled lady who spoke in a grandmother's cadence kept them away. Instead they went to shop at Don Cassígoli's, the Italian who wasn't shy about displaying his daughters' curves. . . . Doña Sara said to herself: "The three necessities that no crisis can do away with are those of nourishment, of love, and of God. The first I'll leave to the bakers, the last to the priests, and I'll take care of the middle one. I will sell potions and amulets to find Prince Charmings, to rekindle flames, repair broken plates, calm the cheated lover, attract good luck. . . ." She liquidated the merchandise she had left and filled the place with bottles of every color. They contained only tap water with vegetable dyes, but she had spent entire nights with them reciting prayers that she made up herself. For each "magic potion," the blessing was different.

"When we want love's magic to be strong, we must practice it responsibly. . . . But, to achieve miracles, Alejandrito, the wizards' secret is to have faith in the faith of others. . . ."

The first month, the clientele grew as people visited out of curiosity. Then it started to dwindle. My mother decided to give the business a push by adding to the sale of each potion some white magic tips. . . . Miss Purísima Verdugo, director of the girls' school, entered furtively into what she saw as a den of sin:

"Señora, between the two of us and in the greatest secrecy, I must ask you for a double love potion: not only do I aspire to be loved, but also to love. Because of the name I carry, I am first pure (I'm burdened with a hymen turned to rhinoceros skin), and secondly a tormentor—that is, a castrator—and it has kept me from finding affection. Help me, by God or the Devil!"

Doña Sara packed up a bottle filled with a red liquid that had sunflower seeds floating in it.

"Miss, if you want to love and be loved, the main thing is to have a good relationship with yourself. To start with, change your name. Choose a flower, maybe Rose, and change Verdugo into Casaverde. Gargle an infusion of parsley to avoid bad breath, bathe with this soap of seven perfumes, and each night before you go to sleep, caress yourself before a mirror of the highest quality. Take this piece of magnetic rock, go to church while mass is being said, and place it in the font of holy water while saying: 'Magnet you are, magnet you'll be, to me love and luck you'll bring!' Go to the Police Stadium, take shooting lessons, pistol and rifle, so you can learn to rid yourself of the inner aggression corroding you. There, a man will approach you, intrigued by what you are doing. Invite him for a walk on the beach. Sit down to have coffee at a restaurant, and, when he gets distracted, pour into his cup the remains of a cow's heart mixed with your menstrual blood that you've chopped up using a black-handled knife and put to dry in the oven until it turns to dust. Take seven handfuls of sand from the footprints this person leaves, and put them in the sun covering a fresh chicken's egg. When a chick hatches, that man, who will be as crazy with love as you are, will not stop trying until he wins you. . . ."

Two months later, with the same slyness as before, the slender director came in again; more than a woman she seemed like a stick, and, spilling tears, she implored:

"Oh, señora, after swallowing the potion I did everything you told me to. I got the desired result: I love and I am loved! But the one who came to the shooting lessons and was excited by me was Father Honorato! I couldn't believe it at first, but I went on with the ceremony. He drank the coffee, his sandy footprints produced a chicken, and now he doesn't leave me alone under sun or shadow. The other day, while I was confessing, he raised his cassock, brought his enormous thing close to the grate, and spit his fecund juice right in my face. Instead of crying out against such a scandal I was silent, rocked by spasms of joy. But you will understand, ma'am, a small town is a large Hell, and every eye will come to rest on our sacrilegious passion! Please, give me something to cure love!"

Doña Sara sadly wrapped up a black antidote in which laurel leaves floated.

"Go to mass every Friday for six weeks, and while he is saying mass, without anyone noticing, you must eat a barbecued sheep's heart. Then steal a candle, light it at midnight, write 'Honorato' on a piece of blotting paper, and burn it in the flame saying: 'Black-winged priest, leave my life now, never offend me again, or your soul will fall into the abyss!' After this, your persistent lover will go away."

The woman, stashing the bottle in her purse, burst into convulsive sobs. My mother, exasperated, picked up a broom and started to beat her:

"Cowardly woman! What you give, you give to yourself! What you don't give, you take from yourself! Stop suffering for what you don't have and enjoy what you do! You are an offering, the highest manifestation of love! Be capable of purifying your soul, not to lock yourself away but to give yourself! Everything that seems separate is joined for all eternity: sink into your dreams and find the mysterious path that has no limits! While you advance with your small faith, other forces, much vaster, are working for you! See where desire takes you; if you don't resist, your passions will become sacred. . . ."

The next day, Purísima Verdugo packed her bags and disappeared. No one seemed to miss her. The Minister of Education immediately sent another director, just as thin as the previous one. . . . When Miss Inmaculada Barrera, with extreme slyness, came into Faith Corner to ask for a double love potion, Doña Sara wouldn't wait on her, and she left, cursing. My mother, fatigued, said to me:

"Alejandrito, if she lacks something, it's because she doesn't want it. How difficult it is to truly desire! Few realize that the most important desire is the wish to give freely. I'm going to change the store's specialty: let's leave magic to the magicians!"

SUCCESS

My mother had the idea to open a café thanks to Super-Beggar-Man, the Jobless Crusader, an old man who hadn't worked in half a century. He had put together a costume inspired by Superman comics, but instead of a superhero he was a super-failure. Some gray long johns, a mangy bathing suit, a shirt now become an ensemble of patches, an eaten-away poncho hanging like a cape, some fetid rubber tennis shoes painted red, and his last three locks of hair dyed red. Super-Beggar-Man climbed up onto anything tall—walls, boxes, trucks, windowsills—and from there he would leap onto passers-by, most of the time making phenomenal belly flops, to implore in a nasal voice:

"Not a thing I can do! Everything is impossible for me! Kryptonite takes away Superman's strength, Super-Beggar-Man gets his from loose change!"

With the few coins he obtained, after buying a *marraqueta* roll, he came to see my mother:

"Dear Doña Sara, I only received enough for bread. With my lack of powers I haven't been able to change it into a cheese sandwich. You, who are a witch, can help me." Smiling, she would cut a slice of Gruyere and make the miraculous transformation. The antihero would show his rotten teeth as he pouted: "Any crust is hard for my soft bones, and, though I try to extract a good hot coffee from the other dimension, I get distracted. I hope you can convince the highest-ranking molecules to make it materialize. With four sugar cubes, please!"

The Jobless Crusader dipped the bread into the sweet concoction, and after scarfing it down, hitting himself in his belly rather than his chest (confusing one character with another), he let out a Tarzan cry and left without saying thank you.

"Alejandrito, just like that ungrateful man, we are really all Super-Jobless. We were created to fulfill a cosmic task, but we lost our memory. What was our mission? We live like parasites, sucking the marrow from the planet and doing it no good. Always in anguish, feeling ourselves to be unfinished, we complete ourselves with hope. Someday I'll have meaning, someday I'll be loved, I'll be applauded, I'll turn lead into gold, I'll discover how to not grow old, I'll conquer illness, I'll avoid death! Given that our main activity is waiting, why not make it pleasant?" And Doña Sara threw her amulets and colored water into the toilet, exchanged the counters for tables and chairs, installed indirect lighting, painted the walls and the ceiling blue with clouds, like a palace, and so she inaugurated The Happy Wait. . . . Though she didn't advertise it, she added a good dose of aguardiente to the coffee, and so the place filled up. In addition to waiting tables, Doña Sara sat on a small stage and played guitar, singing languid boleros in a scratchy voice to disguise her golden throat: *"Mientras viva lo amaré, pero este amor solitario, de mi pecho en el santuario, sólo yo conservaré."*

The cripple Gamboa, who had ambitions to run for mayor, learned of the café's success and arrived full of flattery to mask his desire to win a vote.

"Oh, Doña Sara, this time you took fate by the horns: an elegant café was just what Tocopilla needed. You deserve to triumph, because you have all the requirements I read about in an article in *Life* magazine: to be successful it's necessary to be in the right place at the right time, and to be the right person! If I were mayor I would get you the very best imported coffee, and—" he couldn't finish because my mother, disgusted, interrupted him:

"Stop that seductive chatter, and quit repeating Yankee bullshit like a parrot! The only right time is now, the right place is where we are, and the right person is oneself. Wherever we go, we are the right person, at the right time, and in the right place, as long as we are conscious beings. If we aren't, we will say, as you do: 'Oh, I'd like to be somewhere else, others deserve success, not me; my time has not yet come!' *Caramba*, Señor Gamboa, if you're unable to understand that here is your where, now is your when, you are your who, and this is your what, go buy votes somewhere else!"

FRIENDS

At The Happy Wait, time seemed like a sleepy cat; the world came to a halt and a mug of tasty coffee became a universal balm. Half-drunk on the sneaky aguardiente and the rum in the pastries and the boleros sung like lullabies, everyone let pass, like water under a distant bridge, Ibáñez and the massacres of workers and students, the rebellions at the military marina, the coups, the rise of fascism, the greedy speculations of US bankers. Today swallowed yesterday and tomorrow. It also swallowed scandals. . . . Miss Inmaculada Barrera could no longer hide her pregnant belly. Wagging tongues calculated that the mosquito had bitten her in Antofagasta because, according to her, she went there every month to visit her "family." The gossip continued even though the director, troubled by an attack of mysticism, began to go every day, wearing a repentant expression, to confession. The curtain was pulled back when Miss Purísima Verdugo arrived, also with a bun in the oven, and kicked in the confessional door, forcing the priest to lower his cassock in shame. Father Honorato, who also went once a month to Antofagasta, to "buy candles," lived up to his name and honored one of his skinny lovers in the morning, and the other in the afternoon. Faced with such a complex problem, there was no possibility of marriage or abortion. No one wanted to replace the priest with another—in all of his sermons, he cited just one line of the Gospel and told at least a dozen colorful jokes (a precious entertainment in that small town that couldn't even boast of a movie theater)—and so everyone sailed under the flag of ignorance. Called "assistants" by the faithful, the two pregnant women gave birth elbow to elbow and then began to live together, sleeping in the same bed, one to the left and one to the right of the ardent priest. In the afternoons the three of them came, pushing a double carriage, to sit and drink hot chocolate and eat *alfajores*, grateful that, through her magical spells, Doña Sara had brought them together. . . .

My mother also brought happiness to the cripple Gamboa. One day she told him:

"Look, friend, I'm sick of seeing you staggering from table to table, thinking that the only friends you have are the ones whose votes you can buy! You live a lonely life because you think you're a cripple, not a human being. I'm going to fix your foot: it will stop bothering you when I put the compress of a woman on it. Marry Cristina!"

"Cristina? She's crazy!"

"No, she's not crazy, she's a saint, and only a saint could bear such a nasty man as you! Dance with her!"

"Me, dance?"

"Yes sir, a *cueca*! Make the most of your country's marvelous folklore: the cueca doesn't have set steps, you follow the rhythm as you like and move however you want! Raise your arm, wave a kerchief, stomp your feet, feel like a rooster in heat and go steal your hen!"

And my mother started to sing, asking the patrons to move the tables aside and clap their hands. The cripple Gamboa, with his mouth dry and eyes wet, danced for the first time in his life. At each turn, each advance, each wave of the kerchief, it looked like he would collapse. But he was moved by desire because Cristina lowered her ridiculous disguise of a martyr, and she couldn't hide the generous volume of her breasts and her thighs; he always recovered his balance and went on dazzling the female. The object of his advances, covered in sweat, moaning as if in orgasm, put her feet together, opened her arms, raised her eyes until you could only see their whites, and was lifted five feet off the floor. It seemed her intention was to break through the ceiling and disappear into the heavens, but the cripple grabbed hold of her ankles, shrieking:

"Don't go, Cristinita! Tell God to wait for you, I need you more than he does!"

From the saint's open mouth, a stream of saliva poured over the lover's head. He felt he was being baptized.

"Hallelujah, I've only now been born! I'm a new man, I'm not a cripple anymore!"

Suddenly, his beloved fell into his arms, and, after breaking wind, he carried her tight against his chest, walking on tiptoe on his crippled foot to keep from losing his balance, and he headed off to the Civil Registrar. His leg was still short, but his gait would never again be that of a cripple. . . .

I don't want to give the impression that all of Doña Sara's friends were well-off people; she also accepted the indigent. Three of them were her "Three Wise Men": the armless, the mongoloid, and the drunk. The first had been a worker in the salt mines, and an explosion had blown off his arms. Declared useless, he was thrown out of the mine with his pockets empty. He had to sleep on the beach inside a rusty metal barrel. He stayed in there, curled in a ball, his wounds infected, without eating, for eight days. At the end of that period, a great crowd of bees came to land on his stumps. They sucked out the pus and left. He followed them for miles until they reached a honeycomb in a cave in the cliffs. Respectfully, he drank only enough honey to calm his hunger, and then he stayed there to live. In perfect health thanks to the honey, he thought he wouldn't need to ask anyone for anything. But one day he realized he couldn't scratch his back. The unbearable itching kept torturing him, and rubbing against the grotto's walls brought no relief. . . . He arrived at the café desperate. The patrons confused him with a beggar and scorned him, but my mother, noting that his stumps were covered in live bees, murmured:

"He's a wise man."

The armless man looked at her with the eyes of a beaten child, ashamed and unable to tell her his problem. Doña Sara, telepathic thanks to her own sorrowful love, immediately understood the other's pain. She went to him, asked him to turn around, and with intense concentration began to scratch his back. The man fell to his knees; my mother continued. It seemed that the itch, impossible to assuage, had roots that reached into his bones. . . . Suddenly the armless man let out a long sigh of relief, and in rapture he exclaimed:

"Señora, you are a blessing for all of us, the poor needy! I regret having no hands to caress you! Allow me, then, to caress you with my bees!"

She pulled me to her chest.

"My son and I are one!"

Obeying the armless man's thought, the bees left his stumps and came to pass over our faces, massaging us with their soft legs. I felt that sacred letters were being engraved on my skin. . . . From that day on we never lacked honey, because every time the armless man's back itched, he deposited a full jar beneath my mother's fingernails. . . .

The second Wise Man was mentally retarded. They called him Yugivbred, the mongoloid, because whenever he met someone he would shake a stick he'd made into a rattle by attaching bottle caps, and he'd shout his strange name in their face. Doña Sara understood that it was not a name but rather a hungry request: "You give bread?" The idiot always carried on his back a large sack full of all the leftover food he found in garbage cans. The children followed him and mocked him, but he kept them at bay with his sonorous rod. My mother said to me:

"He wields it like a scepter. This king has subjects. We're going to follow him."

We observed him from far away through a spyglass, and we saw him leave town. Struggling under his enormous burden, he moved off along a path that led to an expanse of dunes. On a carpet of rocks, a bathtub awaited him. He took off his clothes, got into it, poured the garbage over himself, and let out a long, sharp whistle. In a few minutes the place was full of stray dogs, half-feral cats, and seagulls. There were at least a hundred animals. All of them set to devouring the scraps, but in an orderly manner, without fighting. Once a piece of food was in their mouths or beaks, each one withdrew to make room for another one in need. Yugivbred babbled in pleasure as he entered into contact with so many beasts.

"You see, Alejandrito? I told you the mongoloid had powers. I knew he wasn't born retarded like that. On the contrary, he was a very intelligent man. Already a labor leader when he was very young, he led a group in the María Helena mines on a strike to demand a raise, and the police beat him until his skull was cracked. No one knows how they cured him in the hospital at the saltpeter mines, but the fact is he came out like that, lacking intelligence, to the delight of his bosses and to our sorrow. You realize that 'idiot' spends the entire day dedicated to finding the food necessary to keep these abandoned beasts from dying of hunger? What an immense amount of love his heart must contain! Now imagine how much love the Creator must have in order to keep our universe alive. . . ."

Doña Sara began to give the mongoloid a sack of fish meal every Friday. Grateful to her, one night when the moon was full he came to find us, to lead us to the dunes and have us get into the bathtub with him, all of us standing up. Shaking the musical stick with tremendous authority, he called to his troops. Under the silvered light, the dogs arrived and ran in circles, in figure eights, in five-pointed stars. They closed in around us, then separated into sixteen lines and remained still, forming rays like a sun. Then the cats arrived, upright, rising up onto their hind legs. It was like a ballet of costumed gnomes. They went to sit on the backs of the dogs. Yugivbred pointed his scepter toward the sky: clouds of seagulls appeared, and after swirling around us like a maelstrom of feathers, they divided into groups to grab hold of the dogs and cats and carry them off, flying toward the moon. The mongoloid made his great rattle ring out. The animals, from the sky, said goodbye to us with a melodious symphony of barks, meows, and caws. . . .

The third Wise Man had been the owner of a small press where he'd printed his anarchist newspaper, *The Worker's Awakening*. The police rode their horses into the place, broke the linotype, threw acid on the press, stomped on the boxes, and arrested him. To make him squeal on his accomplices, they used pliers to yank out his teeth. He resisted thirty-one times. Then he confessed, and felt guilty he hadn't been able to lose his full set of teeth. When they let him go one week later, scorned by the families of his comrades—all imprisoned or deported because of him—and hating his solitary incisor, proof of his snitching cowardice, he started to drink essence of turpentine. The poisonous liquid turned him into a human rag. He came to the café with his back bent and his eyes on the ground, as if he didn't deserve to occupy the space that surrounded him, to beg Doña Sara for alms so he could continue erasing himself with turpentine. She caressed his contracted mouth and told him:

"Behind these tightly shut lips, you hide a treasure. The little snitch has died. You are a Wise Man, a diamond and not coal. They pulled out your teeth, but not your message. Make of your fall an ascension." And she gave him twelve bottles of wine. The man sat down in the plaza, and after caressing the bottles for a long time, he started to drink the twelve liters they contained. As he got drunker, his tooth grew longer and longer. Then its tip swelled to become a clapper.

"I'm a bell!" he cried, and, knowing that any political discourse would be censored with police beatings, he summarized his rebellion in four cries: "CUCARACUCA! CUCARACAY! TUMBATUMBITA! TUMBATUMBAY!" And repeating that mysterious incantation ceaselessly, he started to stomp the asphalt harder and harder until the street began to shake; then the houses vibrated, the windows broke, and finally the police station collapsed.

The cops thought they were at the epicenter of an earthquake. The possessed man's cries became shouts of triumph. Then there was a snap in his throat and he lost his voice. He opened his mouth and vomited a magma of words made matter that, like a black river, slid off down the street. Caught on his widowed tooth, he was left with only one word: "Cucaracuca." From then on he was forced to express himself only with that. . . . He came on Fridays, the day of alms, and when he received his bottles of wine, he said cucaracuca instead of thank you. My mother would kiss his forehead and told him:

"You are a golden bell: when you die you will be raised to the highest tower in heaven. From there you will ring out, freeing the angel that lies imprisoned in every being!"

THE CANTINA

From the pier to the main street, 21 de Mayo, there was a dark alley down which many decent Tocopillans did not deign to travel. Among backsides of stores and the crumbling ruins of walls that had become lizard dens, yawned the maw of a cantina: The Emergency. Even at noontime, shadow reigned there. The customers, stealthy, damp shadows with their clothes covered in fish scales, seemed to have emerged from the depths of the sea. Amid a cloud of rough tobacco rose sounds of glasses, the mooing of sperm whales, plopping of soft bodies, sticky steps. . . . Attracted by that strange delight that the neighbors called sin, I approached the dive, pretending I was looking for a lost cat. I saw a boy my age go in, barefoot and dirty, carrying a shoeshine box under his arm. I deliberated for a good half hour, then decided. My pigeon heart, keeping me alive with the calm rhythm of its faint beats, eliminated any idea of danger from my spirit. To me, men were every bit as good as animals. When I went into that gloomy place where the thick smell of bitter wine transformed into a fog, my innocent appearance was like an insult. Stevedores, stokers, drivers, rough bodies, callused hands, noses eaten away, scars, baleful eyes, garnet teeth. They all stopped drinking and looked at me, depositing on my person a bottled-up hatred. The owner, skinny and greenish, practically a dwarf, with a defiant smile, lifted up the little shoeshine boy.

"This little darkie is our champion! We're going to see if the pale-faced dandy knows how to fight! Damned kids, spit on your hands and get to punching! The first one who cries, loses!"

I kept on smiling beatifically. The shoe shiner went into a rage and came at me with a rain of blows. Luckily, in his nervous ire he'd closed his eyes, and few of his blows landed. Accustomed as I was to Doña Sara's kindness, I didn't even think of fighting, only of escaping, more out of pity than of fear. Unable to conceive of evil, I saw them all as victims of a hateful demon. They crowded together to keep me from leaving, and shoved me toward my contender. He, thinking me a coward, added kicks to his punches. I fell on my behind, bleeding from my nose. The drunks applauded.

"Bravo, he's got the chocolate flowing!"

I found no way out but to start crying. They burst out laughing.

"You won, Luchito, give this intruder fag a kick in the ass, and let him go!" They started to lift me up, but the green dwarf stopped them.

"No, that's not all! Take this broomstick, Luchito, and beat him till he shits himself!"

The proposal was accepted and celebrated with long swigs of beer. I made a desperate but useless effort to get my intestines working. The first blow was to my mouth, and broke a tooth. The pain exploded in my head like lightning. And in the middle of that flash, the Rabbi showed himself: "Don't be afraid, I'm your friend, let me take over!" I didn't try to block him because, though I had never seen him, I'd always felt his presence. He took control of my body, and with precise movements he eluded the little savage; making the most of the boy's wild impulses, he threw him like a stupid bird through a window into the street. Before anyone had time to react, he faced down the fools:

"Negative mitzvahs: number one hundred ninety-four, it is forbidden to succumb to gluttony and drunkenness; number two hundred fifty-two, forbidden to use mocking words toward a stranger; number three hundred, forbidden to beat a person without legal authorization; number three hundred and three, forbidden to humiliate your neighbor in public! Impure sinners, let me through or Jehovah will set this shack ablaze!"

Openmouthed, terrified not by the threat but by the precise gestures and adult voice that came from a seven-year-old child, they moved tremblingly away. . . . "Alejandrito, tell no one about this, or they will think you are possessed. In any case, the children at school shun you, calling you Pinocchio because of your curved nose and white skin. What can you do? You will always be from another place, another time, with a double self! We're going to share this noble body for many years; let me be your only friend!" When I arrived at The Happy Wait, my mother saw my broken tooth and realized I had gotten into a fight. She brought me at a run to the dentist. Calm now, I told her everything except the part about the Rabbi. She told me:

"I'm sorry I didn't teach you in time how to be invisible. People who have not developed their consciousness, for lack of an inner life, see each other as prey. They find mental waste to be an exquisite food. If you want to survive, you have to pass unseen. If they see you it's because you see yourself. You think of yourself as one thing or another, you form a permanent image of yourself, and that is what they devour with gusto. . . . Look at this wall! It looks impenetrable, right? But if you stop thinking of your hand as an object and you feel it as it really is, pure energy, you can put it right through the place that offers no resistance, where the wall is not a wall but a void." Doña Sara sank her arm into the thick cement up to her shoulder. Then, without any effort, she removed it. "It's the same with your mind; empty of personal thoughts, impelled by a heart free of possessive feelings, it will penetrate into any person through the point where he is not a person. You will pierce him, and he, no longer an obstacle, will let you pass without seeing you. I'm going to show you!"

She brought me back to The Emergency. By then the afternoon was turning to night. Inside the cantina, enormous, hoarse insects were singing obscene songs.

"Don't see yourself, don't identify with any part of your body or mind, let nothing of yours belong to you, be one with the impersonal eye. Come!" And together we went into that lair. . . . We passed among those sweaty men so full of pain, exhaustion, disgust, hatred, loneliness. No one noticed our presence. "You see, Alejandrito? Now that you're convinced, I'll tell you the main thing: if you learn to make yourself totally invisible, when death comes for you, it won't see you and will pass you by."

THE GOODBYE

The children at the public school didn't like me because they couldn't stand the fact that I could fluently read sentences that they had so much trouble deciphering. When I went home, for lack of friends I played with my lead soldiers by myself, without even Basilio's company. The monkey had grown shy since my father had gone, and when I'd try to approach, offering him tasty fruits, he always tried to bite me. The Rabbi said to me: "What are you doing here, playing with these military toys made only so that from an early age you get used to the idea of giving your life in battle to protect shameful business interests? We'd be better off going to the municipal library! Wonderful worlds await us there. Reading, you'll realize that the only honest toy you have is your brain." The Caucasian's voracity was inexhaustible. Forcing me to sit in that somber place for six hours a day, he read, through my eyes, an enormous number of volumes. One fine day the librarian, his face astonished, patted me on the head. "You've read all the books!" he said, and he gave me a lollipop. . . .

When Doña Sara, who barely knew how to read, learned of my achievement, she decided to leave Tocopilla.

"Son, we're going to Santiago, for two reasons. First: this town cannot offer you what you need for your cultural development. In the capital there are very good bookstores and libraries. Second: if your father hasn't returned yet, it's because he can't. It's clear his plan has failed: Ibáñez is alive and hiding out in Argentina, maybe making plans to come back: that kind of egomaniac has to die before it lets its prey go free. Jaime isn't dead; if he were, my heart would tell me. He's probably been expatriated or thrown in jail. In that great city we'll be able to find people who could know where he's ended up."

"What about Raquel Lea, Mama?"

"For the moment she's all right where she is. When we find Jaime, we'll send for her."

It wasn't too hard for her to sell the café to Baltra. He had decided to be what he was, and, dressed as a woman just like his mother, he enlivened The Happy Wait by singing romantic songs in a falsetto voice. When Basilio saw Baltra's new personality, he found unexpected affection for him, and, jumping vertiginously and imitating human laughter, he served cups of coffee and helped the business succeed. . . . One shining morning, before our ship set sail, Doña Sara took me for a walk through the streets of the port we had loved so much.

"Look at everything very closely, eat it all up with your eyes. Life is astonishing: everything passes, nothing remains, and yet all you love is engraved on your soul. It's like a robbery. You leave this Tocopilla, but the Tocopilla you have known, the one of your childhood, will never leave you, you'll carry it with you in its entirety. Your memory will conserve it like an immutable temple. You will walk down its streets and enter every one of its houses, you'll learn about the intimate lives of the people you have captured, you'll realize that everything, absolutely everything, from the biggest hill to the smallest rock, every bird, every corner, has something to tell you. You don't hear it now, but later on this town will become your Teacher. Yes, Alejandrito, it contains all the answers. . . . I don't know how many years you will live, but if you reach old age and you come back to visit, beneath the countless changes you will find it just as you left it. But that time, instead of robbing it, you will return everything it gave you. Because for those we feed on, in the end we become food."

CALLE MATUCANA

In Santiago, for lack of money, we settled into a worker's neighborhood; that is, an impoverished one. Matucana was a dirty street along which a cargo train passed, at any hour of the day, blowing smoke and whistles and very often tearing apart a drunk worker, especially on Saturdays, the weekly day of rest that translated into minimal purchases in the stores and maximum spending in the bars. There, entire families—women, men, children—wearing the occasional new article of clothing, dedicated themselves, in order to bear this bitch of a life, to stupefaction, guzzling wine with strawberries. Late at night, like a slow pachyderm, the wife and children would walk in a closed group down the street carrying the father, now a snoring trunk, saturated with alcohol. . . . In the mornings, rabbit-sellers congregated along the road. The animals had maroon mouths gaping open in their bellies amid a cloud of flies, revealing black viscera that looked like olives. Out of superstition the bumpkins never shooed the flies away, believing that the slightest gesture against them would bring even worse luck than usual. Undaunted, my mother opened a little store in that populous neighborhood, and called it The Fight (against high prices). Its sign showed two bulldogs fighting over a pair of underpants that stretched out, proud and unbreakable. She decided to sell a little of everything, from *yerba mate* to long underwear, including her love potions and lice poison. . . . One day, the communist workers at the neighboring press decided to go on strike: imitating their Mexican comrades, they unfurled a red and black flag and sat down to block the entrance to the building, believing themselves protected by the strike flag. The goal of that guard was to be sure that no "scabs" sent by the bosses could take over the work. . . . Soon, the train came barreling along, braked, and stopped. A swarm of police got out, and, vomiting ferocious curses, they threw themselves into the fray, breaking heads and backs with their batons. A shot was fired. The few workers not groaning under the hands of their aggressors fled in all directions. The ones who were left, blood streaming, were kicked into the bulletproof train cars. After a long whistle, the locomotive started moving. Pale as a plucked chicken, a cadaver was left lying in the street. The ambulance took two hours to come and get it. . . . Doña Sara, scandalized, made no comment, but the next day, for the first time in her life, she started reading a book: *The Complete Works of Karl Marx: Volume I.* She began to talk about workers breaking their chains, and then she exclaimed:

"I'm going to help Pancho!"

Pancho, the window washer, was humble and subservient, but a drunk. Doña Sara gave him clothes.

"Here, comrade: take off those rags and dress like a human being!"

The man looked uncomfortable but splendid with that suit of English cut, shoes, socks, and hat. But then, Pancho disappeared. He came back a week later wearing the same rags as always. He'd sold the new clothes to buy wine! Doña Sara held back her tears and dressed him again from head to toe. The comrade disappeared again, only to return drunk. My mother invoked Marx, and gave him clothes once more. Again the dipsomaniac disappeared, and this time he came back naked and hiccuping.

"*Hic,* where are my new clothes?" Doña Sara continued to be generous. Pancho returned dirtier than ever. "I demand my suit, with a little handkerchief in the pocket!"

This time my mother pointed toward the door and cried:

"Out! You will have no more clothes, you stubborn drunk!"

The man got furious; removing one hand from his front and the other from his back, unashamed at showing his privates, he went out into the street and threw stones through every one of The Fight's windows. The police came and took him away. Doña Sara, dismayed, told me:

"I made a mistake. Better than giving things to those in need is to give them work, so that through their own efforts, they can earn enough money to escape humiliation.... Sometimes dependence creates habits in us, and we stop feeling gratitude and start making demands. Oh, we live as if life belonged to us, without realizing we could die any second!"

THE BROKEN CHAIN

Doña Sara decided to change the name of The Fight and its emblem of two bulldogs tugging at a pair of underpants, to The Broken Chain, showing a worker with hands twice as big as his head destroying links in an iron chain. For after reading Marx, she had dug into Engels, Lenin, Bakunin, and Trotsky, listening endlessly to *La International* sung in Russian. She began to talk with her customers:

"The capital and the workers' conquest must . . ."

The neighborhood was so poor and the workers suffered from such a lack of culture that Doña Sara's words revealed a whole world to them. One afternoon, a commission came to visit her.

"Madam, we have named you the queen of the seventh revolutionary cell!"

Doña Sara raised her arms in joy, and every Saturday she began to give her ten subjects thirty bottles of wine, considering her social duty to be thus satisfied.

"There's no one like Doña Saruca, hooray! Hic, hic!"

But one day they said something else.

"Doña Sara, the Party is going to have a parade! The cells of all the neighborhoods have flags, except for ours!" My mother promised to sew one. In her enthusiasm, she decided to create the most luxurious emblem possible, using felt, satin, gemstones, sequins, golden thread, and letters in relief filled with cotton. She worked tirelessly.

"My luxurious flag is going to stand out above all the rest, which will be ordinary and ugly!"

And the day of the great parade arrived! The groups of the different labor sections of the city gathered, without government permission, in Plaza Almagro, waving their red flags to the beat of circus bands. Although they were made of ordinary cloth, the wind conferred such elegant movements on them that they became waves in a marvelous sea of red. But the members of the seventh cell complained, humiliated: their flag was so heavy that not even a hurricane could make it wave. When the parade started they had to drag it behind them like a dead wing, because not even with their twenty arms could they have carried it the whole way. Then the cops came and the beatings began; they fled, and abandoned the flag among the wounded. For a long time they forgot to visit their queen on Saturdays. . . .

"Alejandrito, what a shame, I was wrong again: we must not adorn, but rather honor! A job done to win applause is different from a job done out of pure love for the task."

THE SEWING ROOM

In addition to working her eight obligatory hours standing behind the counter, my mother, allowing herself no more repose than a brief nightly sleep, spent most of her free time in the sewing room. It was a small room, with a window in the ceiling through which you could see only a single star that Doña Sara had baptized "God's Little Hope." I would sit on the floor and listen to her talk while she tirelessly sewed calico shirts and long underwear for workers.

Though the space was meager, Doña Sara had managed to make it into a universe. There, every action took on meaning and every object became a symbol. If she had to patch used clothes—she bought and sold secondhand articles—she tried to take a piece from the folds of another garment that had been in use for the same amount of time.

"Look," she'd say. "If I put a patch of new cloth on an old surface, instead of a cure I'd be sewing on a cancer. The young cloth, less adaptable, stronger, would end up fraying the place where I'd sewn it on into a thousand threads. When you grow up and want to change the world, never propose drastic solutions that, instead of helping, will end up bringing chaos. I want you to measure and understand the level of resistance of those you help. Don't push them further than they can stand. . . ."

If by chance a suit was stained, all she did was take a corner of the same garment and rub the spot energetically.

"Look how the spot disappears: the cloth cleans itself! When you have spiritual problems, don't look for help from outside, as it will only confuse you. Cure your being with another part of your being. You are your own doctor: you won't find a better one. . . ."

When her thread got tangled, she blew on the knot to undo it.

"When I blow on the thread I calm it, and the labyrinth loses strength and untangles itself. Never force problems. Stay calm and do what you can. They will solve themselves. . . ."

To thread a needle, she held the thread firm without moving it, and trapped its end with the needle's eye.

"If you can't find something, make that something find you. If you want light, put yourself where there are no barriers between you and the sun. Cleanse your soul so the phenomenon can manifest in you, and, being empty, you will obtain it."

THE FUGITIVE POLITICIAN

The ten comrades of the seventh Communist cell arrived just as Doña Sara was about to pull down the metal curtain; they were sober and their hair was plastered back, they wore clean suits, black shirts, red ties, and carried a bottle of red wine as a gift. After handing her the bottle they stood mutely before her, shifting from one foot to the other. My mother smiled, thinking they were coming to apologize for their ungrateful absence. Shorty Gumucio, electrician and filer of pedestrian calluses, took a step forward, cleared his throat, and said with self-satisfied haughtiness:

"Esteemed Doña Sara, we have decided to forget the humiliation your flag caused us, ahem, as long as, ahem, in reparation, ahem ahem, you agree to house in your domicile an important politician who is a fugitive, cough cough, with the condition you ask him no questions, innocent as they may be! We are counting on you, comrade: say yes!"

I was indignant at such an abuse of trust, and I shook my head. But my incorrigible mother . . . At three in the morning, a man arrived in a cart drawn by a donkey; he was disguised as a peasant, wore glasses, and had a large pot belly. He entered the store like a shadow. The cart driver passed him a bag full of clothes and books and then left. No one spoke. The man stayed standing under the bulb decorated with fly excrement in the sewing room. Doña Sara, with a delicate gesture, offered him the only bed in our house. She and I moved in beside the sewing machine, where we'd sleep on a mattress on the floor. The mysterious character never spoke, never raised his eyes from his thick books (what could he be reading?), never made his bed, never swept, never washed a dish, never smiled in thanks, and ate a lot. The only sounds he emitted were twenty coughs in the morning and the nocturnal explosion of his gases, chronometrical, which indicated it was time to sleep. Once a week the cart arrived, the driver handed the man a packet, and without uttering a word, left. Doña Sara patiently washed his underwear, his socks, handkerchiefs, and shirts, she made him food and smilingly accepted the discomfort that ghost caused her. One morning at dawn, the cart driver said something into the man's ear and he left with him, without saying goodbye to us. Six months had passed! I sobbed with rage. My mother said to me:

"What do you know, child, about what's happening to that man? If he behaved like that it's because he didn't want to leave any traces behind."

"He could have been more polite, Mama!"

"Every day I do the same things for you, and you never thank me! You must know that I took him in because he was you! One day, when you grow up and fight for freedom, someone will come after you and you'll need a refuge. Another mother, then, will repay me for this favor by taking you in, without asking questions or wanting anything from you. I'm sure of it, because I know I'm not unique in the world, and if I'm capable of a generous act, another human being will have to do the same for my son! Maybe at this very moment, someone is hiding and protecting your father!"

TORTURE

Three ex-boxers, blowing smoke from their flat noses, dressed as civilians but giving off the stench of police, came into The Broken Chain and leapt on my mother, putting her in handcuffs.

"Come with us, old lady!"

"And don't resist, because things could go very badly for you!" spat the second. The third brandished a pistol. I was frozen, and the few customers slid toward the street murmuring:

"We're sorry for you, little boy, you'll be left alone. . . ."

Doña Sara, dignified as a queen, asked them:

"Do you have an arrest warrant?"

The gorillas laughed cynically:

"Don't you know that Don Arturo Alessandri has obtained extraordinary powers from Congress? Shut your trap and come with us!"

They took her away in a khaki car. . . . And I was left alone, in the middle of the store, with no idea what to do. Suddenly, the merchandise became a cruel audience. It seemed I could hear laughter coming from the boxes of stockings, the wool sweaters clapped their flaccid sleeves together, the underpants opened their leg-holes to form enormous white smiles. . . . Luckily, the Rabbi came to me: "Have faith! In Samuel, 17-37, it is written: 'Jehovah, who has freed me from the lion's claws and the bear's claws, will also free me from the Philistines.' You won't be alone for long." In fact, very soon the charlatan, a street vendor who sold poison to kill intestinal worms, arrived to share his thermos of hot soup with me. A group of workers from the printing press helped me lower the shutter.

"Don't be afraid, boy, no one is going to rob this place."

A woman who was in mourning for her son—the dead man who had been left two hours in the street—came to iron my clothes, sweep, cook.

"I'll take care of you, my boy, until my comrade returns! And if she doesn't return, there's an empty bed in my house, you can use it until we find one of your relatives! . . ."

It wasn't necessary: early in the morning my mother came back, walking with difficulty, whiter than usual. The blue of her eyes had turned gray. . . .

"Mama, the whole neighborhood helped me, except for the ten drunks in the seventh cell: none of those freeloaders turned up!"

"Don't label people the way you do socks! They're human beings, not 'drunks' or 'freeloaders'! They were right: they need to take care of themselves. The police have infiltrated Matucana with a lot of moles."

She drank *mate* with milk from a mug through a straw (her mouth was swollen and she could hardly open it), and she told us—the woman in black and me—in a thread of a voice about her adventure. . . . They'd taken her to the police station, put a number on her chest, and taken photos from the front, back, and profile; they pressed her fingertips into ink to take her fingerprints, then locked her in an empty cell where there was nothing but a pestilential hole that served as a latrine. After a few hours they took her out, beat her with rubber hoses, and put her back in the cell. Doña Sara believed she was finally going to be able to sleep or rest, but no, they took her out again and beat her again, applying who knows what techniques to soften her up. Then they took her through a walkway that had been dug out under the street to a cushioned room in the basements of the public jail. The floor was covered with water and mud and there was an array of torture instruments, among them a machine to apply an electric current. In that sinister dungeon, four agents waited for her and began to interrogate her: "Fucking whore, you hid a man in your house for several months! Who was he?" With loving sweetness, she replied: "He was my father." They punched her in the stomach, hit her breasts, her back. "Who was that man, you old daughter of a whore?" Without losing her sweetness, she answered them: "He was my husband." They decided to employ the electrical machine. While two of them applied the current, the other two held her down, thinking she was going to struggle. But she left her body behind and watched the torture, floating near the ceiling without suffering. Believing she had fainted, they tried to get her to return to herself by throwing a bucket of cold water over her. "Who was that man, you goddamn bitch? You'd better tell us, or we'll pound your bones to dust!" "He was my son." When they got tired of abusing her, when the day had already dawned, they brought her to the office of a dark man with sunken eyes, with a thin line for an upper lip and a thick steak for a lower one, who spoke with the airs of a boss. However, Doña Sara understood that the real top dog was a man who seemed to be a foreigner, dressed in a tuxedo, who didn't say a single word the whole time she was there. "Look, madam, don't take advantage of the fact that this is a democratic country where the law prohibits us from beating the citizens," the ugly man told her with disgusting cynicism. "Stop playing at being a heroine protecting a good bandit, and tell us who that man was!" "He was your brother." The dark man came furiously out from behind his desk and punched her in the mouth. "Talk, wretched woman! Who was he?" "It was you, my son!" "Crazy old loon!" The gringo in the tuxedo said a few words into his puppet's ear. Right away they let her go. . . . She had to walk three miles from the prison to Matucana. Soon she realized the three ex-boxers were following her. . . .

"Now they're hiding on the corner," said Doña Sara to finish her story. "Alejandrito, those poor men still haven't had breakfast. Bring them these cups of coffee and some slices of cake. We must have pity on them: they don't know it, but they are God."

It was hard for me to obey, but I did it. When they saw me approach, the three brutes looked at me warily, but then, gulping down the steaming coffee and devouring the sponge cake, they smiled at me with childlike expressions. Knowing my mother as I did, I could tell those ultra-secret watchmen would very soon end up sitting in the back of the store drinking *mate* with her.

EXPELLED

Keeping closer to the walls then a shadow, Shorty Gumucio arrived at the store and motioned for my mother to accompany him to the sewing room.

"Sit down, my esteemed woman and queen! Take off your shoes, I'm going to file down your calluses."

"And to what do I owe this devotion, my friend?"

"Ahem, ahem. . . . The thing is that the Party's Political Commission, after much internal discussion, has called an assembly to stop the shoot-outs with those Trotskyite sons of bitches disguised as socialists, and try to advance labor unity through a Coordinating Committee. . . . Ahem. . . . To achieve an integration and calm our quarrels, it was thought that you, such a sweet and good woman, would be just the person to help. Your unfair suffering from treacherous torture will unite us on a common front. . . . What do you say? Will you come?"

"Of course I will! I see it as my duty!"

Shorty began to file down her calluses with sincere enthusiasm.

"Oh, that's great, Doña Saruca! I'll leave the soles of your feet as smooth as a nun's behind! When you walk you'll feel you're flying!"

The meeting was held in a neutral place, the Argentine dance hall. A quartet murdered tangos, while the comrades, in order to throw the police off and because women were scarce, danced with each other, more worried about avoiding a knife in the back than following the beat of the milonga. When the coast was clear, the cacophony came to a stop and the dancers left the stage. My mother was invited up, and amid loud applause she was given two brand-new crutches. Out of politeness, she pretended to be limping and thanked them for the gift, blowing a number of kisses that were answered with a rain of carnations.

"Long live the tortured comrade! Long may she live! Death to the traitor Alessandri and his dog Ventura Maturana! Death!"

Once the unifying indignation was achieved, smiling tensely, the communist leaders came onstage to face the head Trotskyites. They flipped a coin. A communist would speak first. Behind him, his comrades unfurled a large photograph of Stalin. No sooner had he said the first few words than the crowd divided into two fierce groups, separated by a wide path of parquet.

"Friends, to fully unite, we must first be sincere, file down the roughness, think back: you Trotskyites commandeered the name of Chile's Communist Party in 1933 in order to confuse the workers!" Boos came from one group, warm applause from the other. Undaunted by the racket, the red continued his jeremiad, shouting: "Once we unmasked you, you decided to call yourselves the Communist Left, adhering to a nonexistent Fourth International. But the workers didn't swallow that story. Then you moved into the anemic Socialist Party, to take control of positions of power and sabotage the development of popular unity. We hope that today, recognizing your errors, you will accept the principles of immortal communism, receiving through our Party the valuable teachings of the Communist International and its great leaders, Stalin and Dimitrov, who march along the path of Marx, Engels, and Lenin!" The Trotskyites started to take off their jackets and roll up the sleeves of their military shirts. In some belts, the butts of guns shone. The Communists did the same, weapons also glinting at their waists. A young speaker angrily grabbed the microphone from the communist. Behind him, some of his brethren unrolled a large photograph of Trotsky. He yelled and accused Stalin of insanity, of being a murderer, an egomaniac, an idiotic dictator, proclaiming that life, with its constant change, demanded permanent revolution. . . . The groups, looking at each other with murderous rage, advanced and narrowed the path until they were separated by a line an inch wide. The communist leader leapt onto the podium and exclaimed: "Those who are with the Trotskyites stay here, and they will by expelled from the Party; those who are with the Party, come with me! I'm leaving now!"

He only managed to take half a step. My mother's stentorian voice stopped him as, no longer faking a limp, she ordered:

"You are not leaving, nor is anyone else! Stop fighting like little brats! Open those fists and shake each other's hands!" Doña Sara's fury was impressive, and the crowd, like one immense child, obeyed her fearfully. More sweetly now, she went on: "I speak to you as a mother, who just like other mothers loves you with all the love in the world. What good does all that pride do you? If you want to emerge from oppression you must unite. Forget the past, crase the words 'communist' and 'Trotskyite' from your brains and call each other 'brothers.' And, above all, do not venerate foreign idols, inflated dolls, giant substitute fathers who have nothing to do with our modest but authentic reality. . . . Will someone lend me a lighter?"

With furrowed brow, someone handed her one. She placed herself between the two photographs, and, with a couple of quick, precise gestures, set fire to them. The paraffin paper burned in an instant. Stalin and Trotsky were consumed by the flames, though their worshippers tried to extinguish the flames with spit. There was an overwhelming silence. Doña Sara had united the assembly, only not in compassion but in rage. The Trotskyite leader boomed:

"This false cripple has committed an unpardonable sacrilege!"

The communist leader vomited out:

"Shorty Gumucio, you are guilty of having admitted this mad saboteur into our ranks! Take her away from here immediately, and tomorrow, first thing, you must properly expel her from the party! . . ."

My mother and I left amid general scorn; to them we had become invisible pieces of shit, while they, back in each other's arms, danced a tango massacred by the guitars and the singers' voices: *Uno busca lleno de esperanzas el camino que los sueños prometieron a sus ansias.* . . . "Full of hope, we seek the path that dreams promised to our longing. . . ."

First thing in the morning, Shorty Gumucio arrived accompanied by Fatty González and Bones Eremberg.

"Ahem. . . . Ahem. . . . Ahem. . . . Ahem. . . ."

"Stop sweating like a scared horse, Don Shorty, and repeat to me, man to woman, with that parrot brain of yours, the message you've been given!"

"Well, Doña Sara, I hope you have repented for the injury you have inflicted on us. You cannot just burn the people's idols like that. From lack of bread we live on illusions, and they, you understand, are sacred. Because of you, the high leadership has decided to expel me if I do not expel you. . . . Ahem. . . . Cough. . . . The problem is that I cannot expel you because you have never registered with the Party. . . . And so, I and my companions of the seventh cell beg you, right now, by signing this small red card, to join the glorious ranks of communism. . . . Ahem. . . . Understand?"

"Sure I understand, my friends, more than you can imagine. Bring me that pen!"

And my mother engraved her signature on the paper. The comrades sighed in relief. Shorty Gumucio, with solemn motions, tore up the card, threw the pieces to the floor, and stomped on them.

"Comrade, you are hereby officially expelled from the Communist Party, incorporated in the Communist International founded by Lenin! Never again shall you speak to us!" The three revolutionaries, their heads lowered, left without looking back. Five minutes later, Shorty came back and effusively shook my mother's left hand: "Thank you, thank you, Doña Sara! In gratitude for your noble act I'm going to tell you that the Trotskyites have decided to teach you a lesson: tonight they will come and shoot holes in your metal shutter with a machine gun. It would be best if you and your son sleep somewhere else. . . ."

The woman in black took us in. She shared her narrow bed with my mother, and gave her son's bed to me. Late in the night she came in, rested her head on my pillow, and just like that, on her knees, she cried until dawn. To overcome my insomnia, the Rabbi told me: "Yes, time is murderous, but it's ours."

THE EIGHTH CHAKRA

Doña Sara, shunned by the workers in the neighborhood and with the metal shutter of The Broken Chain now a colander, sold her store. Having saved up a tidy nest egg, she opened a boutique called The Eighth Chakra in a central area of town. For, after being repudiated by Marx and Trotsky, she was now reading about Tibetan yoga. . . . She started sewing dresses in the latest styles, copied from Eastern traditions. She spent eight hours a day behind the counter, and another eight in the sewing room, but sales were slight and the money she earned barely bought enough to eat. With great sadness, she started to think about having to sell her lovely business. Doña Sara decided to consult her new friend the Sufi, a beggar who justified his laziness by claiming he had invented paper cranes; lying comfortably on the sidewalk, he spent his days making roses out of toilet paper. Doña Sara asked him whether she should sell the store. The mendicant replied:

"The important thing is not distinguishing good from bad—even cockroaches can do that. He is wise who, between two evils, can choose the lesser, and between two good things can discern which one is better. Much of the solution to a problem consists in clarifying how it is posed. If the problem is not understood, the solution never arrives. Really, the true answer consists of posing the question well. Before getting rid of the place you love, analyze from where the evil comes! Is the neighborhood you're in disagreeable?"

"No!" she replied. "Quite the contrary, it's the most beautiful I've seen!"

"Do the neighbors bother you?"

"They behave very well with me!"

"Does the space suffocate you?"

"Oh, it's large, of course, the perfect space for my needs!"

"Then, good woman, your problem is merely that there is something that eats up your time and doesn't give you much money in return!"

"That's it!"

The Sufi reached this conclusion:

"Your enemy is the sale of dresses! The superficiality of fashion doesn't agree with your deep spirit! That magnificent store has done nothing to you: don't get rid of it; keep it! What you should do is change the genre of the business: stop wasting your time sewing clothes, and start selling something that takes less of your time, gives you more money, and is equal to the measure of your spirit!"

And that is how Doña Sara did not sell the place she loved, but rather transformed it and began, with great success, to sell fruit and medicinal herbs.

THE SMELLY WOMAN

My mother did so well with the fruit store, The Apple of Harmony, that she began to import exotic products from Bolivia, Peru, and the Amazon jungle. There was a kind of pineapple that, if it weren't for a glass bell that isolated it, would have filled the place with an unbearable stench of rot. I couldn't understand how anyone could buy it. Speaking of stench, I remember a woman with deep, almost yellow eyes, dark skin, very well dressed, who began to visit Doña Sara. They sat in the back of the store during siesta time and talked about who knows what, because I could never get close to her: the woman had an illness that made her exude a fetid odor. Everything she touched was permeated by it. One day she forgot her pen. I didn't realize, and I picked it up to finish my homework. I nearly threw up! The repellent smell stayed on my thumb and forefinger for hours! Nevertheless, my mother dedicated a lot of time to receiving her, friendly and smiling. One day, annoyed, I shouted:

"You have to throw her out of here!"

I had never seen my mother so angry: she turned red, shook me for a minute, and then, picking up a knife (I froze), she sliced the bad-smelling fruit in half (oh, what a relief!) and offered it to me:

"Eat a piece of this wild pineapple!"

"I can't, it smells like poop!"

She squeezed my nostrils shut. I opened my mouth to breathe and then she stuck the slice in. . . . Wonderful! I'd never tasted a sweeter, more delicate, tastier fruit! I wanted to eat a dozen.

"See? The sense of smell is not king. I receive that woman because she is the daughter of the deceased Pajarito Baquedano—a friend of your uncle Benjamín—who suffered from the same illness (out of love, we copy not only our parents' values, but also their ailments), and because she writes poems as beautiful as the ones your sister murmurs. Listen: 'I must seek the multiform sphere / that grants light to each ounce of shadow / and a beginning to each of my endings / until I give birth to a shape with a soul.' She is a pure woman, almost a saint. You cannot know how her art comforts my being. Thanks to her I have understood the importance of beauty. You remember the apocryphal Gospel, when Christ and his apostles pass by the rotting body of a dog? While the others hold their noses and flee in disgust, Jesus goes closer, looks at the cadaver, and says: 'He has beautiful teeth!' In this world we are all full of illness, because society itself is sick. If we saw only defects, we would never talk to anyone. We must look for the qualities of every being and forget their imperfections. That is what it means to live with courtesy!"

THE BANANA THIEF

The fruit store, since it had so many customers, needed to be expanded, and so the back room was sacrificed. Since she no longer had a private space, Doña Sara sat in the doorway, enjoying a spot of sun, and, for lunch, she drank *yerba mate* and ate fruit that she couldn't sell because it was already too ripe. One morning she peeled a banana, and was about to bite into it when

a beggar child, seemingly wild, ran at full speed past her and
snatched away the soft fruit, holding it tight. She watched him
flee, looked at her watch, and smiled. The next day, at the same
time, Doña Sara, with her hand slightly extended, presented
another banana. The boy again came running and snatched it.
From then on, my mother displayed the fruit so the little wild
thing would steal it. I said:

"Why do you do it? That beggar is never going to thank you!"

Very calm, she replied:

"You're wrong about something: he's not a beggar. If he was,
he would be here with his hand outstretched, whining plaintively.
He has his dignity: society has treated him badly, and for him that
robbery is a kind of justice. He hates us all. To give him alms would
be to add one more insult. I'm not worried about receiving thanks;
I want to be on good terms with myself and practice my beliefs,
unaffected by praise or insults. The only important thing is that
that boy is hungry, and somehow we must find a way to help him,
without him feeling it as help."

"Look, Mama, I think you're imagining all this; that savage has
never known dignity!"

Doña Sara turned red, but this time she contained her anger.

"Fine, you have to learn, though it will hurt you later. You're
going to feel very guilty! . . ."

Before noon, my mother rolled up a ten-peso bill very thin
and stuck it lengthwise into the banana, so well hidden you
couldn't see it. She sat in the sun, drank her bitter infusion
through her silver straw, and pretended to be about to eat the
fruit. Again the raggedy boy appeared and snatched it. An hour
passed. Suddenly, a rock fell in the middle of the store with a
crash! We jumped. The stone had the bill tied to it. We never
saw the boy again.

FAILURE

When I turned eight, Doña Sara, ever more caught up in her esoteric books, said to me:

"Alejandrito: you're grown up now; I'm not going to give you toys, I'm going to give you knowledge. But bear in mind that more important than what we know is what we do with what we know! Listen: to triumph in life you must learn to fail. Failure is a cruel but marvelous teacher who tells you when you have taken the wrong road. If you aren't proud, you are grateful for the lesson and you change your behavior. For example, yesterday I had a failure: the owner of the pastry shop next door came into the Apple of Harmony to ask me to teach her about Illumination. Illumination (achieving the total awakening of the spirit) is a subject I'm passionate about. So I show her books about Zen, Taoism, Islam, Hasidism, the kabbalah, alchemy, tarot, et cetera. Then I see the neighbor is disconcerted. I ask her what's wrong. She replies: 'It's just that I wanted to learn how to light my bakery well, and I just wanted you to teach me, seeing your magnificent indirect lighting in your fruit shop, how to place the bulbs in the best place! . . .' I'm not ashamed to have told you this, because, thanks to so much reading, I've become a hunter of my defects, and I am constantly stalking them. When I catch one, I feel as satisfied as a lioness with her prey. . . ."

The Sufi, who had come to bring me a gift of a frog of folded paper that could be blown up, bowed deeply to us:

"Forgive me for sticking my spoon into such spiritual soup, but I would like to contribute my own praise for failure. Sometimes losing is winning and not finding what you're looking for means you find yourself. When I was a boy, before my family perished in Algeria, their heads cut off by religious fanatics, my grandfather told me stories before I fell asleep. My favorite one was about the immortal tree. The old man said that in a distant country, in the center of a wonderful garden, there was a tree that never died. I grew up thinking that my only purpose in life was to find that eternal plant. In school, instead of listening to the lessons, I day-dreamed and planned. 'I'll see it someday and discover its secret: I will not die either!' Years later I scoured the planet looking for that tree. I crossed the continents asking thousands of peasants: 'Have you seen the immortal tree?' No one could answer me. After a long time, when I had nearly lost hope, a goatherd who brought his animals to graze on an isolated peak, answered: 'I know an old man who can tell you where it is!' He brought me to a cave where a man as wrinkled as a mummy lived. 'Come, boy' (he muttered with his toothless mouth), 'behind those rocks is the garden you seek!' In fact, there, in the middle of the moun-tains, grew an orchard full of leafy bushes and fragrant flowers. The hermit led me to the center to show me a hole in the ground. 'This is all that's left of the tree!' Dismayed, I said: 'But where is it?' He replied: 'Think about it, boy: an immortal tree doesn't need to reproduce in order to keep life going. It eliminated its flowers, fruits, and seeds! An immortal tree doesn't need leaves, since they only serve to maintain life, taking nourishment from the sun. Nor does it need branches, since the branches only serve to hold up the leaves. Nor does it need a trunk, since that's just for holding up the branches. Much less does it need roots, since those are only for absorbing sustenance. And an eternal tree doesn't need to eat! As you see, my boy, when the tree became immortal, it no longer needed roots or trunk or branches or leaves or flowers or fruits or seeds. Only this hole was left!" The Sufi looked at my mother with a mocking smile. "Maybe I'm lying, but you, Doña Sara, once read to me: 'Buddha said: Truth is what is useful.' Before the uselessness of material existence, like the tree of my story, I am gradually eliminating the superfluous. Maybe one day, when all that is left of me is a toilet-paper flower, I will have achieved the immortality of my soul.... That reminds me, Doña Sara, while I wait for that happy moment, could you not give me some bread, cottage cheese, three or four fruits—five if you like—and a small bill of ten pesos so I can wash down my meal with a little wine?"

THE END OF THE WAIT

Between eight and ten years I did nothing great in school: the Rabbi did it all. He said: "My little friend, the worst thing a human being can do is steal someone's childhood. I don't want your studies to devour all your free time. You go ahead and take walks, play, entertain yourself, and leave the responsibility of exams to me. Fairy tales will be more useful to you than the endless exaltation of military heroes." As usual, I had no friends, but I did have two great temples: the Minerva cinema, where I submerged myself for countless hours and watched three movies every day, and the National Library, a noble French-style building that offered my imagination all the stories and adventure novels that it needed to calm its voracious appetite. The teachers didn't reprimand me because, when I got to school, the Rabbi became king of my brain. Amid a hundred envious children, I seemed to be the best student, but in reality, though I brought home a report card full of the highest grades and praise, in my own memory I retained nothing of the official knowledge. In sum, with my soul deliciously full of Doña Sara, movies, books, and the Rabbi, I didn't feel the need for a father. Innocently, I came to believe I was the son of a virgin priestess who, in her old age, had been inseminated by God.... That

October 24, my birthday, as she offered me the usual strawberry cake, Doña Sara's tears extinguished one of the ten lit candles.

"Oh, my dear boy, everything that begins comes to an end, even sorrow. Those who are absent move further away toward the dark edges of our memory, and as they lose shape they become, more and more, loving energy that spills into the present. Yes, Alejandrito, the dead are the roots of all love! Look at me well: this old woman is not me, she is a shell that has allowed me to bear up, without temptation, through the wait. But day by day cracks appear, caused by a youth that, from very deep inside, longs for the touch of a man. Trying to be faithful, to muffle my desire for life, I submerged myself in the outside world, rejecting anything for myself so I could do good for others. But today I feel, in your tenth year, that the cycle has ended. I'm not your wife, my son, I'm your mother! You are not the son of the Lord, but of Jaime! He left us to kill Ibáñez, but, more alive than ever, that dictator is back now and the Nazi Party is naming him today as their candidate for president. That means it was your father and not the colonel who had his brains blown out! Understand? I cannot go on feeding hope with my flesh and my being. I must give myself to mourning, bury my husband in the sacred center of memory, as I buried my father, and, above all, I must stop loving him in you, as if you were no more than a fragment of his spirit. You are you, he was him, and now I will be me, Doña Sara no longer, but Sara Felicidad!"

When she stopped talking, her mutation began: she undid her bun and let her hair down. I saw fall from her head an undulating river of gold, a waterfall of perfumed amber, a silken jellyfish invading the dull shadow of the everyday with its brilliance! I went to touch that long mane with the movements of a blind person, while my pigeon heart swelled until it became an apple. . . . My hands, sunk in that sublime softness, were also eyes, and ears, and nose, and tongue. The blond filaments tied me tighter than rope. I heard her vertebra creak. Her retracted spine, tearing shirt and bra, began to stretch, one inch after another. My mother grew to be over six and a half feet tall. Her large, pointed breasts perforated the air. Her eyeglasses fell from her face, landing like dry leaves. Through her pale skin, the warmth of youth began to circulate again. It was like seeing a gigantic caterpillar turning into a Venus-butterfly. "Mother of mine, take me flying away, take me out of this world, set my heart on fire, leave me in the middle of the empty night, let me bring light into the world, allow the perfume of your breath to crystallize, to grant every man a skeleton of stars!" My delirium was interrupted by the blaring music of a military march. Outside the store, in the street, the Nazis and the communists were facing off. The former, led by a military band with snares and kettledrums, trumpets, and whistles, uniformed in black pants, gray shirts and ties, plus a thick leather belt with a bronze buckle, waving flags of yellow-white-blue crossed with a red stripe, flogged the asphalt with their boots as they walked. The latter, garbed in similar uniforms only with purple ties, waved red flags with the hammer and sickle. Both brandished guns, and all kinds of bladed weapons. Motionless between the two groups, with his wooden arms open in a cross, a ragged prophet with long hair and beard was trying to stop the combat. The Nazis were trying to get to Mapocho Station, where they would receive the now-general Ibáñez. The communists had decided to block their way. Advancing in opposite directions, both parades shouted that they were the only representatives of the people, both of them railed against selfish plutocracy, both denounced the corruption of the social system, both accused Alessandri of having sold out to British and US imperialism, depriving the country of the benefits of its saltpeter and coal, both announced that their party was the only solution to avoid dictatorship, sacking from foreigners, and Chile's collapse. . . . Finally, the two lines crashed into each other. The first to fall, wounded by a cudgel-blow to the head, was the prophet. He fled the battle on all fours, trying to elude the knives and bullets, and before Sara Felicidad could lower the metal shutter, he slid into the store and fainted onto the fruit. Neither I nor my mother recognized him, but the Rabbi, taking control of my tongue, shouted: "Hallelujah, it's Jaime!" My mother swayed as if on board a ship, then threw herself on the fallen man and licked his bloody skull. Then, amid heartrending sobs, having recovered her language of musical notes, she expressed happiness, pain, passion, disquiet, love. I suddenly felt alone. I ran to hide behind the sacks of walnuts. Outside, trucks full of police shooting machine guns drove past. The communists and the Nazis, all mixed together, fled in every direction. In a great pool of blood lay some young bodies that, united by the red, left no clue as to which of the two parties had offered up their lives.

SIX

BETWEEN THE SUN AND THE MOON

A LONE, NOT A CENT in his pockets, with his hands paralyzed and his memory still pocked with holes, where could Jaime go for help? As soon as he tried to approach a person, he received looks of disgust and gestures of refusal. The city stretched out before him like an immense, hostile animal. His body, too, was hostile. His muscles trembled, his stomach had a burning hole in it, his pasty, swollen tongue barely fit in his mouth, and his throat burned, eroded by thirst. Every one of his cells was pleading for wine. He walked to the Central Station and tried to board a train that would carry him north. The inspectors threatened to sic the dogs on him. For hours he tried to wave down the trucks heading toward Valparaíso. Who was going to want such a monstrosity as a passenger? He went back to the city center, sat next to the door of the University of Chile, extended his hands to show the now deteriorated Chilean flag, and he began to sing the national anthem with exaggerated pride. But instead of *"Puro, Chile, es tu cielo azulado, puras brisas te cruzan también . . ."* (Pure, Chile, is your blue sky, pure the breeze that blows across you, too"), he howled: *"Rico Chile soy un hombre hambreado, sucios piojos me pican la sien. . . ."* ("Rich Chile, I'm a poor, hungry man, filthy fleas are biting my head"). He received a few coins before the doormen could shoo him away. He wanted to buy bread and cheese, but his feet dragged him to a cantina. The alms became a liter of acidic wine that he introduced into his body in a single gulp. The heat that it unleashed in his belly proclaimed the alcohol as the absolute master of his soul. A stupid happiness made him dance a few steps, and, emboldened, remembering the hunchback's letter, he turned his steps toward Santa Lucía Hill. Behind some rocks he found the cave, a stinking niche where a dog was already living. The canine, who was lying among excrement, pigeon skeletons, and pieces of dry bread, first growled at him in fear; but then, when he lay down beside her, she considered him to be another animal, and she started to lick his face with intense love. Jaime, shaken by convulsive sobs, embraced the dog, then leaned his face over a crust, softened it with his tears, and devoured it. The cold obliged him to press tighter against his friend. Soon, both of them were snoring.

Jaime was standing looking into the dog's deep, ancient eyes. The point of light that lay in the depths of the left one began to grow; it filled her eye socket, spread out along her snout, and then covered her whole body like a silver skin. From her back grew two large wings. The animal stood up on her back legs, now become an angel. She showed him two glasses, one with wine and the other with milk. Jaime knew he had to choose one, and foresaw that if he made a mistake, the luminous image would change into a demon that would waste no time devouring him. He drank the milk. The angel-dog told him then: "Praise be to God, for he has guided you toward the Mother: you've returned to your origin!" The luminous claw of the index of her right hand-paw grew long and sharp as a scalpel. She lifted Jaime to float in the air, and opened his chest from throat to belly button. Then she extracted his heart, and with her long tongue began to lick the clots of blood until she cleaned the organ of all resentment. The ceiling of the cave opened up, showing a constellation of seven stars. The apparition breathed in the fragrant air that came down from the heavens, then blew into an artery until the heart, swollen, beat with happy energy. "I have transmitted faith to you, never again will you doubt, certainty will sail through your blood!" She placed the heart back in its place, and with the caress of a wing, closed the wound and flew away.

When Jaime woke up, the dog wasn't there. Before leaving forever she had left a white cheese in his unfeeling hands. Jaime devoured it. He felt full of energy. The dream had made the alcohol disappear from his veins. He had no need for wine. He decided to look for work, sure that he would find it: hadn't the angel-dog granted him faith?

✝

Hiding his hands in the torn pockets of his military coat, he walked with dignity through the streets until he reached the outskirts of the city. After a few hours he came upon the carpentry workshop Holy Timber, where an old man was sanding chairs.

"Allow me, sir . . ."

"Halt right there, friend, there's no sir here! If the Holy Carpenter was not proud, why should I be? Let the grass dry out, the flower wither; but the word of our Lord lasts forever! Call me José, just so. What can I do for you? Judging from the way you look, I guess you're in need of a coffin." The old man let out a childish laugh and went on sanding the wooden chair. Jaime stood before him in silence. After a while, the carpenter murmured, without taking his eyes from his work: "'Psalm 136:23: He remembered us in our low state, His love endures forever . . .' On the table at the back there's an empanada. Go on, get it and eat it!" Jaime took his hands from his pockets. The old man made the sign of the cross. "'If I forget you, Jerusalem, may my right hand forget its skill.' Psalm 137-5. My brother, your forgetting has been great! What are you punishing yourself for?" Jaime fell to his knees before the good man.

"Please, José, sainted man, give me work!"

The man put his chair aside and got up from his stool, went to the back of the workshop, came back with the empanada, and fed it to Jaime himself.

"Two are better than one, brother mine! You will help me sand the wood!" With great skill, he tied a piece of brick wrapped in sandpaper to each of Jaime's hands, then deposited a board on his lap. "Sand with your soul, brother, all Jehovah's paths are mercy and truth!"

When the sandpaper wore out, José very respectfully untied the pieces of brick from Jaime's hands and replaced it with new sheets, murmuring phrases from the Bible, which he knew entirely by heart. He let my father sleep beside him on a sack filled with sawdust, and every day, after work, he placed some bills in his pocket. After six months, Jaime had saved up enough to buy passage on a ship. Finally, he could return to Tocopilla and hear Sara Felicidad's melodious voice saying, between her abyssal moans: "I inhale when you come so that you come even more, and when you withdraw my soul follows you, so that you do not go as far as the place where you can be without me, because I am only the softness that adapts to the gift of your hardness, a living clay mold that at every touch takes different shapes, and conforms to the idol that grows, expands, burns, palpitates, is prolonged in your hands, now claws, that dominate my thighs. Under the pressure of your fingers and the thrusting of your hips, my skeleton forms. As you possess me, I grow around you." With a feeling of happiness that emerged from suffering like the white tip of a dark iceberg, at the end of the week he said goodbye to Don José, who with his never-ending smile, quoted Psalm 7:

"You brought happiness to my heart." And kissing Jaime's hands, he added: "Go with God, my son."

Light and practically dancing, he walked toward Mapocho Station to take the train that would carry him to the port. Between Avenida Matta and San Diego, he saw a commotion around a cargo truck. He approached, pushing the gawkers gently out of the way so he could stand in the front row. One of the vehicle's enormous wheels was crushing a man's head! It was so heavy that the entire brain had shot out of the open skull and landed a yard away. There it was on the dirty pavement, like a vulnerable pink mollusk. Beside the cadaver, a woman was on her knees, six pale children clinging to her as she looked with deranged eyes at the morbid crowd.

"He worked, I took care of the children. . . . And now what are we going to do? We have nothing. . . . Help, please!" The spectators didn't move a finger; they stood there and stared at the blood. Jaime, who could now slightly move the tips of his thumbs, pulled out his little bag of money and placed it before the woman's knees. Then he walked off without looking back.

He returned to the workshop, having decided to work for another six months. He was afraid José would turn him away, but instead he said:

"'A broken and contrite heart you will not despise.' Psalm 51-17." And he tied the sandpaper to Jaime's hands.

Grateful, Jaime sanded his boards better and better. When the wood left his hands it was so shiny objects were reflected in its surface. The old man, every night before sleeping, read him a page from the Bible with intense emotion. Jaime again managed to save the price of a ticket.

"This time is for real, José. I have a wife and children. I know they're waiting for me. I'm going home."

"'And all peoples on earth will be blessed through you.' Genesis 12:3. Go with God, my son!"

Even happier than the first time, Jaime ran toward Mapocho Station. He was a small piece of metal, and Sara Felicidad a gigantic magnet. Her melodious voice was saying: "My desire calls you from my belly, where my center of gravity vibrates as if all the Earth, with its valleys, its mountains, its jungles and oceans, were concentrated there. I tremble from my hips to my pubis and I feel as if my skeleton were melting and raining into the throat of my sex, which, swollen, seems to drown. You are the key to that locked door. When you rest your hardness in my aqueous world, my lips open like a flower that grows and breathes. I accept and absorb you without the shadow of an obstacle so that in my dark depths your burning extremity will deposit divine strength in a liquid pearl." Intoxicated by his desire, he got distracted and wasn't able to dodge a mattress that was thrown from a third-floor window. He crawled with difficulty from under its bulk, and, unable to brush from his coat the dust that formed the shape of a large rat, he stood up and realized that the sidewalk was full of old, ordinary furniture. There was a bed, a dresser, a table, half a dozen chairs, lamps, kitchen utensils, and an anemic sofa where an old couple was sitting, watched over by a group of armed police. From above, in haste or contempt, a trio of movers threw out the window notebooks, packages, clothes, cushions, all of it old, all of it gray, all wrinkled. That pair of octogenarians had been unable to pay the rent on their apartment, and they sat there in the middle of the street, their eyes cloudy, looking panicked, their tense faces displaying the shadow of a future now become a murderous snake. None of the police, movers, or spectators showed an ounce of pity for them. Those desolate old people were just two more old, gray, and wrinkled objects. To top it off, a drizzling rain began to soak everything. The woman got up, took an umbrella from the wardrobe, and opened it over her husband. They interwove their fingers on the curved handle and began to cry with tears as fine as the shower. . . . Jaime approached them, and with intense pain took out his little bag, and, showing them the money it contained, offered it to the old couple. They accepted it, stuttering words of thanks. Pretending to be deaf, he turned around and headed back to the workshop.

"'A friend loves at all times, and a brother is born for a time of adversity.' Proverbs 17:17," said the good José. And, without asking for any explanation, he set Jaime to sanding.

Another six months, the longest he'd ever lived, polishing those aromatic boards! What had before been splintered and hostile, had now become friendly wood, lively, conscious, like an animal that only lacked words. Each piece had its own character, its subtle message, its discreet teachings. The dust that came off of them entered his lungs like a balm to absorb the poisonous residues of the capital's air. Thanks to Don José, who on Sundays invited him to walk up the imposing San Cristobal hill, he began to love the trees, and, because of that, to distinguish one from another. The leaves transmitted to him the song of their shapes: spear-shaped, oblong, elliptical, oval, interwoven, smooth, spiky— a whole world! Oh, those araucarias stretching out their great, hard leaves, over a thousand years old, the male and the female separate, sensing each other from afar, converting the atmosphere and the insects into the vehicle of their caresses, yes, for ages living an inextinguishable love, in spite of the distance, just like him and Sara Felicidad! He realized that all the trees, different as they may be—cypress, carob, plum yew, cinnamon—sank their roots into their woman's sex: she was the origin of the forest, and he a lost traveler trying to reach her green heart. Don José laughed on seeing him atop the hill, waving his arms like wings. However, Jaime did it with conviction: someday, the miraculous wind would come and carry him off across the twelve hundred miles separating him from his female!

At the end of another laborious six months he again saved the money for the trip. This time the old man told him: "Psalm 32:8: 'I will instruct you and teach you in the way you should go; I will counsel you with my loving eye on you.'"

He closed the workshop, put on his Sunday suit, and went with Jaime to Mapocho Station, determined not to leave his side until he got on the train to Valparaíso. The carpenter's old age kept him from taking very long steps. Jaime calmed his impatience and adjusted his stride to his friend's; José, to fill the time, started a conversation:

"Dear brother, you who are so eager to reach the train station, tell me: what's the shortest way between two points?"

Jaime immediately answered:

"A straight line!"

"Brother, that is the ideal solution, but in everyday practice, the shortest way is the one that offers the least resistance."

"That is true, José."

"But if we want to be psychologically exact, the shortest path is the one we know best, because, being free of anxiety, it tires us less. And even better: the most beautiful path is also the shortest, because as we move forward, the pleasure makes our energy grow. You see? However you, walking like a tortoise because of this poor old man, take the fastest route of all: the path of love. . . . Even if it takes an entire lifetime to arrive, right now you are at your goal. Love makes the two points into one. You are here, she is there, but there is no separation between you. 'The law of their God is in their hearts; their feet do not slip.' Psalm 37:31."

No sooner had the old man finished his sentence than they both fell to the ground. A strong earthquake shook the street. Cracks appeared in walls. A crevice rumbled open in the sidewalk. The tall buildings, swaying, vomited a swarm of terrified citizens into the street. "Earthquake!" The tremors decreased in intensity after some interminable seconds, and the terrifying bellowing that came from the earth's guts went quiet. Some men of humble appearance came over to the carpenter and embraced him.

"Brother José, Psalm 55:5: 'Fear and trembling have beset me; horror has overwhelmed me'!"

The old man answered:

"Same psalm, 6: 'Oh, that I had the wings of a dove! I would fly away and be at rest.' Brothers, doves rest only in their loft, where they are fed by their Master. This earthquake is a sign. Let us gather in our temple to fervently sing our psalms."

Don José took Jaime's arm, and without asking his consent, led him a few blocks until they reached a big house converted into a protestant temple. The asphalt still creaked with slight shudders. The area filled with faithful men, women, children, some four hundred souls who communicated among themselves citing phrases from the Bible. José, not letting go of Jaime, advanced through the considerable crowd, who opened way for him with great respect. He went up onto a stage and began in his faint, worn-out voice to intone:

"Listen, oh God, to my prayer. . . ."

Everyone continued in a loud chorus:

"And do not hide from my plea. . . ."

As they all went on singing, their voices grew in intensity, losing the anguished tones and filling with confidence and happiness, growing into a thundering and euphoric musical waterfall:

"Cast your cares on the Lord and he will sustain you; He will never let the righteous be shaken!"

The parishioners, without stopping their song, got up from the chairs and started to dance and fall into a reverie. Jaime's heart sped up:

"But José, my good friend, should I believe what my eyes are seeing? All the chairs of this temple are the ones that you and I made!"

Because of the noise, the old man had to bring his lips to one of my father's ears to make his weak voice heard.

"So they are, my brother! Who would be interested in buying so many chairs of humble wood? The day you arrived I had decided to live off my savings, and with the boards I'd accumulated in the storeroom to make the four hundred chairs my temple needed. God sent you. You worked with me for a year and a half, and you helped me fulfill my promise. In the first six months, I gave you as payment a third of my savings. In the second, another third, and now you have the rest in your bag. I have nothing left. When I left to go with you to the station, I closed the workshop forever."

Jaime felt a knot form in his throat, looked at the shining chairs, made, sanded, and varnished with love, and he wanted to say something to the old man. But he managed only a long, hoarse, deep sigh. The carpenter raised his arms and exclaimed:

"Brothers, the earthquake has ended! We're going to jump twenty-six times to give thanks for the Lord's mercy!"

The excited believers started to jump, counting out loud: "One! Two! Three. . . ."

The temple began to shake more than it had in the earthquake. Don José, with unexpected energy, jumped like a child.

"Four! Five! Jump, brother, your hands are paralyzed, but your legs aren't! Praise be to God! Eight! Nine!. . . ."

Jaime jumped and jumped. It seemed to him that each time he jumped higher, as if attracted by an external force on high.

"Close your eyes, brother, and you'll feel you reach the stars! Seventeen! And even further, to paradise itself! Twenty-one! And further still: to the loving heart of God! Twenty-six!"

Everyone fell into their seats, sweating and happy. The carpenter collapsed, finished off by a heart attack. Jaime pressed an ear to his chest. He got up, sorrowful:

"Brother José is dead!"

Amid the general silence, a venerable matron stood on a chair.

"'And with you, Lord, is unfailing love; You reward everyone according to what they have done.' Our brother's is a beautiful death: at the twenty-sixth jump he reached God's heart, and there he stayed! For each free chair he gave the temple, he deserves a paradise! God shall grant him eternal life in four hundred heavens! Alleluia!"

"Alleluia!" everyone exclaimed, and they passed around a hat to contribute to the burial. When it finally reached Jaime, he saw the few coins there: his friend would go to rest in the common grave. . . . With another long, hoarse, deep sigh, he dropped the money for his ticket into the hat, and, his pockets empty again, he went out into the street. A strong wind was blowing. He faced in such a way that the current would blow at his back and he let himself be carried along with the dry leaves of the trees down Alameda de las Delicias. He felt light. Sara Felicidad was with him.

The wind brought him to Mapocho Station. He started to laugh. He walked to Parque Forestal, which spread out over many blocks like a sensual green stain. He walked slowly under the tall trees, breathed in the scent of grass with delight, sat on a bench and looked at the pairs of students in the shade of the branches, intertwined in an interminable kiss, and let the hours pass. Thoughts came to him that he once would have found absurd, but that today produced a subtle pleasure in him, as if instead of his old brain, full of shadows, he now possessed a brand new, luminous one. Looking at the world with his head down, ordinary concepts turned upside down: "The sense of life is the life of the senses. . . . The idea of reality is the reality of the idea. . . . We don't make love, love makes us. . . . If we bring something to light, it's because the light brought it to us. . . . The essence of knowledge is knowledge of the essence. . . ." Then he made decisions that were really more like metaphors: "I must teach my wounds to sing! I will turn to stone so that any saint can build a temple on me! Here is what I was finding and could not seek!" He went on like that, with great pleasure in spite of his growing hunger, saying random phrases that, as soon as he murmured them, dissolved into oblivion. "For the bird to reach the stars, the tree sinks its roots to the center of the Earth. . . ." He played at splitting in two, a disciple and a master. He asked questions that he answered himself: "How does one change to stop doing the same thing? We all do the same thing always: we never stop changing! Why can I never know myself? It is totally improbable that the fish will become aware of the water before the moment it leaves it! Who am I? A statue of salt cannot sink into the ocean to see how deep it is!" Finally, he imagined the epitaph for his grave: "No start, no end, who lies here?" Suddenly, in a mute explosion, night arrived.

Trembling with hunger and cold, his coat dampened by a light fog, he got up and went to urinate behind an oak tree. Four shaggy youths, drunk and stumbling, came over to Jaime and began to urinate as well, trying, with their long streams, to go further than him. After losing, they embraced him, letting out exaggerated cries of jubilation:

"Oh, champion of the yellow arc, great Walt Whitman, you have abandoned Parnassus to come visit us! We, humble Chilean poets, welcome you! Save us, please! Here we are, returning every second from a trip on which we didn't find our treasure, back to the Present, home, with our hands empty, as if doing were the reason for doing, as if to stop were to stop being, and the only way of living were to create utopias!"

Jaime, with pleasure and embarrassment, went along with the game and replied:

"From nothing, being nothing, and falling toward nothing, we must force ourselves to be born and awaken!"

The poets, hearing such words from that madman's mouth, broke off laurel branches and made him a crown, and brushed the mud from his ragged coat.

"Oh, exquisite seer, you will come with us to inaugurate the statue of the Invisible Man!"

They brought him to the old statue of a hero of the Independence, climbed onto the marble pedestal, covered the manikin with a sheet, and with loud cries, as if the park in that late night were full of listening people, they announced the monument's unveiling. Pulling back the white cloth, with searching gestures, they palpated the air in front of the effigy as if they saw nothing. One of them declaimed:

"We are officially inaugurating, in this distant island of the southern hemisphere, the statue of the Invisible Man, cruel homage to the millions of nobodies who populate its streets. And with you now, the distinguished poet, Walt Whitman!"

The shaggy boys applauded and made Jaime climb up onto the dignitary's shoulders. My father, suddenly beset by an ancient suffering, recited in a voice that came from the furthest corner of his kidneys:

"No one has ever said anything, we have been always mute, these animals that come out of our mouths are not words! No one has ever seen anything, what we call the eye is a black sheet: there is no light, we have dragged ourselves since distant times through a tunnel! No one has ever heard anything, and if you think about it, there is no Time: we never saw this sculpture made with the steam of blood! That Chinese puzzle lying in the street was never deformed by the rain! The porcelain doll with whom I slept for years never decayed! We never collected fly wings to make a portrait of our souls! We have never spoken dead man to dead man! No one has caressed us with a thousand hands! No one has written anything, ever! I repeat: no one has written anything, ever!"

The poets were silent for a long time. Jaime slept with his eyes open, looking toward the bright star of dawn. With sudden respect they took him down from the patriotic hero as if he were a dead bird, and they poured rum into his mouth. Jaime took a few minutes to leave the reality of his dreams and enter the illusion of wakefulness.

"Come and eat with us, poet, at the fortune-teller María Lefèvre's!"

They crossed the park and the street and came to an ancient building, where they went down a cement stairway that seemed to serve as a cat shelter and into a basement lit only by candles. Lying in her wide bed, a woman between fifty and sixty years old, dressed in a Chinese robe and accompanied by a naked teenager, was reading from *The Zohar* to the rhythm of a soup bubbling in an iron cauldron.

"Boys, everything you brought to eat, throw it in the magic pot!"

They pulled from their pockets a couple of onions, a packet of noodles, some pieces of chorizo, and a handful of rice. They threw the provisions into the soup, which was half water and half wine, and they poured themselves some mugs of the appetizing juice. Jaime drank greedily, burning the skin of his lips.

"We brought you this bard as a gift, María!"

In an impressive voice, like a hoarse sailor's, the woman said to Jaime:

"How glad I am that my poet friends can see the diamond that lies within the heart of the poor! Each human being is a gift! The basement of Lefèvre, your humble servant, is open to all ... writers, bandits, police, cardinals, sinners, philosophers, crazy people, from sunset to dawn: the night is my kingdom.... Here, the soup boils ceaselessly, like life; and like life, it nourishes but sometimes burns.... Sit on my bed, on my throne. I'm going to read your cards!" She rummaged under the pillow, took out a yellowed tarot deck, and put it on the floor. "Mix the cards slowly with your left foot! From that unique disorder, your destiny will emerge!" She gathered up the cards and spread them over a black handkerchief. "Choose three.... Let's see: The Hanged Man, The High Priestess, The Wheel of Fortune.... You are in the first one, hanging from one foot, looking at the world upside down, entering like a root into the unknown to absorb the Being.... Unmoving, unable to choose, accumulating knowledge and feelings, in gestation.... Those hands behind the back hide the cause of your illness.... Beside the Hanged Man waits a woman who for love has become a virgin, cloistered, waiting for you, converting her desires into the ruled lines of a sacred book the color of flesh, her sex. In the Wheel of Fortune, in what goes down and up we see the end of a cycle. The monkey, going down, has his hands tied like you. The hare, going up, has its ears blocked like you. Both of them fear the truth. The sphinx who balances at the top of the wheel, like you has a sword piercing her heart. If you want to recover your lost world, you must accept a feeling that you reject, so that your hands are paralyzed. . . . Let's see, choose another card. . . . The Emperor! Who is the powerful tyrant who ties you to shame?"

Jaime fell to the floor foaming from the mouth, and, shaken by epileptic spasms, he cried:

"Carlos Ibáñez del Campo!"

María Lefèvre took off her Chinese robe and threw it over my father. As soon as that silk covered him, his convulsions stopped. The woman, naked and showing the stretch marks on her belly and her flaccid breasts without shame, lay down beside Jaime and took him in her arms.

"You cannot go on like this. You must face the monster, understand why you love him so. . . . It's natural to be afraid, but to be a coward is an illness. This afternoon I heard on the radio that the representative Jorge González von Marées, head of the Nazis, has officially proclaimed General Ibáñez as candidate for the presidency of the Republic. Tomorrow there will be a great parade, and all the Nazis, in their meticulous uniforms and carrying banners, will go to Mapocho Station to receive the candidate as he arrives from Argentina. . . . Go with them, my poor dear, approach the man you consider the cause of your illness, and, like a fisherman with his nets, observe your emotions as they develop. Don't hide the truth! Whatever it is, if you are able to bring it into the light, it will become food for your soul! Come, choose one last card. . . . The Judge! You will be reborn, with the help of a woman, a boy, and a being who is dead but speaks as though alive. The reading has ended! In the soup there is a whole chicken. Fish it out with this spear and eat it. When you wake up tomorrow, around two in the afternoon, run to follow the parade."

The fortune-teller gave him room at the foot of her bed. While the teenager strove to possess her, Jaime, rocked by the bed's swaying, felt his eyes slowly close. When he woke up, the soup was still bubbling in the cauldron. The four shaggy youths, each in a corner of the basement, were sleeping soundly amid notebook pages covered in poems. The fortune-teller, bedecked with twelve cats, added her snores to their purring. The teenager, naked as always, with a pink ribbon tied in a bow around his member, served him a plate of steaming carrots:

"Finish eating and go right now. The parade is about to start. Señora Lefèvre gave me this card for you, the number seven, The Chariot. She asked me to show you how the character, without reins, lets himself be driven by the horses. Understand?"

"Thank you, friend, I understand: we don't arrive when we struggle to reach a distant, separate end, but rather when we understand that the end is part of us, and we trust that we will be brought to it."

Jaime went up the stairs trying not to bother the dogs, cats, and rats that were sleeping curled up one against the other, and running the length of Parque Forestal, he reached Plaza Italia, where, in that exact moment, the people were crowded in the streets to see the exotic parade begin. It was preceded by a black truck from whose roof a speaker was shouting: "Rebirth of the pride of the race! Work and social justice for all! War with communism! Eradicate politicking! Freedom from the economic yoke of international Judaism! Chile for the Chileans! Chileans for Nazism! Nazis for Ibáñez!" Flanked by rows of police on horses, accompanied by a military band, flags held high, a large number of young people, proud of the dun-colored shirts they sported, some of them with supposedly ferocious dogs that were clearly street mutts, walked with their arms outstretched toward Mapocho Station. Jaime fell in behind them, and adapting to the rhythm imposed by the military band, he followed them. To avoid suspicion, he raised his paralyzed right hand. After a time one of the leaders, who wore a patch with two crossed stripes as a sign of his rank, came over to him and said:

"The Roman salute is made with the hand outstretched, friend!"

"I can't, sir: it's all dried up!"

"Then lower it, it looks like you're making fun!" And that's what my father did. The other man, disbelieving, felt his hand to verify it was paralyzed. Convinced, he returned to the ranks. . . .

Jaime noticed that, little by little, the police were covertly leaving. When none remained, one of the truck's tires blew out. Something told him a metal spike had been intentionally placed in the street. The unsuspecting youths, on finding themselves deprived of their loudspeaker, began to shout their slogans themselves. Soon those cries mixed with others that were coming from the opposite direction. A Communist parade! Jaime understood that the battle was imminent. And if it happened, he would never have the chance to get close to the dictator. . . . He ran desperately toward the head of the parade, passed it, and with his arms outstretched like a cross of rags, he planted himself equidistant from the enemies, believing his vulnerability to be a powerful motive for the two groups to stop. It was not so. The clash of fanatical youths was ferocious. He received a cudgel to the head, fell to his knees, and was trampled by the proselytes' boots. Across the street, through all the discord, he saw a fruit store with a sign that said The Apple of Harmony. He crawled toward it to seek refuge. He collapsed in a faint amid the pears and oranges.

†

When the Rabbi, taking control of my tongue, cried: "Hallelujah, it's Jaime!" my mother, who had just gotten rid of Doña Sara to be Sara Felicidad once again, felt an immense happiness and at the same time a deep shame. Having followed the path of hope for an eternity, she had given up just an inch from the finish line. After promising to wait for him forever, to believe in his return despite the years, the misery, illness, and death, she had fallen into the hormonal trap, desire had conquered her like any cat in heat. That miserable Jaime who fell into her arms should have found a devoted Doña Sara. He should have been the one to let down her hair, it should have been his passionate embraces that lengthened her spine, his caresses that recreated the tautness of her skin, and his kisses that blessed her mouth so that her words would be music again. How could she, who had believed him dead, tell him she loved him? What is death? With utter certainty it is not an end: we are something before we are born and we will be something after we perish, and in those two somethings love is present, the effect precedes the cause, love exists before birth, and will continue after death. . . . Knowing herself to be a traitor, weak, with counterfeit faith, affected her balance: she swayed as if she were on a ship in high seas, then fell onto the wounded man and licked his skull. Stretching her bloodied tongue toward the ceiling, she let out some heartrending moans that contained two immense sorrows: one that she had contained over all those interminable years of waiting, and another for having lost all merit out of animal weakness. The intense pain that pierced the center of her joyful heart, a rotten pit in a peach of sweet pulp, made her understand that the importance of time did not depend on its length. In just one second, she had lost everything. . . .

While the machine guns barked outside, Jaime slowly opened his eyes, saw his Sara Felicidad shining, shaken by a sob of love, and he felt like a ship lost in the storm finally reaching its longed-for port. He was flooded with happiness, but also with shame.

"Do not kiss me, my love, I don't deserve it! I failed! I had him in my hands, but I was incapable of blowing out his brains! I made you wait, I sacrificed you uselessly, I don't deserve your fidelity, I'm a coward!" And he fainted again.

†

My father had a concussion and was unconscious for six months. Large black circles grew beneath his eyes. The Rabbi told me: "They're like Venetian gondolas. . . . But beauty does not exclude danger. If it is the shine of truth and that truth is poisonous, the brilliance can become one of Death's disguises." Waiting for the edema in his encephalic mass to dissolve, my mother, silent, patient, beautiful, whiter than ever, cut my father's hair, filed his nails, fed him pureed food and juice, took care of his urine and excrement, bathed him, perfumed him; she treated him as if he were a God-child.

In that environment, few were the sounds that were tolerated. At times you could hear the rasp of a broom, others the whistle of water coming to a boil, the cottony rhythm of the knife cutting vegetables or the buzz of the inevitable flies that, as they flew past each other, wove a vibrating macramé. Words were entirely forbidden. If by chance it occurred to me to utter a sentence, my mother looked at me with widened eyes, as if that breach could unleash an avalanche. I had no recourse but to talk, in silence, with the Rabbi. That's what we did at night, when my father's snores invaded the sacred silence like a horde of vandals.

"My dear host: because I live inside you, I feel how you suffer. Throughout your childhood you had a sainted mother, exclusively to yourself. From one day to the next, the priestess transformed into an empress in love with an intruder you are required to call Father. That half-dead man runs you out of the bedroom and takes for himself the attention and the body of the woman you love. Now you are obliged to sleep behind the sacks of fruit, solitary as your soul. (I count very little for you in terms of caresses.) However, all that happens in the material world is for good, if you are good. If you are bad inside, all that happens outside, even if it seems wonderful, is for bad. . . . You are good in your essence, you'll see that things will work out. You will learn to share; you'll realize how incomplete your spirit felt with an absent father; between your mother and you, he will supply the difference; you'll be able to stop being a child, and you'll know the nobility of an adult mind. . . . Listen to this little story: A dark frog swallowed more and more fireflies, unconcerned by the bitter taste, until through the skin of his swollen belly, a sublime light began to shine."

"I like your story a lot, Rabbi, but think about this: when the frog was dark, the herons didn't eat it. When it gave off that sublime light it became easy prey for raptors."

"You're trying to seem smart, Alejandrito, but intelligence without heart leads to error: if the frog is a monk and the light in his belly is illumination, the bird of prey is God (blessed be his name). And to dissolve in His mouth is happiness."

"Yes, Rabbi, but that's not the absolute conclusion. If the frog's belly shines, it's because inside it the fireflies are alive, and if it wants to keep that sublime state, it must not digest them. For that same reason, God, who swallows the frog, doesn't do it for its intrinsic darkness, but rather for the borrowed light; it's the light that interests him. In conclusion, God will swallow the illuminated ego but he'll keep it in his sainted breast, for eternity, just as it is. The fusion with the Lord, in this case, is pure myth."

"Oh, how stubborn you've turned out, you blasted child! God (blessed be his name) created the light and sent it to travel the world. The fireflies swallowed it, the frogs swallowed the fireflies, the herons swallowed the frogs, and God (blessed be his name) swallowed them all! And that's how the light, the brilliance of

Truth, returned to the Truth, because beauty and God (blessed be his name) are one and the same entity."

"Very nice, but what a waste of time! If God disguises himself just to return to himself, this whole world is no more than—"

"Be quiet, and do not blaspheme! Beauty does not have an explanation. We'd do better to change the subject!"

Our discussions were interminable, the months sped by, until one day, without the Venetian boats and in full use of his mental faculties, Jaime got up from the bed. The first thing he said was:

"Where is Sara Felicidad? Go get her, Benjamín!"

It was normal for him to ask first of all for the woman he loved; still, I was very offended. During his illness, there had been many times when my mother had to attend to customers, and I'd been the one to give him his soup. Scarcely did he recover a hint of consciousness, he spat the food into my face, saying furiously:

"Don't bother me, Benjamín! You're not my mother!"

And now that he'd recovered his senses, he still forgot my name. With my chin held high and proud, I told him:

"That's not my name! I'm not your brother, I'm your son. And if your memory isn't too dented, my name is Alejandro!"

Immediately he took me in his arms and tried to caress me with his claws, but he only gave me painful scratches.

"I'm sorry, my son, I'm still confused. In a couple of days you'll see that everything will return to its natural course. Know that I love you. Though for the moment my heart seems like a rock, inside it is full of ambrosia, connected to the fountain that never stops flowing."

My mother, at last hearing the beloved voice, ran the customers out ("Closed for holiday"), asked me to leave the store's back room, to stuff cotton in my ears, or to go for a walk, and she gave herself to my father. Mouth to mouth, sex to sex, breast to breast, the two hearts started to beat with such intensity that the pyramids of apples collapsed and the ripe grapes fell from their stems. I took two pounds of birdseed and went to the plaza to feed the sparrows. The Rabbi had taught me to stay still and hold my hand outstretched with a little mound of seeds in it. If I managed to eliminate the words that came to my mind, thinking they were clouds that an implacable wind swept from the blue sky, and if I did the same with my emotions, imagining they were leaving me through roots that grew from the soles of my feet, the little birds would land on my hand, then on my arms, then on my head, and finally I was covered in those warm little bodies as if I were a tree of gray feathers. I think I was like that for three hours. When I returned, the pounding of hearts and the rocking of the bed were still disturbing the order of the fruit. The floor was covered with it. Silent, I crossed that sugary carpet and, like a shadow, I slid into the back room: my father's body and my mother's, harmoniously intertwined and covered in a sweat that, on reflecting the blue of the walls in every drop, turned them into the infinite sky, never stopped moving with the grace of an octopus dancing in the ocean's depths. Jaime's roars were like those of a lion in the zoo: they united freedom and imprisonment. The oboe moans that rose like a torrent from Sara Felicidad's throat were darkened by a great sadness. In the moment of final pleasure, the octopus rose up and floated in the air above itself. Then it collapsed onto the mattress, kissing itself and crying. Jaime babbled:

"I don't deserve your love, my swan," and for a long time, in one continuous sentence uttered while he exhaled and inhaled, where the words fused tail to head, he told her of his lamentable adventure. "I failed at the last minute! I was incapable of finishing what I'd started! That's why my hands are paralyzed! Never again can I caress you!"

"I'm the one who doesn't deserve your love, my sweet! At the end, when you were just a few yards from me, I despaired. I didn't keep my promise to wait for you forever. Oh, that you can't caress me with your hands is a punishment I deserve!"

They cried and cried and cried. The tears, instead of falling, went to land on the ceiling, and they accumulated there, shining like stars. I couldn't stand that sorrow, and I took off my clothes and went to lie down with them. My mother embraced me like a shipwrecked survivor clinging to a life raft. My father, jealous, gave me a look of hate that then, regretful, he disguised with a smile. He told me, sweetening his harsh voice:

"Benjamín, your mother and I have serious business to discuss. We told you to go outside."

Feeling I was being expelled from paradise, oppressed by an infinite sadness, I got dressed. I was about to leave the back room with my head hanging, when the Rabbi, indignant, took control of my brain. Making my body adopt the precise movements of an adult, he faced Jaime and Sara Felicidad:

"Enough of this nonsense! I can't let you ruin the magic of this encounter with delusions worthy of the worst unbelievers! Starting with you, woman: how is it possible that you, a true believer, so pure you deserve the love with which God (blessed be his name) protects every second of your existence, can think you are traveling life's path abandoned and alone? Precisely because Jaime was a few yards from you, He Who Knows All (blessed be his name) sent you the order to bury Doña Sara and go back to being Sara Felicidad, to receive your husband not only with the beauty of your spirit but also that of your sublime body. If you accept that your will belongs to the All-powerful One (blessed be his name), you will recognize that the change in appearance obeyed a divine order. Stop blaming yourself and recognize that it was the effluvia of the nearby male that awoke in you those desires of a thirsty woman. If your husband had been truly dead, you would have been buried, and no third-rate Romeo would have been able to pull you from the wise old woman you had wrapped yourself in. . . ."

On hearing these words, my mother felt the steel ring imprisoning her heart break. Letting the Rabbi's words fill her, she happily moved her body closer to my father's.

"As for you, Jaime, what I have to say to you requires that you listen to me, and believe once and for all that I exist, that I'm not an illusion created by your father's madness or an inconvenient and aggressive ghost. I'm sure that the blows life has given you have served to soften the rational heart you built with such rage. I knew your father deeply, the shoemaker so saintly and at the same time so weak, so dedicated to suffering humans and so absent from his family, giving himself to everyone and to you, nothing, except for my presence: I was the hateful legacy you received, a Rabbi come to tear down your atheist world with his fits of mysticism. . . . I also know you deeply, since for a good number of years I shared your organism. Listen: you complain of not finishing what you started. . . . Your immense pride is equal to Sara Felicidad's immense humility: it makes you believe, like her, that you walk the path alone; you don't realize that we are all accompanied. God (blessed be his name) walks ahead, beside, behind, above, and below us. No one ever starts anything, because all is done in Him (blessed be his name), and He (blessed be his name) has no beginning. What you did, others had begun, and what you didn't finish (nothing finishes because everything is in Him, blessed be his name, who is infinite, and there is no end), others will continue as long as time lasts. . . . You believe you didn't shoot Don Carlos Ibáñez del Campo because you considered him to be the father you had always wished to have,

an upright, atheist, powerful, implacable man, as you could have
been if the enlightened shoemaker, instead of giving to others and
leaving you in misery on his death, had concerned himself with
obtaining earthly triumph. That false Russian didn't even leave
you a nationality. The dictator kept an entire country under the
soles of his boots; you didn't even have a square yard where your
cadaver could be buried. Pulling the trigger became patricide for
you. However, sparing his life is not sufficient cause to paralyze
your hands and make you lose your memory. A detestable feeling
that you couldn't accept made you, in the absence of an earthly
grave, bury yourself in forgetting. You wanted to die because you
realized that you were as much a criminal as the man you had in
your sights. Yes, Jaime, you saw very clearly that, deep down, you
were also a murderer. And what is worse, a cowardly murderer. You
sought out Ibáñez not to make him your victim, but to thank him
for being a good executioner. He was the one who made your most
fervent wish come true, and that's why you couldn't finish him off.
It would have been like blowing the lid off your own brains! I had
the chance to observe you since you were little: Benjamín's arrival
was a catastrophe in your life. That weak, effeminate boy took over
Teresa, your mother, obliging you to commit abominable mischief
to get an instant of attention from her, even if it took the form of
a whipping. Remember how many times you tried and failed to
eliminate your little brother? You broke his skull by throwing a
stone at him, you forced him to pick up a cobra, you invited him
to swim out to sea in hopes he would drown, you threw yourself
at him and took his space, you kept him from speaking, cutting off
his words with mockery and shouts, you started fistfights with him,
knowing that his lack of manhood would keep him from defending
himself. . . . You tried, later, taking advantage of the sick fascination
the weak feel for those who torment and scorn them, to corrupt

him with alcohol. . . . You felt his declared homosexuality like a shameful stain in the middle of your face; that he lived with your mother almost as a conjugal partner drove knives into your heart. Oh, how you refused him, how you hated him, how you forsook him! Finally, believing yourself to be indignant over his death, very deep down, you were grateful to the dictator. If you had been in his place, you also would have drowned all the fags in the country, including Benjamín. When you found him at the bottom of the sea, it didn't occur to you to free his cadaver to give it a decent burial. No, you left it there knowing it would be devoured by the fish, and the only thing you brought back to the surface was the treasure he kept in his little metal box: you robbed him of his poetry. . . . And so, first you refused him, pretending not to understand him; then you made him into the foundation for your actions and, at the end of all your trials, you so incorporated him into yourself that he became part of your bones. It struck you as good that they would confuse you with Walt Whitman, you accepted that role of poet as the confirmation of the total displacement of your brother. Once poetry was definitively yours, Benjamín was finally eliminated!"

Jaime's face turned red, thick drops of sweat grew on his forehead like a crown. Now that he was hearing the truth, it seemed he had always known it. With profound humility he said to the Rabbi:

"Go on, please. . . ."

"Finding yourself back in your home, sick, with a lover converted into a mother, again the interference appeared: Alejandrito demanded his rights as prince consort, trying to usurp your rightful place. You immediately fell again into the error you committed since he was born: you considered him a copy of your brother, never your son. That's why you can't stop calling him Benjamín, without realizing that behind that substitution of names is hidden the desire to kill him. . . . To relieve you, I should reveal that in the dark zone the idea of death does not exist. Since the spirit has not seen anything die, it does not accept the concept. To kill, for it, is to make disappear, become invisible. And the weapon it uses is to ignore, to brush aside more and more the existence of the condemned one. Little by little the voluntary omission erases him, and that is how your son becomes your brother to end up a stranger, a shadow, nothing. . . . Jaime, if you want to recover the use of your hands, you must recognize four debts: the desertion of that poor hunchback, the atrocious poisoning of Grenadier, the abandonment of Benjamín's cadaver at the bottom of the sea, and the lack of affection for your son. Are you willing to pay them? I trust that you are, because you have changed. You no longer wish that an egomaniacal military man were your father, and you know very well that Alejandro the shoemaker, with one hand crippled by the sewing machine, had the greatest of powers to leave to you: the power to help! Misfortune is a beautiful teacher, and it has taught you to honor your father."

†

Jaime felt that his heart was opening into multiple petals. Before, what he'd desired most was not to change, to persist in being what he thought he was, incessantly repeating hypnotic circles, rejecting everything different. Then he decided to change, to leave one personality for another, opposite one, to go turncoat—that is, to modify his appearance while conserving the same ideas. Then came the transformation, the awakening, the disgust at himself, the discovery of sublime emotions, thoughts, and desires that made him feel he was dragging the past like a rotten organ. That transformation, on passing through the chrysalis of suffering, had to conduct him to transmutation: a being that blesses all that enters into the field of his gaze, an essential stone that with its mere presence turns simple metal into gold, demons into angels. From there to adoration would be no more than a step: full of light, he would know how to see the light in others, he would find a world at his level, he would participate in an angelic choir, impersonal, always changing, forged in Creation, which is continuous, eternal pleasure. Jaime shook his head and returned to the fruit store: the world went back to being itself, but without anguish. Even the smallest parcel of unreal reality was swollen with happiness. Shame had been supplanted with a fervent devotion. . . . With the same musical voice as Sara Felicidad's, he said to the Rabbi:

"I'm sorry. Everything you have said is true. I am willing to pay those four debts, but I don't know how to do it. I beg you, with the healer's wisdom you have acquired over so many centuries of immaterial existence, tell me what to do."

The Rabbi created a complicated ceremony to remedy the lack of paternal affection, which we fulfilled detail by detail. It was about giving me a series of knowledge, to which every human being has a sacred right, but that, out of ignorance, had not been transmitted to me. I was going to go back in time to be born again.

They sat me naked in the highest place in the room, atop a closet. I was covered by a veil that conferred on me the quality of an unborn spirit. I had been asked to awaken inside myself the urgent need to materialize. Then, convinced of my desire to live, I would cry out two magic words: "Father! Mother!" On hearing them uttered in an emotional tone, Jaime and Sara Felicidad would enter the room naked to stand on opposite sides of the bed, their backs to each other, indifferent. I had to create desire in the woman. I whispered to her:

"Let the insistent request from the depths of the galaxies enter your flesh, give the infinite universe the chance to endure, let your sex echo the ocean, open your legs, and before the male appears, allow me to enter so I can nest in your ovaries and choose the man who will be my father."

And Sara Felicidad fell onto the bed and slowly separated her alabaster legs. There in the center, under the little forest of golden hair, I saw the damp doorway, like a marine animal that was angelic and ferocious at the same time, mysterious and pink labyrinth imbued in sacred love, revealing itself in its incommensurate desire to swallow. From there, I exercised my will and called to my father:

"Turn slowly, moving like a nocturnal butterfly from absolute darkness toward the light of the moon. Observe well this body of living marble, and obey the call of the cathedral opening between her legs. It asks you for blood: let it move through your veins and accumulate in your phallus. It grows, gets hard, advances, strikes the flint and makes the spark fly that will light the ovaries, so that my soul, an old phoenix, will burn in them, and from the ashes my body will surge anew. Give me the chance to take shape once again."

Then my father moved closer to my mother, and with sweet slowness, positioning himself so that from atop the wardrobe I could see the act of love, he penetrated her, while she, with the same delicate slowness, absorbed him. In spite of my father's tensed hands, the caresses they gave each other drew marine currents on their bodies, planetary trails, dances of remote races, letters from sidereal alphabets. They said to each other:

"We unite to obey the call; we belong to each other thanks to the child who will be born from this enchanting encounter. He wants to be born, and we want him to be born. And, for that, we will give each other intense pleasure: he will not be the son of duty or frustration, but of a shared orgasm."

The harmonious movement of their hips accelerated until, nearing the cosmic explosion, they called me. I pulled the veil off, descended from the wardrobe, and went to lie in a fetal position between their burning bodies. Their bellies whipped my flanks until two cries, braided together like an unbreakable rope, announced the pleasure that would bring me into this world. . . . My father withdrew and I settled on my mother's belly. They covered me with a sheet soaked in warm water. There, every five minutes meant one month. I imagined I was growing for nine times five, forty-five minutes. The two of them, meanwhile, made plans for my future. Jaime, bringing his mouth close to the damp bulk, said:

"He will be a little man, similar to me, but his own personhood. He will grow like a plant in the direction he chooses. I will only water his soil, give him the chance to carry out his destiny. Oh, how much I will love him! I feel that he wants to be named Alejandro, like my father. Before, I rejected him out of resentment, but now that I have forgiven and asked forgiveness, I have recognized that name and cleansed it of hate; I accept it as a transmission of love."

Sara Felicidad, stroking me through the sheet, murmured:

"I must birth you without effort: the cosmos and I created you like a beautiful fruit; your body will be strong, your intelligence limitless, your heart generous. To your eyes no images will be forbidden to see, your ears will be able to hear without censure all the ideas in the world, hands that will know how to caress and transmit to the other's skin the song of the soul, nostrils that will know how to appreciate the divine perfume of everything that exists, a consciousness that will be able to discern under the veil of words the incessant miracle of life. . . . Prepare yourself, my son, the moment has come to enter this world that awaits you as a savior."

With Jaime's help she crouched down, and giving great sighs of happiness she pretended to be birthing me. She didn't forget the pain, but she showed it with satisfaction, without transforming it into suffering. I came out spinning in a spiral like the planets. My father received me in his arms and pressed me to his chest. For the first time, in a voice so sweet it seemed like a woman's, he called me Alejandrito, and I, also for the first time, pronounced the word that all those years he had hoped would emerge from my mouth: "Papa." Then he placed me on my mother. With a hungry mind, I appropriated her left nipple and began to suck. Up until then everything had happened as in a theatrical ceremony, but then, by my mother's sainted heart, a miracle happened: her breast filled with milk and I could, for a long time, taste the nectar I'd been deprived of during the first months of my life. For ten years, though I hadn't realized it, my body had demanded its due. Now, finally satiated, I could eat earthly food without that constant feeling of distaste and the threat of vomiting.

Jaime and Sara Felicidad had tied one end of a red cord around my waist, the other end around my mother's; once I felt satisfied, they cut the cord. They caressed me, bathed me, sang to me, dried me, sprinkled talcum powder over me, they made me grow, dressed me in new clothes. And, the three of us embracing, we went to a café where I had to eat ten pieces of cake, one for each year of life. . . . Jaime's two pinky fingers recovered their flexibility.

✝

Seeing the one she loved—no matter if he was her father or not—torn to shreds, his intestines hanging from a tree, was the definitive push that started the poor hunchback on a downward spiral. Something had to be done to offset that horror inscribed in the collective unconscious. For the Rabbi, violence led to violence and love to love. Cruel acts were ephemeral, but they were accompanied by ghosts passed on from fathers to sons for generations. "For I, the Lord your God, am a jealous God, punishing the children for the sin of the parents to the third and fourth generation. . . ." Exodus, 20:5.

Jaime had to go to the market and buy a hundred caged birds with red breasts, each one symbolizing a piece of the torn body. Then my mother and I went with him to the police station, which by then had been rebuilt. Along its gray walls, on the sidewalk and in the trees, to the astonishment and curiosity of the police, he placed the hundred cages. Then, one by one, he opened them. The birds shot out, but didn't disappear from sight. They waited for their companions, circling and twittering raucously. When there wasn't a single prisoner left, they formed a happy flock that traced the outline of a human being, and they disappeared in the direction of the mountains. . . . Jaime's ring fingers recovered their flexibility.

†

But how could he balance out the murder of Grenadier, that innocent horse who had died in the throes of horrendous pain? Eye for an eye, tooth for tooth, life for life? Would it do any good for Jaime to poison himself? Sara Felicidad, in that case, would follow him to the grave, and Raquel Lea and I would be orphaned; four more victims would not resuscitate the noble animal. Jaime had to repent to add conscience to the world. He would win the forgiveness of God (blessed be His name) or in any case himself, through a great penance. . . . The Rabbi made an astral visit to Linares and saw that the little farm had been purchased by perfume makers and was now planted with lavender. Since there was nothing to steal there, and the plants grew without need of being watered, a caretaker passed by to look at the fields only once a week. This would allow Jaime, unmolested, to carry out his act.

My mother and I went with him in a truck driven by the Sufi (he turned out to be an excellent driver), to drop him off seven and a half miles from Linares. From there, carrying on his back a five-foot-tall plaster Christ, he walked on his knees toward the farm. Though he was wearing knee guards, after a couple of miles his meniscuses were swollen and he was hounded by horrible pain. He began his march at six in the morning, and he reached the lavender field past midnight. While we cleaned and dressed his wounds, he drank three liters of water and devoured a roast chicken. Then he went to place the Christ in the ruins of the burned stables. It wasn't a crucified Christ, but rather a triumphant prophet, with a long white toga and a red stole, his arms outstretched to encircle the world, his chest open to show a heart in flames. Seeing him like that, standing amid the black rubble, Jaime understood the Rabbi's message. The burning of the houses and the horse's cremation had turned into a blazing heart, lighting the world with its mercy. . . . Next, we went with him to walk down the fragrant and violet avenues, toward the little wood where he had cultivated the poisonous grass. After he had pulled it up by the roots, we helped him deposit there, in a circle, twelve hives full of hardworking bees. What had been a field of death was now a cradle of life. . . . Hobbling, my father crossed the fields to find the place where the beautiful beast used to roll around and joyfully breathe in the bitter perfume of the grass. We handed him a shovel. He began to dig his grave. He finished when the sun was starting to come up. He lay down in the hole and we covered him with damp earth. From the dark mound emerged two white tubes he had sunk into his nostrils so he could breathe. Scarcely did the first ray of sun shine through, the swarm of bees invaded the lavender bushes with deafening, sensual buzzing. The Sufi brought a basket full of provisions from the truck. We spread a blanket beside the grave and began to eat breakfast. Then, lulled by the insects' song, the purifying smell of the lavender, and the thick heat, we took a long nap. Jaime had to stay buried all day and all night, given over to nothingness, letting the last traces of hate, rancor, and uncertainty dissolve. The Rabbi had told him: "For you to be born again, the old you must die. In this tomb you will let your entire skin fall off, the closed concept that you have had of yourself, in order to accept your limitless being, that which does not possess a name, or age, or race, or borders. . . . Make yourself one with the earth. Grenadier's hooves once passed over it. Absorb the memory the dust conserves of his harmonious pace, his galloping steps. Open your soul so the equine soul can enter. Your victim will take on meaning as he becomes spiritual nourishment. He must help you transform the world." As soon as the sun rose, we hurried to dig Jaime up. He collapsed, numb. Following the Rabbi's instructions, Sara Felicidad massaged him with lavender oil, good for curing burns. The middle fingers of Jaime's hands recovered their flexibility.

The hundred birds, the truck rental, the twelve hives, the plaster Christ, had all cost my mother a large part of her savings; the rest of it she invested in the trip to Tocopilla. The fruit store was closed with the sign SUDDEN VACATION. The Marú set sail from Valparaíso, and, sped along by the Humboldt current, it wasn't long before it reached Antofagasta. From there, the same dilapidated bus as always, after shaking and tossing us sixty miles along a road full of rocks and holes, deposited us right in front of the Municipality. Jaime scarcely gave us time to shake the red dust from our clothes and hair, and then he dragged us up the stairs toward the Mayor's office. Two fat policemen, with the eyes of children and cheeks colored by wine, carrying unnecessary machine guns, didn't even ask us who we were, and let us through.

We surprised the cripple Gamboa sitting at an enormous desk, reading the adventures of Prince Charming in *Pulgarcito*, a weekly children's comic magazine. He saw Sara Felicidad first, and he was stunned.

"But Doña Sara! What's happened to you? You look so different.... Has something bad happened?" Strange: for that gentleman with his belly girdled, gray hair darkened with walnut dye, and a disguised limp, a person who had regained her youth was sick! Then, as if his arm descended from the sky, without noticing his semi-paralysis, he condescended to shake Jaime's right hand. In passing he patted my head, leaving the mark of his sweaty hand on my hair. "What does this happy family have to tell me? What can the mayor—by unanimous vote—of this beautiful port do for you? Doña Sara, have you seen how now, thanks to your initiative, Don Pancho is covered in pepper trees? Also, I have you to thank for this...." He showed them a hand-colored photograph of Cristina sporting a muff of silvery fox fur—in this torrid clime!—and three little girls of the same age, with the same face, all dressed the same. "Destiny brought us triplets! According to Cristina they're a feminine holy trinity: mother, daughter, holy spirit, that is, Jehovesa, Jesusa, and Gabriela! In truth, leaving protocols aside, you, ma'am, changed my life when you cured me of my limp. Only then could I achieve my two dearest dreams: love and power." He pointed to an enormous, autographed portrait of Alessandri. "I have great influence in the government. Ask me for whatever you like!"

Jaime replied:

"Mr. Mayor, sir, we did not come to ask for anything, but to make an offer.... Near the coast off Tocopilla, only a few yards out to sea, there lies on the ocean floor a sizable treasure. Since I know the exact site, I want you to give me the necessary means to extract it, load it into a boat, and bring it to the port, in the greatest secrecy, of course. The group of police that does your bidding at the Municipality would be very convenient for our purposes."

"A great treasure underwater? It must be gold in a pirate ship! A fortune! And you say we would keep it a secret?"

"Of course, Mr. Gamboa. My share would be one per thousand."

"One per thousand? You mean that of every thousand dou-
bloons, you would give me nine hundred and ninety-nine?"

"That's right. I'll keep only one."

"I accept the deal! When do we start?"

"Right now!"

The cripple placed at Jaime's disposal a tugboat, a big barge,
and six police; in addition, he paid Don León and his team of
divers. Jaime was the first to descend. The cemetery, after over
seven years, had changed its appearance: the enchanting dance
was now a nightmare. The fish had devoured the meat, and all that
was left were skeletons in rags, no longer upright like princes and
queens, but bent, twisted, mutilated. Most of them were missing
their heads: the skulls, unmoored from the cloth, lay beside the
chained feet. He recognized Benjamín as the only skeleton in a
tuxedo. With great care he unshackled him from the chain, put
his bones in an oilcloth bag, and then tugged on the rope three
times so they would pull him up. Hugging his package tightly, he
ordered the police to organize the team of divers to extract the
whole cemetery. Many hours passed before the last of the thousand
skeletons was brought on board. The Rabbi's plan was being carried
out to perfection. "Jaime, all of this is to cure you. You must have
faith and complete the actions I recommend to the letter. In this
lower plane of reality I am the solitary healer who helps you, but
in higher planes, a crowd of immaterial doctors is working for you,
because as you faithfully follow the prescriptions that they dictate
through me, you help yourself. And on helping yourself you fall
into the grace of God (blessed be His name), who celebrates his
creatures building themselves up instead of destroying themselves."
It so happened, to confirm these beliefs, that at the very moment
when Jaime was accumulating his macabre cargo, on 5 September

1938, in Santiago a hundred Nazi youths who were determined to unseat President Alessandri through armed revolution, directed by their leader Jorge González von Marées—using a radio apparatus from afar, incurring no risk to himself—invaded the central house of the University of Chile. They took the rector prisoner, locked the doors, and began to shoot from the windows at the police, who responded to their pistol fire with machine guns and grenades. Another part of the group, more numerous, took control of the building of the Workers' Social Security office, across from La Moneda Palace, to barricade themselves on the seventh floor and start shooting toward the Palace with their few rifles and an old machine gun. These youths, idealistic and naive, were sure that the navy would be swayed by Carlos Ibáñez del Campo's presence in the country, and would rise up and come help them bring down the Government. Much to the contrary, the commanders in chief of the army, the air force, and the police complied with the president's orders, and they attacked the scanty band of revolutionaries in large numbers. The police and soldiers destroyed the doors with cannons, invaded the occupied buildings, and quickly forced the youths to surrender. They piled them into the Social Security building, and, without the slightest pity and in cold blood, turned them to face away and perforated their backs with bullets. Four boys who were badly injured pretended to be dead, and miraculously they survived. The story of the massacre scandalized the entire country, and the candidate of the oligarchy, Gustavo Ross, lost a great many votes. On the other hand, the general, who had countless Ibáñistas supporting him, saw before him an unexpected opportunity to rise back to power, for lack of an opponent. . . . Jaime, then, showed his cargo to the cripple Gamboa.

"What, Don Jaime? This is the promised treasure, bones and skulls instead of gold and diamonds? You've tricked me! Tell me what you've brought, and if your explanation isn't satisfactory I'll throw you in jail, along with your wife and offspring! I give you my word as mayor!"

"Look, Mr. Gamboa, I promised a treasure and I'm keeping that promise: these remains will be the trampoline of your great political career. More than a thousand homosexuals, my brother among them, were ordered drowned by then-president of the Republic, Carlos Ibáñez del Campo, understand? You will fly to Santiago, and, in your position as mayor, you will be immediately received by the general. You will show him these photographs of the remains. You will tell him that a witness who saw the death flights presented you with the photos, and that this citizen is willing to not reveal this abominable crime to the press, as long as he abandons his candidacy for the presidency. Also tell him that if he tries to assassinate me, an accomplice who is unknown to you will send these photographs to all the media outlets of the country, along with my statements narrating the abominable drownings and asking for the guilty man to be tried for crimes against humanity! If you protect yourself well, General Ibáñez will also buy your silence and will promote you quickly in the political world." When he heard this, the cripple Gamboa blinked greedily.

In the first week of October, a statement from Ibáñez appeared in the papers in which he withdrew his candidacy and left his followers as free agents. The fifteen thousand Nazi votes, along with those of other Ibáñistas, were added to those of the Popular Front and led to the triumph of the left's candidate, Don Pedro Aguirre Cerda, a mustached individual with the eyes of a good man and the nose of a drunk. Jaime's happiness was immense, and his index fingers recovered their flexibility.

†

In turn, my father's thumbs recovered life when my father fulfilled the last of the tasks the Rabbi gave him: to go at night, like a thief, to the General Cemetery, climb a wall, open his mother's grave and put Benjamín's bones inside the casket.

The Rabbi was insistent that this healing act had to be done unlawfully, with the danger of catching a bullet from the guards, who at night, having drunk more than their share, shot at any shadow they saw.

"You must demonstrate your sincerity by risking your life!" On uttering this phrase in the Rabbi's voice, I fainted. That period when I was constantly possessed by the disembodied man had been so intense for my childish brain that, at the edge of agony, I collapsed before my parents. Only then did they remember that I was a child. The Rabbi, on changing my voice, my rhythm, my gestures, had imposed himself like a real being, erasing me almost completely. I spent a week in bed, cared for, caressed, fed, lavished with chocolates and flowers. . . . The thing that did me the most good was my father's affection. Jaime was no longer himself. His transformed spirit, like holy water, was invading every cell of his organism: his skin grew soft, his eyes shone, his hair waved silkily, his body gave the sensation of being surrounded by a warm aura. To be caressed by those hands that were now almost entirely alive was a powerful tonic, and it made me, at the end of seven days of convalescence, leap out of bed and exclaim:

"All that apparently begins must apparently be finished! I'm going to call the Rabbi again!" Immediately I seemed to grow, my voice turned hoarse, my gestures became precise and my face, as though transparent, let the Caucasian's oriental face show through. "You will go to Cajón del Maipo, and in the foothills you will gather certain wildflowers and woody vines that I will indicate. You will boil them for a full night in holy water in a copper cauldron, and you will drink a green soup that, when you ingest it, will awaken in you very useful hallucinations. In reality they will be signs from the parallel world, that of the so-called dead who, though we do not see them, have as much existence as we do."

At midnight, Jaime drank a liter of the green concoction, and carrying a pick, a shovel, and the sack of bones, he set off for the cemetery. He saw that the streets of Santiago near the cemetery were full of the dead. They strolled down walkways with their dogs, cats, chickens, in compact groups: thousands of relatives, genealogical trees of ten or more generations, dissolved into each other, accompanied as well by their servants and friends, all deceased, making use of the things, the scenery, without realizing their own emptiness, haughty, vomiting toward the city the contempt they felt for themselves. . . . But who the hell doesn't have contempt for themselves? To every millimeter of consciousness corresponds an infinite horror. . . . Jaime repeated to himself again that those visions and ideas were produced by the brew he'd drunk, yes, but they were his and no one else's. What he was seeing and thinking as he walked toward his mother's grave, weighed down by Benjamín's bones, was his own interior. . . . In the wide avenue that led to the General Cemetery, there were so many dead people agglomerated in a dense fog that he had to move through them circling his arms like windmill blades. On the walls around the burial ground, that magma accumulated layer by layer over centuries had formed a slippery skin. He had to stack up garbage cans so he could climb over it. He put his feet on the shoulders of an angel who was pointing toward the future with lyrical hope, and he jumped down to the path edging the graves, trying not to spill his brother's remains. He thought it would be easy to find the Jewish section, but a pack of black clouds refused to let the moonlight through. He wandered for an eternity, trembling and sweating, until he found a square of old graves with inscriptions in Hebrew and old Spanish. It began to pour freezing water, wrapped in a hot fog. He managed to make out a blurry name: Teresa. Finally, his mother's grave! Frenetically, he deposited his burden on the wet rocks and wielded the pick and shovel. With great effort, he opened the grave and then the casket. The rain began to break up the putrefied remains. Quickly, he deposited the bones inside and closed the lid. There was a clap of thunder and a series of lightning flashes while the downpour began to diminish; an old woman rose up beside him, then sat down elegantly in her sealskin coat and a little straw hat covered in tortoiseshell flowers. The flashes of light showed through her transparent body. She said to him, in a friendly but long-suffering voice:

"I do not understand, sir, why you have filled my coffin with so many filthy bones. I don't think I deserve that profanation. I was a decent woman, I never hurt a soul."

"One moment, ma'am, there's something strange here! This grave is my mother's!"

"No, it's mine, and you are not my son! Unless your last name is Feldman. . . . because I'm Teresa de Feldman. Who were you looking for?"

"Teresa de Jodorowsky."

"Oh, now I understand, you made a mistake because of the dark! Your mother lies two hundred yards further on, in block B, path 153."

Jaime apologized profusely, gathered up the pieces of Benjamín, and closed that grave as best he could. When he finished the unpleasant task, from the emotional tension or the effects of the green syrup, he was beset by cramps. Diarrhea was imminent. He ran to block B, holding it in with all the strength of his soul.

He barely made it to stand before his mother's grave. The incipient dawn let him read her complete name. With no time to find an appropriate place, he pulled his pants down right there, and, squatting down, let a fetid stream escape. The pain was unbearable. He fell to sit in his own magma. He cried.

"Mamaaaaa!"

Blinded by his tears, he didn't see her appear. He realized she was present only when his exhaustion made his sobs more infrequent. Her voice slipped in during a pause, the voice he had kept locked in the oldest drawer of his memory; the voice that, in spite of her distant tone, had been the balm of his childhood sorrows. It was musical, sweet, the bearer of an angelical peace, the auditory shroud in which he wished to die, the exact copy of Sara Felicidad's sung speech. When he heard it, he bawled even harder: he had traveled from woman to woman pursued by the absence of that voice. His mother had never caressed him, it's true—maybe his anxious baby's body had repelled her—but she had sung to him in Russian, bringing her lips to his right ear. What did it matter if it wasn't out of love, but only so he would fall asleep more quickly and stop pestering her! She spilled into his soul the supreme pleasure of that whisper, the definitive end of anguish!

"My son, little Jaime, you're sick, let me help you!"

"I've sullied your grave with my excrement, and you still want to help me?"

"Your health is more important than all these tombs. First let's stop that diarrhea, then we'll talk. Eat a prickly pear from the bush that grows beside my gravestone. Be careful, don't prick yourself!"

Hypnotized, he obeyed. He peeled the fruit, and, nearly choking, he swallowed the sugary pulp almost whole. Immediately, the cramps stopped. Only then did he dare look at his mother.

He had two memories of her: the first was from before he turned five years old, in Russia, where she was a weightless princess, slender, with amber hair, a body as hard as rock and covered with a fragrant skin, so white she could be compared to the sail of a ship. Yes, it was her voice that every night transported him to the magical world of dreams. . . . In the second memory, from five years on, in Chile, she appeared as a dumpy monster, always wrapped in a girdle to hide her droopy belly and fallen breasts. The words emerged from her mouth converted into strands of acid shouts, and her skin, covered in freckles, was like giraffe leather. . . . He was repulsed at the thought of seeing her again like that.

Half-closing his eyes to let the minimum of the image through, he faced her. How she had changed! Her white hair, pulled back into a bun, was surrounded by a golden halo. Her thin body undulated with gentle gestures that seemed to be part of the movement of the clouds. The incandescence of her eyes didn't terrify him because it was tempered with a kindness so intense it seemed to come from the depths of eternity.

"As you can see, my boy, I died nearly in peace. It's been a long time now since I should have left this world, but I haven't been able to for one single reason: I have a debt with you. I've stayed here waiting for you. How wonderful that you have finally come, bringing me your brother's remains, which means you have forgiven us! Let's talk. . . ."

"What about all this shit?"

"Don't worry, the rain is starting up again and will take care of cleaning it. You should also let it wash you, because you smell pretty bad."

"Enough, your devotion is late in coming, I'm a man now, and you should have behaved like this when I was a child! But no, you only worried about that weakling Benjamín!"

"When you were little I lived like a mute violin, closed up in my black case. Clouded over by fidelity to that half-being who was your father. A poor shoemaker bled dry by a demon he called God, he couldn't even see that I was unsatisfied; others didn't exist for him. Understand me well, in that time neither Alejandro nor I were in conditions to comprehend reality—that is, the other. We could only communicate through images that we projected ourselves. We never knew each other. As children, we had both been given the status of stray dogs. The pain of that abandonment locked us in towers with no doors or windows, and the same thing our parents did to us, we did to you. Benjamín didn't count, because since he adhered to me like a mollusk, in reality he lived like a prolongation of me, one more organ, and never an autonomous being. But none of that meant that your mother didn't love you: I carried my repressed tenderness as a punishment, two immense wings breaking my bones as they beat within a space surrounded by walls. I admit, many painful years had to pass. I had to grow old and finally die, so that in the grave, I could realize that I loved you, with sorrow, with regret, and that, in a muffled way, I had never ceased to lament your absence. It's true that I deserved it, but when you cut me off, when you found Sara Felicidad, it was brutal: you banished me to oblivion! When I was laid to rest under the gravestone beside your father's coffin, before my flesh had even rotted away, I tried to go visit you in dreams; I wanted you to know my love, I wanted you to come and see me in the cemetery, I sighed to die again, only in your arms. As I was agonizing in the small puppet theater I had with Benjamín, I thought of you, but there was so much I wanted to say to you that I didn't know how to do it. So I left you as my legacy three phrases. . . ."

"Liar, you left them to my bald brother! He kept that inheritance a secret for himself, he would never share it with me!"

"Poor Benjamín, my victim: after they murdered my lover, in the time when I hated men, he was my companion, and he eliminated women from his life; he slept with me in the same bed and used my robes, because in private he only wore feminine clothes! He was also victim of my jealousy: everything he obtained I took from him. Not only did I insinuate that he should get rid of the hair on his body, I also obliged him to remain locked up in our apartment without ever going out into the street. He was forced to put sleeping powder in my milk to go and visit his friends. I made him my slave. Until the day I died, I sucked his blood! That's why he was so stuck to me, trying, obsessed, to take back the Being I had stolen from him. Do you understand now why he took your three phrases?"

"What good does it do me to understand, if I am still curious to know them?"

"Do you want me to tell you? Are you finally willing to receive something from me?"

"Wait, I'm not ready yet! First I have to forgive you, and I want you to forgive me at the same time. In the game of misfortune, the torturer and the victim always end up exchanging roles. . . . But how stubborn I've been: I've turned thirty-seven and I'm still complaining! How could I have been so unaware? How did you never realize that I wasn't asking for food, but for tenderness? How could you shut yourself up, painful as your life was, in your personal universe? How could you not see me, or hear me, or touch me? Why did I hear your bitter voice wake me up every morning by saying 'Stinking boy, go take a shower!' Why did you make me guilty of so many imaginary crimes?"

"Understand, Jaimito, that there is no difference between a dream and life. We provoke what happens to us. But the first blow comes from far off, a voracious feline that climbs up from the roots of the tree to devour the bird that nests in the top branches. I slept for years convinced I was a simple wife, clean, discreet, attentive, humble, obedient, fertile, and religious. I woke up when the swollen waters of the Dnieper River drowned José, my adored son. I was blinded by an intense rage against God that, step by step, aided by my lack of will, turned into hatred. An impotent hatred that I never wanted to break away from. That absurd desire for revenge, impossible as it was, built up in my heart until it broke it. Forgive me, my son! As I emerged from the emotional fog, thanks to my death, I gradually realized your absence; first I wondered who you were; I didn't remember your body or your face, only your wavy hair; then I reproached myself for not knowing you. Then I imagined you with all the qualities we lend to the disappeared. I suffered for years, waiting for you to come. The anxiety to hear your voice at times made my bones bleed. Finally, to my desperation, exhausted by the seemingly useless wait, you went back to being what you had always been: a vague shadow. You have the right to hate me. . . ."

Teresa, as she spoke, was gradually losing energy. Slowly, she fell into her grave. Jaime stopped feeling sorry for himself and for the first time realized how his mother had suffered, how frustrating her life had been. . . . He approached the stone where she lay, sat down next to her, and let her white head rest on his belly, lifting her clothes to uncover, between her belly button and clitoris, a broad scar. He wanted to tell her so many things, give her affection so she could go to the other world peacefully, but he couldn't utter a word. He kept mutely rubbing that suture, more and more, with such pressure that he tore it. There emerged a torrent of blood that went on flowing from the stone bed to the ground. The path became a red pool. Jaime shook his head, sweating. The blood and the scar disappeared, but not his resentment. He knelt before the dead woman and tried to take her hands, but his eight living fingers closed, trapping only air. If he wanted to join himself to his mother, he had to leave his body. Since he knew he was under the influence of a drug, he controlled his hallucinations, lowered his defenses, dissolved his edges, and stuck his head, hands, torso, and finally his legs through the wall of flesh. Suddenly he left the man on his knees behind and found himself standing, transparent, before the ghost. What a relief to find himself free of necessity, desire, emotion! To get drunk on the joy of shining, any memory now converted into phosphorescence! It was not mother or son or woman or man, only two fireflies dissolving slowly into each other. They began to vibrate. Now there were no more limits between her essence and his, and those sphere-shaped waves were the song in which their impalpable marrow united. They spread out at a torrential speed, moving together toward infinity. They sailed along an invisible edge, conquering the thirsty blackness beat by beat to flood the abyss with light. Love became for them a meaningless word. They consumed the structure of the syllable, transforming it into a shooting star, absurd happiness to be beyond the limits and disappear into indifference. . . . Suddenly Teresa, making a tremendous, harrowing effort, recovered her individuality.

"No, my son, separate yourself! You don't want to disappear in me. Don't dig into me, don't fill me. You are responsible for your body, you're not going to abandon that faithful animal: this dream is yours but it's only a dream; our union could lead to the death of your flesh. Don't make me a murderer! Go back!"

With a strong shake she sent my father back into the dense world. One by one, each hungry cell took control of a fragment of his soul. The dark flesh swallowed his light. He saw two plucked angels appear: cold and heat. His senses stabbed him, dividing his unity into various answers. He took on weight, and was again the man kneeling before his mother's grave.

"Please, wait! Don't go without telling me your three phrases!"

Losing her human form, looking more and more like a jellyfish, she stammered:

"If you want . . . to find the light . . . look for the root . . . of the shadow! You are a star: shine without fear . . . of overshadowing . . . the planets! Do not desire . . . anything for yourself . . . that is not for! . . ."

She couldn't finish the third phrase. She separated a small halo from her astral matter that rained down as dew. Jaime was happy to receive an unfinished inheritance. "It does not begin, it does not end, what is it?" A great peace flooded the cemetery. The first rays of sun drove the fog away. Hundreds of birds began to sing. That innocent music healed the wounds of his open heart. Teresa had finally dissolved in the world. Her kindness purified the air. Wherever he went, she would be with him.

†

He could move his thumbs normally. His hands were alive again! He opened the grave, pulled out the nails in the coffin, and with infinite tenderness placed Benjamín's bones beside his mother's, taking care that the two skulls were temple to temple. Then he put everything back the way it was. In spite of all the noise he made, the guards didn't appear. They were surely somewhere sleeping it off. He emptied a large vase and filled it with water from a nearby spigot. Beside it he found a wheelbarrow with brushes, brooms, rags, and bars of soap. He began to clean the grave until the stone was shining. The effect of the syrup was wearing off. No ghosts were wandering the place. However, far away, sunk beneath the dusty gravestones, he heard voices complaining of their abandonment. He decided to clean all the graves. Though he hadn't slept, he felt full of energy. He soaped, scrubbed, swept, rinsed. He finished his task as the sun was going down. The cemetery, reddened by the moribund sun, shone like a necklace of immense rubies. . . .

†

Sara Felicidad and the Rabbi were waiting for him in the The Last Goodbye café, across from the cemetery. When he arrived, after kissing my mother and caressing her body with his large, open hands to show her he'd been cured, he thanked the Caucasian for his advice and apologized for having rejected him for so many years. Then, with great affection, he said:

"My good friend, at the risk of offending you, I hope you'll understand, I'm going to ask that for a while, a couple of years maybe, you don't appear. I have a great debt to my son and I want to repay it. Give me the chance to be a father. . . ."

The Rabbi, without a word, vanished. I didn't see him again until I turned twelve years old. . . . To complete our family's happiness, the three of us traveled to Arica to get my sister.

In the store called The Six Bs (*Bueno, Bonito, Barato, Básico, Bendito, Blanco*: Good, pretty, cheap, basic, blessed, white), my grandmother Jashe, her sister Shoske, their husbands Moisés Latt and César Higuera, my aunts, Raquel First, Raquel Second, and Raquel Third, married in the same order to their first cousins, Jacobo First, Jacobo Second, and Jacobo Third, dark Sephardic Jews, without children, all lived in that enormous six-floor store where everything was white, from the food (cheese, milk, eggs, rice, chicken breasts, fish fillets) to the clothes and kitchen articles, to the toys (a collection of ghosts imitating human activities: aviators, divers, diggers, doctors). Raquel Lea, with her pacifier in her mouth at ten years old and weighing over two hundred pounds, dragged herself around the store like a fish out of water; she was filled not with fat, but with poetry. The river of metaphors had never stopped flowing. And since she was forbidden to utter her verses, they accumulated in her flesh, every day more swollen. When Jaime, after cursing his in-laws, took the gag from my sister's mouth, she recited louder and louder, faster and faster, and as the impetuous river of words flowed out of her body, she grew thinner.

"But precisely of that which keeps us from speaking, we must speak, sink the tongue into the invisible and turn words into mirrors, sail inside them knowing they are crew-less ships, with no interest but the enigma of what or who turned them into ghosts, a dense but impalpable presence that we must approach with a blind man's steps, in this universe where all is approximation and miracle of stone, of flesh, of endless trajectories, of gods sunk into darkness. With steps of the blind we will sink our white cane into the ubiquitous center, there where the eternal origin throbs, giving burbling life. Of it we can say nothing, that's why the darkness is our guide. If we accept ignorance, it becomes a lamp: under the apparent vacuity of the words crouches divine brilliance. . . ."

†

As the poetry came out of her lips, Raquel Lea recovered her beauty and happiness. Later, I realized that just as I lived in eternal unity with the Rabbi, she was visited by Rubi Grugenstein. That's why stones danced in her verses, why they spoke of metals, sang of geological layers, revived the gods of the Incas, Aztecs, Paracas, and Mayans. It was the redhead's spirit that convinced my sister, the day she turned fifteen, to go live in the Amazon jungle. There she made friends with a native tribe and breathed into her nose the dust of the sacred beetle. Suddenly the tree trunks turned transparent, and through them she saw a Peruvian coming toward her, Luis de Gallo, a tall and thin man with a noble forehead, who taught her how to speak Quechua with the tribespeople. After they had a child, Dayal, they set off on a crusade through South America to foment the Poetic Revolution. I've never seen her again. I remember her last words:

"Wrapped in the void like a thick coat, in a felt chrysalis as my wings prepare to emerge, I will finally populate the spheres of my eternal absence!"

†

Jaime and Sara Felicidad, to recover their lost years, decided to live without separating for a single second. Together they worked, ate, went to the bathroom, slept. They even united their voices: they could pronounce identical words in duet. Such was their happiness in life, and they attended their customers with such good humor, offering them first-rate merchandise, that The Apple of Harmony had to expand. When they saved enough money, they left me living in a good pension house to continue my studies, and they went off. to Patagonia with the intention of recreating, using Przewalski's horses, the Tarpan breed, with thick hooves and abundant hair able to live near the poles. By now Jaime has turned a hundred and Sara Felicidad ninety-five. . . . It seems that, amid their savage hordes, they have not grown old. . . . It seems that she is pregnant again. . . . So it seems. . . .

ABOUT THE AUTHOR AND TRANSLATOR

ALEJANDRO JODOROWSKY was born to Ukrainian Jewish immigrants in Tocopilla, Chile. From an early age, he became interested in mime and theater; at the age of 23, he left for Paris to pursue the arts, and has lived there ever since. A friend and companion of Fernando Arrabal and Roland Topor, he founded the Panic Movement and has directed several classic films of this style, including *The Holy Mountain*, *El Topo*, and *Santa Sangre*. A mime artist, specialist in the art of tarot, and prolific author, he has written novels, poetry, short stories, essays, and over thirty successful comic books, working with such highly regarded comic book artists as Moebius and Bess. Restless Books has published three of Jodorowsky's best-known books for the first time in English: *Donde mejor canta un pájaro* (*Where the Bird Sings Best*), *El niño del jueves negro* (*The Son of Black Thursday*), and *Albina y los hombres-perro* (*Albina and the Dog-Men*).

MEGAN MCDOWELL is a Spanish-language literary translator from Kentucky. Her work includes books by Alejandro Zambra, Samanta Schweblin, Lina Meruane, Mariana Enríquez, Álvaro Bisama, Arturo Fontaine, and Juan Emar. Her translations have been published in *The New Yorker*, *The Paris Review*, *Tin House*, *McSweeney's*, Words Without Borders, *Mandorla*, and *VICE*, among others. Her translation of Zambra's novel *Ways of Going Home* won the 2013 PEN Award for Writing in Translation, and her translation of Schweblin's *Fever Dream* was shortlisted for the 2017 Man Booker International prize. She lives in Santiago, Chile.